ALSO BY RICHARD PAUL EVANS

A Perfect Day
The Last Promise
The Christmas Box Miracle
The Carousel
The Looking Glass
The Locket
The Letter
Timepiece
The Christmas Box

For Children
The Dance
The Christmas Candle
The Spyglass
The Tower
The Light of Christmas

✷ RICHARD PAUL EVANS ✷

THE *Sunflower*

DOUBLEDAY LARGE PRINT HOME LIBRARY EDITION

SIMON & SCHUSTER

NEW YORK LONDON TORONTO SYDNEY

This Large Print Edition, prepared especially for
Doubleday Large Print Home Library, contains
the complete, unabridged text of the original
Publisher's Edition.

SIMON & SCHUSTER
Rockefeller Center
1230 Avenue of the Americas
New York, NY 10020

SIMON & SCHUSTER and colophon are registered
trademarks of Simon & Schuster, Inc.

Manufactured in the United States of America

ISBN: 0-7394-6016-1

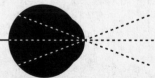

This Large Print Book carries the
Seal of Approval of N.A.V.H.

✦ ACKNOWLEDGMENTS ✦

I'd like to thank the following for making this book possible:

My brother Van for all three trips to Cuzco, Puerto Maldonado and the jungle. Carolyn Reidy and David Rosenthal for welcoming me back. Sydny Miner (It's always a joy working with you). Team Sunflower: Kelly Gay, Heather McVey, Karen Christofferson, Fran Platt and Judy Schiffman (Judy, I'll check your boots for spiders any day). Karen Roylance, for all your assistance and all-nighters (and Mark for putting up with it). Dr. Brent Mabey for technical assistance and New Year's in the E.R. Dr. Michael Fordham, whose insight led me to this story. Carolyn Anderson and Mary Williams for first-hand dengue information. Jessica Evans. Those in Peru who helped me with my research: Leonidas, Jaime and Terry Figueroa, and Gilberto. Laurie Liss. And always, my best friend and companion, Keri.

To Van

Perfect love casteth out fear.

✦

1 JOHN 4:18

T H E
Sunflower

CHAPTER

One

El Girasol (the Sunflower) is sanctuary, as much to me as to the orphan boys we rescue from the Peruvian streets. But I have considered that it might be more. For in a world where evil seems to triumph more often than not, El Girasol is evidence that we might be something better— evidence that we might be good. So while few will ever know or care about the work we do, the worth of this little orphanage is far greater than the number of boys we save. For perhaps it is us, not them, that have need of saving. And to that end the Sunflower is more than a place. It is hope.

✳ PAUL COOK'S DIARY ✳

Going to the jungle wasn't my idea. Had the thought actually crossed my mind, I would have immediately relegated it to that crowded portion of my brain where things *I should do someday but thankfully never will* are safely locked away to languish and die.

The idea was my daughter McKenna's. Three months before she graduated from high school, her sociology teacher, a graying, long-haired Haight-Ashbury throwback who had traded in his tie-dye T-shirts for tweed jackets with leather elbow patches presented to his class the opportunity to go to South America on a humanitarian mission. McKenna became obsessed with the idea and asked if I would accompany her on such an excursion—kind of a daddy-daughter date in the Amazon.

I agreed. Not that I had any real desire or intention of going. I figured that she would soon graduate and her mind would be occupied with other concerns. I never believed it would really come about.

I should have known my daughter better. Four months later I found myself standing with her and a dozen of her former classmates in the Salt Lake City airport boarding a plane for Lima, Peru.

Unbeknownst to our little group, we had entrusted our lives to novices. We were the first group our expeditionary guides had actually led into the Amazon—a fact we discovered twenty-four hours later deep in a jungle teeming with anacondas, jaguars and hand-sized spiders. Several times in the course of our expedition, our guide, an elderly Peruvian man, would suddenly stop, lay his machete at the foot of a tree, then climb above the jungle canopy for a look, each time descending with a somewhat perplexed expression.

After our third complete change of course I asked our guide (as tactfully as one being led through a jungle must) if he knew where he was going. In broken English the old man replied, "Yes, I have been here before . . ." then added, "when I was six."

During our hike we came upon the village of an Amazonian tribe, the Los Palmos.

Overjoyed to learn that they were neither cannibals nor headhunters, we soon noticed that the population of the village included no young men, only women and the elderly. Our guide asked one of the natives where all the young men had gone.

"They have gone to town to kill the mayor," she replied.

"Why?" our guide asked.

"The mayor has said we can no longer cut the rainforest trees. We cannot live without the wood from the trees. So our men have gone to kill him."

"Do you think that's a good idea?" our guide asked.

The woman shrugged. "Probably not, but it's how things are done in the jungle."

There was something refreshing about her logic. I've never been overly fond of politics, and the image of painted tribesmen carrying spears and bows into town hall delighted me—certainly something we don't see enough of in Salt Lake City. I still wonder how that all turned out.

Two days into our journey we ran out of food. For several days we lived on jungle fruit and the piranhas we caught in the river.

(Piranha doesn't taste that bad—kind of like chicken.)

I remember, as a boy, sitting spellbound through a Saturday afternoon matinee about a school of piranhas that terrorized a small jungle village. These Hollywood piranhas swam in conveniently slow-moving schools that cinematically frothed and bubbled on the surface, allowing the hero a chance to swim across the river and rescue a woman just inches ahead of the churning piranha death.

The piranhas we encountered in the jungle were nothing like that. First, Amazon piranhas are nearly as ubiquitous in the jungle as vegetation. Drop a fishing line in any jungle river and within seconds it will be bitten. Usually in half. Second, there are no warning bubbles.

Adding crocodiles, electric eels and leeches to the mix, we decided it best to just keep out of the water.

After several days of traveling we reached our destination, a small village where we established our clinic. The Quechuan natives were waiting for us.

The goal of our humanitarian mission was threefold: teach basic hygiene, fix teeth and correct vision. I was assigned to the latter. The optometrist who hiked in with us would conduct an eye examination, then hand me a written prescription for eyeglasses that I would attempt to fill from the bags of used eyewear we had packed into the jungle.

I remember one patient in particular. He was an elderly man, small featured and sun-baked, his skin as leathery as a baseball glove. And he had just one eye. As he was led from his exam to my station, the doctor handed me a blank prescription.

"What do I do with this?" I asked.

"Find the thickest lens you can find," he replied. "He's all but blind."

I knew the pair. Earlier, as I was organizing the glasses, I had come across a pair of lenses so thick I was certain they were bulletproof. I retrieved them and placed them on the little man's face. I soon learned that he had not just one eye, but also just one tooth as a broad smile blanketed his face. "*¡Puedo ver!*" he exclaimed. *I can see!*

It was my daughter's job to tend the children as the doctors treated their parents. Indelibly etched in my mind is a sweet mental picture of my daughter as I looked out to see her running and screaming in mock terror from a throng of bare-chested little boys, who were laughing so hard they would occasionally fall to the ground holding their stomachs.

As we left the village, the children gathered around her and she hugged each of them. We sat together in the back of the bus, and she grew very quiet. After a few minutes I asked her what she had learned from this experience. She thought about it a moment, then said, "We love those whom we serve."

We moved on by boat up the muddy Río Madre de Dios past the camps of the illicit gold miners scarring the forest with their bulldozers and sluices, eventually coming to a small clearing in the jungle. An airfield. Boarding a cargo plane, we flew south to Cuzco, where we took buses up into the Andes Mountains to a rundown hacienda.

The hacienda had been magnificent once, with elaborate tiles and intricate woodwork. It had a stone courtyard, a balcony and a bell tower. But the opulence of centuries ago was gone now, and what remained, rotting and looted, provided barely adequate shelter for the orphan boys it now housed. The place was called El Girasol—the Sunflower—and it was in the business of saving street children.

Among all the people we encountered in this mystical land, it was here that we met the most memorable: an American by the name of Paul Cook.

I was told by one of our guides that Paul Cook had once been a successful emergency room physician. Up until one Christmas Day when everything changed.

One night, after we had completed our day's tasks, we sat around a fire recounting the day's events as darkness closed in around us. Gradually our group retired to their sleeping quarters and I found myself alone with this quiet, intriguing man. We talked mostly about America; about the NBA, current movies, the Oscars and whom I thought would win the next presidential election. When I had satisfied his curiosity about current events, I asked him what prompted him to come to Peru. He just stared into the fire. Then he said, without looking at me, "That's a long story."

"No clocks in the jungle," I said.

Still gazing into the fire, he smiled at the use of one of his own favorite phrases. After a moment he said, "I'll show you."

He led me through the labyrinth of the hacienda to a small windowless cell with a wooden floor and a high ceiling. The room was as austere as any I had seen in the orphanage and was lit by a single lightbulb hanging from a cord from the exposed rafters. There were a few simple pieces of furniture: a small tin washbasin, a crate for a desk with a wooden chair and a bed that was just a mattress on box springs set on wooden blocks.

And there were books. Lots of books, visibly well-read and stacked in sloppy piles against the wall. I scanned the titles. Classics and bestsellers, *Reader's Digest* compilations, medical journals and crossword puzzles, biographies and thrillers. Books in Spanish as well as English. There were a few love stories.

On the wall above the books were two framed photographs: one of an elderly couple I guessed to be his parents, the other of a beautiful young woman whom I was to learn was named Christine. The most peculiar adornment to the room was a movie poster: a moody, black and indigo poster of a man kissing a woman beneath a title written in Italian: *Cinema Paradiso*.

Paul let me take in the surroundings for a moment before motioning for me to sit on the bed. I noticed that he had something in his hand—a hand-sewn leather pouch. He untied its drawstrings and took from it a small toy soldier and handed it to me. Then he sat down next to me and commenced his tale. An hour or so later, when he was done, he looked weary and spent and I could sense the walls rising again in his demeanor, as if maybe he feared that he had shared too much. He restored the soldier to its pouch, hanging it by its drawstrings to a nail on the wall.

I asked if I could share his story. He showed little interest in my request but said he would sleep on it, a reply I also understood as my dismissal. Three days later, just a few hours before we were to fly back to Lima, he agreed.

It's been said, *Seek not your destiny for it is seeking you.* Paul Cook's story reveals, as well as any I suppose, that this is true. It was equally true for a young woman named Christine, who went to the jungle looking for anything but love.

This is their story.

CHAPTER

Two

There are times, it seems, that God throws a cosmic switch that moves the tracks beneath us, hurling our lives headlong in a new and uncertain direction. Of these times just two things are certain: It's best we don't know what's ahead. We can never go back.

✦ PAUL COOK'S DIARY ✦

CHRISTMAS DAY, 1999
ST. PAUL, MINNESOTA

I've got to move to Arizona, Paul thought as his wipers struggled to keep up with the snow. He had underestimated the intensity of the storm; the blizzard had hit a little after noon, just after Christmas supper. He had left the warmth of the fireplace and his fiancée's arms around two, allowing nearly an hour for what was usually a thirty-five-minute drive. It was almost half past three as he pulled his Porsche off the snow-packed streets into a reserved parking space behind the E.R.

He hurried in, brushing snow from his shoulders as he entered the back door and walked to the locker room. Inside the room another doctor was changing into street clothes. He glanced up as Paul entered, relieved to see his replacement. "You made it."

"Barely," Paul said, removing his parka. "The roads are crazy."

"You should see the E.R."

"Bad?"

"Like a Wal-Mart on the Saturday before Christmas. Except everyone's sick or bleeding."

"And why are you leaving?"

"I've already put in a double shift. I'm the walking dead. For the last four hours it's been just me and Garrity."

Paul hung his coat in a locker, slipped off his shoes and pants and pulled on a pair of scrubs. "Where's McVey?"

"Down with bronchitis."

"Convenient." Paul slid his shoes back on. "What are we seeing today?"

"Usual Christmas joy—suicide attempts, family brawls, accidents from all those new toys they got to hurt themselves with. And your usual snow-blower incidents."

Paul shook his head. "I'll never understand what possesses someone to stick their hand into a snow blower."

"I started my shift with an eight-year-old with a candy cane stuck up his nose. Makes you wonder how our species has survived at all." He pulled on a ski parka. "How's that gorgeous fiancée of yours?"

"Mad that I had to work on Christmas."

"Don't worry. Some day she won't care."

"That's the day I'll start worrying."

He smiled wryly. "I've seen your fiancée. Get used to worrying." He walked to the door. "Take care."

"Drive carefully. And Merry Christmas."

"Maybe next year," he said.

Paul stowed his pants in the locker, shrugged on his white coat, then went to work. The center of the E.R. bustled with activity as nurses and techs crowded in and through the same small spaces. Paul hailed them. "Merry Christmas all."

The charge nurse looked up from her terminal and sighed with relief. "I was afraid you wouldn't make it. Merry Christmas, Doctor."

"Merry Christmas to you."

Marci, an R.N. with red hair and a freckled complexion, walked by wearing a hair band with velvet antlers. She stopped and smiled at him. "Merry Christmas, Dr. Cook."

"Merry Christmas. Which reindeer are you?"

"Vixen," she said, tilting her head.

Paul smiled as she walked off.

"More like Rudolph," the charge nurse said snidely.

From where he stood, Paul could see the waiting room with its display of seasonal decorations: paper snowflakes hand-cut by children from a nearby elementary school and potted poinsettia plants scattered throughout the room, their leaves bright crimson against the dull gray of wall and carpet. In one corner of the lobby was an artificial Christmas tree decorated with white lights and strands of pink metallic beads.

In the waiting room the chairs were all occupied and people leaned against walls or sat on the carpeted floor. A long line had formed in front of the triage desk.

Paul squirted antibacterial lotion on his hands and rubbed it in. "Looks like we're a little busy."

The charge nurse looked up at him. "You think?"

He walked back to the patient charting room. Dr. Aaron Garrity was sitting at a computer terminal dictating from a chart. He stopped mid-sentence, shutting off the computer's recorder.

"Hi, Paul. Merry Christmas."

"Thanks. You too." He clipped a radio to his belt. "It's just us today?"

"Outgunned as usual."

Paul crossed the room to a computer terminal flashing the names of admitted patients. "What have you got?"

"Four fevers, a wrist-slasher, two overdoses and a woman whose husband didn't like Christmas dinner so he cracked her skull . . ."

Paul frowned. "Peace on earth, good will to men."

". . . and a man who stuck his hand in a snow blower."

As Paul looked over the screen, a nurse walked in.

"Hi, Dr. Cook."

He looked up to see Kelly, a petite young nurse with an infectious smile and blond hair. Kelly was both competent and pleasant and he was always glad to see her on his shift.

"Hi, Kell. Merry Christmas."

"Merry Christmas. I'm glad you made it safely. How were the roads?"

"I would of made better time with a dog sled."

She smiled.

"Who else is on call?"

"Marci, Ken, Jean, Paula, Gary and Beverly." She touched his arm. "We have a woman with a laceration in H, it's only level four, but she keeps getting bounced back. She's been here for almost three hours."

"Probably lost her Christmas cheer by now."

"She's been surprisingly patient, but I feel bad for her. I've cleaned up the cut and put on a temporary bandage, but she needs sutures."

"Do you have her chart?"

"Right here." She handed him a clipboard. "She cut herself slicing the Christmas ham."

He examined the chart. "How big is it?"

"The ham?"

He looked up and a smile rose on his lips. "The laceration."

Kelly blushed. "Sorry. About two and a half centimeters."

"Let's go see her."

The woman was twenty-something, dressed in black, tight, low-slung jeans and a long-sleeved pink T-shirt. She had darkly lined eyes and spiky, brunet hair. She was sitting upright on the examination table, holding a gauze pad around her finger. The blood had stained through the bandage and she glanced up nervously as he entered. He greeted her with a warm smile. "I'm Dr. Cook. I'm sorry you've had to wait so long."

"It's okay. It's really busy."

He walked to her side. "I understand you decided to serve your finger for dinner."

She slightly smiled. "I was cutting a ham and the knife slipped."

"How long ago was that?"

"About three hours ago. I came as soon as it happened."

"Let's take a look." He gently pulled back the bandage. The laceration was about an inch long and looked like it went clear to the bone.

"You're pretty brave. I'd probably be howling about now. Before I give you an anesthetic, I need to see if you have nerve or tendon damage. I want you to extend your finger like this." He held his forefinger out in demonstration. She obeyed.

"Now hold it stiff, don't let me bend it." He pushed down on the top of her finger, which she successfully resisted.

"That's good. Keep holding it out and I'll check blood flow."

He squeezed the end of her finger until it was white, then released. It quickly turned pink again. "Blood supply is good. Just one more test."

He took the paper clip from her chart and bent it out so its two ends were extended. "Close your eyes." He touched her finger with the two prongs. "How many points do you feel?"

"Two."

He moved it down her finger.

"And now?"

"Two."

"Good. You can open your eyes."

She examined the paper clip. "That's pretty high-tech equipment you've got there."

He smiled. "Nothing but the best for my patients. Kelly, get me three cc's of two per-cent plain Xylocaine."

Kelly had already prepared for the shot. "Here you go."

"Thank you." He took the syringe and turned back to the young woman. "You missed all the vital stuff. So all I need to do is sew you up and send you home. Let me

have you lay your hand down, palm up. I'm
going to give you a digital block to numb
your finger."

She turned away as he slid the needle into
the palm of her hand. She said, "I feel so
dumb. I work at a floral shop and cut flowers all day and I've never had an accident."

"Accidents happen. Dumb are those who
do it on purpose." He took the needle out.
"Just one more."

She bit her lower lip as he slid the needle
back into her palm. She asked, "Do you see
many suicides?"

He nodded. "Especially this time of the
year." He stood, breaking the needle off into
a disposal pack. "It will take a few minutes
for that to numb. I'm sorry to make you wait
again, but I'll be back in just ten minutes.
Promise."

"Thank you."

He walked back to the charting room and
wrote down the details of his visit, then
scanned the screen for his next patient. Another nurse, Ken, was inside the room. Paul
asked him, "Have you seen Mrs. Schiffman
in G?"

"About ten minutes ago."

"Let's go see her." He grabbed a chart and

walked to the fourth door. A blond woman in her mid-thirties lay on her back. She was wearing a hospital gown and her foot was elevated about five inches off the bed. Her husband, a red-faced, barrel-chested man with a beard and a large belly sat next to her reading *Car and Driver.* He looked up as Paul and Ken entered, his face screwed up with annoyance. "It's about time someone came. Doctors think their time's more valuable than everyone else's."

"We're a little busy," Paul said, then turned to the woman who was clearly embarrassed by her husband's temper. "Hi, I'm Dr. Cook. How did you hurt yourself?"

"I was carrying my boy out to the curb when I slipped on some ice. I think it's broken."

He examined her leg. An enormous bruise blackened her ankle, which was swollen to almost twice its normal size. He felt around it, pressing in spots. "Does that hurt?"

"Yes."

"And here?"

"Ow! Yes."

"Sorry." He turned to Ken. "Let's get a complete set of X-rays on this." He said to the woman. "I'm guessing that you have a type A fracture of the fibula. In English that means you've broken your leg. But we'll need X-rays to be sure. Have they given you anything for the pain?"

"No."

"Are you allergic to anything?"

"Valium."

He lifted the chart and wrote on it. "Ken, let's give her ten milligrams of morphine with fifty milligrams of Phenergan IM." He touched her arm. "I'll see you when I get the X-rays back."

"Hey! You're not leaving?" the man said.

"There's nothing I can do until I see the pictures. But Ken will take good care of your wife for now."

The woman flushed but said nothing. The man grumbled as they walked out.

"Sweet guy," Paul said. "Let me know when the pics are up."

"You got it."

"And take this, please." He handed the chart to Ken, then walked back to room H. The young woman smiled as he entered.

"I told you I'd be back. Are you numb?"

She nodded. "As a brick."

He smiled at her choice of words. "Good. The miracle of Xylocaine—greatest discovery since the bikini." He took a suture pack from the cupboard. "Let's sew you up and get you out of here." He sat down next to her and pulled on some latex gloves. "All right, lay your hand on this." He guided her hand over to a padded armrest. "Just relax. First I'm going to apply a small tourniquet. Fingers tend to bleed a lot and that makes it hard for me to see." He rolled a small rubber ring down her finger. "You'll feel some pressure, a little tugging, but you shouldn't feel any pain." He hooked the needle through the flap of flesh. She jerked.

He looked up. "Did you feel that?"

"Sorry. I'm just a little jumpy."

"Try to hold still."

"Sorry."

He hooked the needle through the opposite flesh and tied the first stitch.

"How many stitches will this take?"

"Six or seven." He sensed her anxiety. "You're a florist?"

"Yes."

"Where do you work?"

"Hyde Floral. It's just a few miles from here, on Ninth."

"Across from the Honda dealership."

"Right."

"I've bought your flowers before."

"Cool. Your next order's on me."

"Thank you. What's your name?"

"Lily Rose."

He looked up. "Really?"

"I know. It was my grandmother's name. Lillian Rose. I get razzed about it every day at work. I guess I'm in the wrong line of work."

"Or the right one." He pulled a thread up and tied it. "It's nice to meet you, Lily. Though next time we'll meet at your place."

"No argument here."

"Whom were you cooking for?"

"My family. We get together once a year to remind ourselves why we stay away from each other the rest of the year. If you're off soon, you're welcome to join us."

He smiled. "Tempting."

"It would make my mother's Christmas. She's always wanted me to bring home a doctor. And a handsome one at that."

Paul smiled. "Thank you."

Just then Kelly stepped into the room. "Doctor, paramedics are in transit. We have a child with respiratory distress."

He continued suturing. "Where's Doctor Garrity?"

"We had a code blue on the floor. A woman went into arrest while delivering a baby."

"What's the ETA?"

"About two minutes."

"Is the child still conscious?"

"Yes."

"What's his oxygen saturation?"

"It's dropping. It was eighty-eight percent at the house, now it's down to eighty-two."

Paul frowned. "What happened?"

"Possible aspiration of an unknown object. The parents and the paramedics tried the Heimlich, but it didn't help."

"Tell the paramedics to get an IV going but don't delay transport."

"I'll call."

Paul looked up at Lily. "I'll have to leave when the child arrives. I don't think I'm going to finish this in time. Will you be okay?"

"Yeah." She was quiet for a moment. "When I was a teenager, I was babysitting a neighbor kid when she choked on a cinnamon bear. She finally coughed it out, but it scared me to death."

Paul tied off another suture. "Choking always scares me."

Just then Ken entered the room. "Dr. Cook, we've got a cardiac arrest in transit."

Paul groaned. "When it rains, it pours. What's the ETA?"

"Five minutes."

"Status?"

"Paramedics are performing CPR. A forty-two-year-old male who was out shoveling snow when he collapsed."

Kelly stepped in behind Ken. "Doctor, the ambulance with the child is here."

He set down the needle, lifted the scissors and snipped the tourniquet. He looked up at Lily. "I'll be back."

"Good luck."

He said to Kelly, "Wrap her with some gauze, then come help me." He walked out into the hall as the paramedics brought in the child. He was a small boy of three or four. His face was bluish and his eyes were open and wild and a large paramedic struggled to hold him as he flailed wildly, the end of the IV tube whipping with his motion.

"What's our oxygen saturation?" Paul asked.

"Seventy-nine."

"Give him to me." Paul put his arms

around the boy and began the Heimlich.
Nothing.

"Get him on the table. Get him moni-
tored."

Just then a woman burst through triage
into the E.R. screaming "Where's my boy?"

The triage nurse had unsuccessfully tried
to grab her arm as she passed and she was
now following her. "Ma'am, we need you to
stay out in the lobby."

"Where's my boy? I'm not leaving my
boy."

Kelly arrived. "Dr. Cook, the boy's
mother . . ."

"Let her back."

Kelly shouted down the hall, "This way,
ma'am."

The woman ran to where they had gathered around her son. She grew even more
panicked at the sight of him. "Do something . . . please!"

Paul asked, "Do you know what he swallowed?"

"No. He was just playing under the tree."

"Were there small ornaments?"

"I don't know. Just take it out! Take it out!
He can't breathe!"

Paul turned to Kelly. "We've got to sedate him. Give me one milligram of Versed."

She injected it into the IV but the boy continued to fight against the men holding him.

"Saturation dropping," Kelly said.

"The Versed's not enough. What's his saturation?"

"Seventy-five."

"Great," he said caustically, "I've got to find out what he swallowed." He turned to the mother. "How much does he weigh?"

"Uh, uh, thirty pounds."

Paul did the math in his head. *One milligram per kilogram.* "Kelly, get me fifteen milligrams Succs."

Just then the sliding doors opened and a frigid gust of wind flooded the hall. Two paramedics in thick boots tramped inside pushing a stretcher with a man strapped to it. Marci walked up, her antlers gone. "Doctor, paramedics are here with the cardiac arrest."

"Where's Garrity?"

"Still on the floor."

"You're going to have to help me, Marci. What room's open?"

"D. Delta."

"Take him there and keep the CPR going. What's his rhythm?"

"V-tach."

"Have the paramedics shocked him?"

"Two hundred, three hundred and three hundred sixty joules."

"Give him a milligram of epinephrine, wait one minute and if he's still in V-fib, shock again with three hundred and sixty joules. Kelly, where's the Succs?"

"It's ready."

"Saturation's fallen to seventy," Ken said.

"Get me the intubation kit."

"Right here."

"Okay, guys, let's do this. Give him the Succs, Kell."

Kelly pushed the syringe. Within moments the boy went completely limp. The woman screamed, "You killed him! You killed my boy!"

"He's not dead, ma'am. Medic, please take Mom to the family waiting room."

"I brought him in alive! He was alive! I love you, Stevie."

"He's still alive, ma'am," Paul said, "He's going to be all right."

The paramedic took the woman by the arm. "I need you to come with me, ma'am."

"I love you, Stevie. Mommy loves you," she sobbed as she was led away.

Paul inserted the laryngoscope into the boy's mouth and lifted his jaw, exposing the vocal cords.

Marci walked back into the room, "Doctor, we need you, the patient just vomited and the paramedics can't get him intubated."

"I can't leave, suck out the vomitus and bag him until I can get there. Kelly, get me the . . ." Kelly handed him the forceps before he could finish. He reached down the child's throat. There was a spot of color among the vocal cords. "There it is."

"Doctor," Ken said, "Saturation's at sixty-eight." Just then the heart monitor started beeping. "He's bradycardic," Ken said.

"What's the rate?"

"Thirty."

"Ken, start CPR. Kelly, two-tenths milligram of atropine IV and get a six ET tube." He clamped the forceps on the object and slowly worked it out of the vocal cords. It was a small toy soldier. He dropped the toy and forceps on the bed tray. "Ken, where are we?"

"Nothing."

"Tube, Kelly."

She handed him a narrow, plastic tube. He passed it between the boy's vocal cords, then stopped to listen. "Breath sounds, end tidal CO_2 are good. Kell, hyperventilate him."

"Doctor," Ken said, "he's in V-fib!"

Paul felt for a pulse. "I'm going to shock him, Ken, the pads."

Ken pulled the boy's shirt up and stuck pads to his chest, clipping wires on with alligator clamps. "Ready."

"Charge to twenty joules, all clear." The tiny body jerked.

They all looked to the monitor. Nothing.

"Charge to forty joules, all clear." Another jump.

"Saturation's up to ninety, Doctor," Kelly said.

"We've got oxygen, if we can just get this heart beating."

"Still nothing," Ken said.

"Ken, CPR. Kelly, epi two-tenths milligram IV."

Ken began massaging the boy's chest. Paul stared at the monitor, "Come on, come on."

"Come on," Kelly echoed.

Paul turned back, "Forty joules. Again. Clear."

Marci was again standing at the door. "Doctor, what do you want to do with your patient in D? We can't intubate him, we've shocked him six times, three doses of epinephrine and we're up to a hundred and fifty milligrams of lidocaine."

A bead of sweat rolled down Paul's temple to his jaw. "Are there any other docs in the hospital who can help us?"

"We've paged overhead but no one's responded. We've called Dr. Mabey at home, but he can't get here for twenty minutes."

"This will be over in twenty minutes. Ken, continue CPR. I'm going to D for thirty seconds."

He ran the forty feet to D. Inside the room a slightly overweight man lay on his back, his shirt cut off of him. There were two paramedics; one of them was pumping on the man's chest while the other watched. Camille, the respiratory therapist, was holding a mask over the man's face and compressing a large bag to force oxygen into his lungs. Paul quickly scanned the cardiac arrest record trying to analyze what had been done and what still could be done. All looked to him, their eyes revealing their helplessness.

"Marci, give him another milligram of epi, wait a minute and then, if there's no change in rhythm, shock him again with three hundred sixty joules. Set me up for an intubation. I'll be right back."

Paul ran back to the other room. The boy's face was an ugly blue. "Where are we?"

"Still in V-fib," Ken said.

"Shock him with another three hundred joules."

Kelly looked at him. "Three hundred?"

"I mean forty." They exchanged glances. "Forty. Clear."

The body jumped.

The monitor stopped beeping. "We've got rhythm," Ken said.

Paul grabbed the boy's wrist. "We've got a pulse. Kell, call Primary Children's, we're going to need a pediatric ICU, let's see if they can get a helicopter through this storm."

"Saturation up to ninety-five percent," Kelly said.

The color was slowly returning to the boy's face. Paul exhaled in relief. "Good job, guys, good job. Stay with him, I'm going back to D."

Paul ran back to the other room. The team was still working on the man but visibly distressed. Marci looked up: "We can't get his heart beating, and we still can't get him intubated."

Paul took the tube and successfully maneuvered it into place.

"Good job, Doctor," Marci said.

"That's why you make the big bucks," one of the paramedics said.

"Let's shock him," Paul said. He grabbed the paddles. "Marci, three hundred and sixty joules. Clear."

The body heaved.

"Anything?"

The paramedic shook his head.

"Atropine?"

"We've maxed out."

"CPR, now. Marci, more epinephrine, two-tenths milligram."

She injected the steroid into the IV.

"He's not responding," Paul said. "I'm shocking again. Three hundred sixty joules. Clear."

The body heaved again but as quickly settled.

It's like trying to jump start a sofa, Paul thought. "He's not responding to anything."

The monitor flatlined.

"He's asystole!" Marci said.

"I'm shocking again. Three hundred sixty joules. Clear!"

Nothing. Paul looked around the room. "Have you seen any pulse at all?" he asked.

"Nothing," replied a paramedic.

"No, Doctor," said Marci.

"How long has he been arrested?" Paul asked.

"We picked him up forty-three minutes ago," the paramedic said. "The call came in fifty-six minutes ago."

Just then the sound of a helicopter landing shook the windows. Paul looked at the man. He was dead and had been for half an hour. Paul exhaled in frustration. "Let's call code."

Marci glanced at her watch. "Time of death sixteen twenty-seven."

The Life Flight crew passed outside the room. Just then Kelly stepped in. "Doctor, the boy's heart rate is down to forty, we need you."

Paul turned to Marci. "I'll see the family when I'm done." He hurried back to the boy.

Halfway down the hall the red-faced man from room G stepped in front of him. "Hey, we've waited long enough. What about my wife's X-rays?"

Paul's temper flared as he walked around him. "Get back in that room. I'm trying to save a life."

The man timidly walked back to his wife. The helicopter crew stood outside the boy's room, waiting. "Trip's delayed, boys," Paul said. He glanced up at the monitor as he entered. The boy's heart rate had dropped four more points. He called out, "Atropine, two-tenths milligram IV."

V-fib again appeared on the monitor. "What's going on here?" he mumbled to himself. "Kell, charge to twenty joules. Clear." The body jumped.

"We've got a beat," Ken said.

"For a moment," Paul answered as the rate began sliding. "We're keeping him alive with epinephrine. How's saturation?"

"He's fine, doctor. Ninety-five percent."

Dr. Garrity looked in. "I'm back, do you need help?"

"I can't hold a heart beat. We're maxed out on atropine and we're up to three milligrams of epinephrine. Any ideas?"

He shook his head. "You're doing all you can. We've got a car accident coming in, with level-two multiple injuries."

The heart monitor started beeping again.

"V-fib, doctor."

Paul began giving the boy CPR. "Come on. Come on, hang in there. Kelly, let's try one more time. Epinephrine, two-tenths milligram IV."

"Done."

"Charge to forty joules. Clear."

The body jumped. For a moment the heartbeat returned, but no one rejoiced this time. It almost immediately began to fall.

"Hold," Paul said. "Hold, hold." The monitor started beeping. Paul looked around the room. "Anyone have any ideas?

No one answered.

"Come on, Kell, one more time two-tenths milligram epi IV."

She again injected the IV. "Done."

"Ken, charge to forty joules. Clear."

The body jumped. This time the monitor did not move but continued to bleep.

"Again," Paul said angrily. "Charge to sixty joules. Clear."

The little body bounced nearly a foot high but to no effect.

"Nothing!" Paul shouted. The monitor beeped. "Again. Charge to sixty joules. Clear."

Again the body jumped. Again the monitor showed nothing. To continue shocking the boy seemed cruel. For a moment they all stood silently as the room's hyperactivity dissolved into the lethargy of defeat. After a moment Kelly touched his shoulder. "Shall I call code, Doctor?"

Paul didn't move.

"Doctor?"

He covered his eyes with his hand and breathed in and out deeply. "How long has it been?"

Kelly glanced at her watch. "Thirty-seven minutes."

Paul looked up at the boy's perfect, peaceful face, then over at the small toy soldier lying on the tray. His voice cracked. "Call the code."

Kelly said softly, "Sixteen forty-two, patient expired."

Paul stood there, frozen.

Marci stepped into the room behind Kelly. "Doctor, the man's wife and children are waiting to hear from you."

Paul continued to stare at the boy as if

he hadn't heard her. Then he said, "I need a minute."

As everyone watched, Paul walked over to the corner of the room and sat down on the black vinyl-capped stool, laying his face in his hands. Then his body started to tremble. He began to cry.

Kelly's eyes began to water and she brushed tears back from her cheek. "You did everything possible," she said. "It was in God's hands."

A moment later, echoing down the hall came the cry of a woman looking for her child.

CHAPTER

Three

Hope grabs on to whatever floats.

✦ PAUL COOK'S DIARY ✦

FOUR YEARS LATER, OCTOBER 22, 2003
DAYTON, OHIO

Christine Hollister placed the veil over her auburn hair and looked at herself in the hallway mirror. Beneath the ivory veil she wore gray sweatpants and an oversized University of Dayton sweatshirt, the combination as incongruous as a butterfly in winter. In just seven more days she would wear the veil for real. The thought simultaneously thrilled and stressed her. There was still so much to do before the wedding.

She laid the veil on the kitchen counter and picked up her wedding planning notebook. The binder was neatly categorized, alphabetized and indexed, pockets bulging with articles and pictures cut from bridal magazines, and notes and business cards.

She leafed through the book, stopping

occasionally on pages not yet crossed out. *The caterer was set—almost—still needed a deposit. And they needed to order more éclairs. Mom promised she'd take care of that. Better call and remind her.*

The videographer had left a message about music. *Nothing with vocals,* she thought. *Piano would be nice. Rachmaninoff, what was it? From that Jane Seymour–Christopher Reeve movie.* She wrote a note to herself in the page's margin.

Flowers. No roses. She hated roses. Her wedding bouquet was made of red sunflowers and daisies, as were the centerpieces at the guest tables. The cake, satin white with three tiers, was also decorated with fresh sunflowers. Even their wedding announcements had not escaped the flower's presence: parchment with ivory vellum over sheets watermarked with sunflowers. No one could doubt she loved sunflowers.

She stopped at a picture of the bridesmaids' dresses cut from *Modern Bride.* Dark navy, satin, A-line silhouette, middle-of-the-calf hemlines. She drew a line through the page. Her maid-of-honor had finally picked up her dress, her bridesmaids were ready. Now she just had her own dress to worry about.

Her wedding gown had been her great-grandmother's. It was cream satin charmeuse, embroidered with crystals and pearls.

According to the bridal magazines, cream (or candlelight, as they called it) was ideal for fair skin like hers. The dress was stunningly beautiful but had obviously been made for a woman of another era. The hips were fine, the bust small but sufferable, the waist downright impossible. She had, out of necessity, worn the gown for her bridal photos. The waist was so tight that she would have screamed, she told the photographer, if she could draw enough air into her lungs to do it properly. She had always thought that she had a small waist, and she wondered if women were really so much smaller two generations ago or if they just had more effective corsets and higher tolerances for pain.

Now the dress was at the seamstress's, and she considered checking on it again to make sure it would be done on time but was afraid to. The last time she had phoned, the seamstress told her that she would have had the gown done if not for her incessant calling.

On the bottom of one page she'd scrawled: *Remind Martin to get his father and Robert in to the tuxedo rental.* She crossed it out. She'd just call them herself. Lately, it seemed that every time she discussed wedding details with Martin he became irritable. In the last week they had gotten into several small tiffs and just yesterday she had called Jessica, her best friend and maid-of-honor, in tears. Jessica had reassured her that quarreling before the wedding was as much a part of the process as choosing flowers. "Nothing to ruin a marriage like a wedding," she said.

Not that she was making it easy on Martin. Christine had fantasized about her wedding day since she was ten and was so insistent on every detail that there were times when she felt more like Bridezilla than Bride Beautiful. All things considered, Martin had been remarkably patient—as well as smart, successful and handsome. Wedding stress aside, she was a lucky woman.

Christine's wedding plans matched the fantasy in her head in all but one point: she had no one to give her away. Her father had died two years earlier of cancer, but even if he had lived, she wouldn't have asked him. Her parents had divorced when she was nine. While her mother had never remarried, her father had married within a few months to a younger woman with two small children. With time he became a stranger to her. He didn't even attend her high school graduation, just sent her a check for fifty dollars that she had angrily thrown away.

She looked at her watch. Her bachelorette party was tonight and Jessica said she'd be by to pick her up at six. The thought of the party made her anxious as well. Even though Christine had made her promise not to do anything too wild, she knew that her request might simply have encouraged Jessica to do just that. It was Jessica's ongoing quest to get Christine to "let her hair down."

Christine and Jessica were proof that opposites attract; if Christine was silk, Jessica was leather. Christine never had more than one boyfriend at a time, while Jessica never settled with less than a bevy of them as she found them "more manageable" that way.

Both women were beautiful but in different ways. Christine's beauty was more classic—the kind of look you'd admire in a fifties movie but wouldn't know what to do with offscreen. Jessica was more playful—bare midriffs and Daisy Mae shorts. Men moved quietly around Christine, like she was a porcelain figurine. Jessica never spent a weekend night home.

And both women, in their own ways, envied the other. Christine envied Jessica for her fun and brashness. She envied the way life seemed to bounce off of her. And while Jessica relished making fun of Christine's propriety, she envied her too for her steadiness and clarity, for everything she was not.

Christine set the notebook on the table, went to the stove and turned on a flame beneath the kettle. She planned to lose six pounds before the wedding and was halfway there, living on herbal tea and spinach.

As she was taking the tea caddy from the cupboard, someone knocked at her door. She crossed the room and opened it. Martin stood in the hallway.

Martin was an immaculate dresser, and even though it was the weekend, he wore perfectly pressed slacks, a bright polo shirt and a tweed jacket. "May I come in?" His voice was tight.

"Of course. What's wrong?"

He didn't answer and she stepped into him, wrapping her arms around him. He pulled her to his chest. After a moment he said softly, "We need to talk."

She stepped back and looked into his face. Something in his expression frightened her. "What is it?"

He stepped into the room, walked over to the kitchen table and sat down, momentarily resting his face in his hands. Christine walked over and turned off the stereo. She felt her stomach twisting in panic. "Do you want a Coke?"

"No."

"Something stronger?"

"No."

She sat down across from him at the table. "What's up?"

He was quiet for a moment then looked up into her eyes. "I can't do it, Christine."

"Can't do what?"

"Get married."

For a moment she stared at him, not believing he could really be serious. Her throat went dry. "Did I do something?"

"No."

"Then what didn't I do? I don't understand."

There was no reply.

Her eyes began to fill with tears. "Is there someone else?"

"No." He stood, looking awkward. For a moment he stared at the carpet, then he looked up at her, his face bent in pain. "I'm just not ready for this. It all happened too fast . . . It was like the Christine bridal train just picked up speed before I could jump off."

She felt numb. "That's what you want? To jump off?"

"No, it's not what I want. I mean . . ." He again exhaled in exasperation. His voice softened. "I can't do it, Chris, I just can't do it *now.*"

"The wedding's a week away; the invitations have been sent. My bachelorette party is tonight."

"I should have said something earlier."

She looked at him sharply. *"Earlier* would have been better." She dropped her head on the table. "I can't believe this . . ." She began to cry.

"Hey," he said softly. He reached over and touched her hair, but she pushed his hand away. He walked around the table and squatted down close to her. "I love you, Chris . . ."

"And this is how you show me?"

"Would you rather have found out after we're married that I wasn't ready? You want me to fake being happy?"

She covered her face with her hands. "I thought you *were* happy." Her voice cracked. "I thought you wanted me."

"Of course I do. Just not like this." He stroked back her hair. "What do you want me to do? You want to just go ahead with this?"

She glared at him. "Right, my dream wedding." She pulled the ring off her finger and threw it at him. It fell on the floor. "Take your ring and go. Just leave me alone."

He took a deep breath, rose, then bent over to lift the ring. "I was hoping you'd understand." He walked over to the door. "I'm really sorry, Christine. I know it seems cruel. And I know it's not fair. But marrying you, when I feel like this, would have been even worse." He paused for a moment, then opened the door. "I'll call you later."

She didn't look up at him. "Please. Go away."

When the door shut, it felt as if her heart had been closed in it. Desperation rose in her chest and she wanted to run after him and beg him to stay. Instead she fell back onto the table and sobbed uncontrollably.

Across the room the teakettle began to whistle.

CHAPTER

Four

*American culture is a curious thing.
We fret over a sport star's twisted
ankle or the ill-fated marriage of
celebrities, yet lose no sleep over a
hundred million children living
in the streets.*

✦ PAUL COOK'S DIARY ✦

ONE WEEK LATER

Of all people, why did this have to happen to Christine? Jessica thought as she pounded on Christine's apartment door. Christine hadn't answered her phone for two days. Now she wasn't answering her door. "Christine, it's Jessica." She rapped again with the back of her hand. "C'mon, Chris, open up. I know you're in there."

Christine's next door neighbor, a squat, elderly woman with thinning, disheveled hair, looked out the crack the security chain allowed. *The Price Is Right* blared from behind her.

"No one's there," the woman said. "No one's been in or out for days."

"Her car's downstairs," Jessica said.

"Didn't say it wasn't. But I haven't heard a peep from that girl since that boy dumped her."

"Thank you for sharing," Jessica said flatly. The woman's eyes narrowed, then disappeared behind the door.

Christine wouldn't do something crazy, would she? Her chest constricted with the thought. "Christine, open up! Now!"

Inside the apartment Christine lay in sweats across the top of her bed. A harsh sun streamed through the room's partially drawn blinds, and she rolled from it toward her radio alarm clock. She had awoken to Jessica's pounding, not sure where she was until consciousness flooded in thick and unwelcome. Today, especially today, she didn't want to see anyone.

She leaned out from the bed, her face inches from the dull glowing face of the clock. She groaned, then rolled to her back, covering her eyes with her forearm. It was already a quarter to one. Somewhere in her mind, fragments of an earlier schedule remained. She wasn't supposed to be in bed. She was supposed to be standing in the church in her perfect gown, perfectly coiffed, with her perfect groom. She should have been Mrs. Martin Christensen by now.

The thumping came again, followed by

Jessica's voice. "Christine, I'm going to call 911 if you don't answer."

"I'm coming," she shouted hoarsely.

She rolled out of bed, pulling her long hair back from her face as she stood. Her room was a mess, cluttered with clothes and cans and Styrofoam containers. For the last week she had pretty much subsisted on Diet Coke, ramen noodles and licorice. She picked her way to the front door, unhooked the security chain and opened the door.

The expression on Jessica's face was a mixture of relief and anger. "I called you twelve times yesterday."

"I'm sorry."

"Can I come in?"

"Yes."

Jessica stepped inside, surveying the room in awe. In all the time she'd known Christine she had never seen her apartment in this state. Christine was the kind of woman who fretted if there weren't vacuum lines in the carpet.

"Wow, this looks like my place." Jessica shut the door behind her, then put her arms around Christine. Christine lay her head on her shoulder and began to cry, softly at first then growing into a sob.

"I'm sorry, honey," Jessica said, rubbing her back. "It's not right."

When Christine's crying slowed, Jessica stepped back slightly, and they stood forehead-to-forehead. "It's going to be okay, honey. It's all going to work out for the best." She parted the hair from Christine's face. "When was the last time you ate?"

"I don't know."

"Oh, baby," she sighed. "You go shower. We're going out for lunch."

"I don't want to go anywhere," Christine said.

"I know. That's why we are. There's a half-price sale at Lord and Taylor. You know how shopping brings you out of a funk." She smiled, "And I have a big surprise for you."

"I don't want any more surprises."

"Of course you don't. But you'll like this one. It's a good surprise. Trust me."

CHAPTER

Five

*A patient once told me that a trip to
the mall was twice as effective
as Prozac.*

✦ PAUL COOK'S DIARY ✦

When Christine emerged from her bedroom, the kitchen blinds and windows were open, filling the room with light and cold, fresh air. Jessica walked over to the counter and poured a cup of coffee and carried it to her. "Drink this. It's a little strong."

"You're acting like I have a hangover."

"I know."

Christine took a sip from the cup and almost gagged. "That's awful."

"At the office they call it jet fuel."

"They're being kind."

Jessica smiled. "So what have you been doing the last three days—besides not answering your phone?"

"TV," she said. She looked around. "Why did you open the windows?"

"It smells like three-day-old ramen."

"It's cold in here."

Jessica shut the window. "You look nice in that blouse. Is that new?"

"No. I just haven't worn it in a while. Martin didn't like it."

"Again, Martin proves he's an idiot." She looked at her watch. "Let's go, honey. Bargains wait for no woman."

✦

It was after three when the women sat down at the crowded mall café, surrounded by shopping bags. Light Christmas music played in the background. As soon as the waitress left with their orders, Christine said, "I think it's wrong playing Christmas music in October."

"That one store had a Frankenstein cutout with a Santa cap," Jessica said.

"It's just wrong." Christine sipped her water. After a moment she said, "Thanks for getting me out of the apartment."

"You're welcome. You okay?"

"No. Not really." She looked into Jessica's eyes. "It's just so humiliating. I feel like I should be on one of those talk shows, *Women Who Got Dumped at the Altar . . .*"

Just then the waitress returned. As she set Christine's salad down, Christine said, "I'm sorry, I wanted the dressing on the side."

The waitress frowned. "My fault. I'll get you another salad."

"Is this the raspberry vinaigrette?"

"Yes, ma'am."

"I think I'll just have vinegar and oil."

"Okay." She turned to Jessica. "Is everything all right with your order?"

"It's great."

"Oh," Christine added, "and could I have a lime wedge instead of a lemon?"

"Of course. I'll be right back."

She took Christine's salad and left.

Jessica shook her head in wonder. "Girl, you are *so* high-maintenance."

"I just like things the way I like them." She took a bottle of antibacterial lotion from her purse, squirted into her palm and rubbed her hands together. "Mall hands," she said. "Want some?"

"No. I'll take my chances."

She put the bottle back in her purse, then lifted her Coke.

Jessica started, "You were saying?"

Christine shook her head. "You spend your life building these romantic fantasies. You don't expect your knight to dump you off the horse a block from the castle. I just don't know what I did wrong."

"*You* didn't do anything wrong. This is about Martin, not you. He'll come to his senses eventually." She lifted her drink. "The only question is whether you'll be dumb enough to take him when he comes crawling back."

"You really think he'll come back?" she asked hopefully.

Jessica instantly regretted her comment. "Really, Christine, Martin was marrying above himself." She took a drink. "It's like I always said, his parents left the second 'A' out of Martin."

"You make him sound awful."

"He is."

Christine's eyes moistened. "No, he's not. He's everything I've ever wanted. If he called right now and said he'd made a mistake, I'd meet him at the nearest justice of the peace."

Jessica frowned but said nothing. After a moment Christine asked, "Do you think it will ever stop hurting?"

"Someday. Not soon, but someday. But hiding in your apartment isn't going to help. The sooner you get on with your life, the sooner you'll feel better." Jessica's expression changed abruptly. "That reminds me."

She reached below the table and pulled a folded brochure from her purse. She laid it flat on the table, smoothing it down with the side of her hand. "There you go. My surprise."

Christine looked at it without comprehension. It was a glossy travel brochure, creased where it had been folded. The main picture was of lush rounded hills with stone ruins of some kind. There was an inset photograph of several chocolate-haired llamas being herded by a small boy.

"What's this?"

"It's Machu Picchu," Jessica said.

"And why are you showing me this?"

Jessica leaned back for emphasis. "Because that's where we're going."

"We?"

"I signed us up. There's this foundation that takes Americans to Peru on humanitarian missions. You work in villages or set up clinics in the jungle for the natives. And, in our downtime, we'll tour the country. We'll see the Incan ruins, climb the Andes, camp at a jungle lodge in the Amazon."

Christine just stared at her. "A jungle lodge?"

"It's unforgettable."

"So is a root canal. I don't want to go to a jungle."

"Why not?"

"Jess, you know . . . my idea of roughing it is a three-star hotel. If we're going to vacation, let's go to Palm Beach."

"This isn't a vacation. They say you'll never work so hard in all your life."

"What part of this am I supposed to get excited about?"

"They say the best cure for a broken heart is to give of yourself."

"I already gave of myself."

"I know, honey, I know." She leaned forward. "But we're going to help street children," Jessica said, her voice softening, "work with babies." She smiled, leaning closer. "You love babies."

Christine crossed her arms at her chest. "Why do you *always* try to make me do things I don't want to do?"

"Because you *never* want to do *anything*. You're too afraid of life. I swear, if it weren't for me you'd never experience anything at all."

"That's not true."

"Name just *one* spontaneous thing you've done this year that I didn't make you do."

"I got engaged."

"You call that spontaneous? You dated for six years."

"Five." Christine glanced back down at the brochure. "I can't afford this anyway."

"It's been taken care of."

Christine didn't like the finality of her tone. "What do you mean, 'taken care of'?"

"Your mother already paid for it."

"My *mother* agreed to this?"

"She sent me the check."

"My mother can't afford this."

"She wanted to do it for you. Besides, it's a lot cheaper than the wedding."

"It would have been nice if someone had asked my opinion."

"If you'd answer your phone, we might have," Jessica said tartly.

"What about your parents?" Christine asked, "Do they want you to go?"

"Are you kidding? The congressman practically started packing my bags. Think of all the political mileage he'll get telling his constituents about his wonderful daughter's humanitarian work."

The waitress returned with Christine's salad. "Does that look all right?"

Christine inspected the salad. The waitress glanced at Jessica, who smiled sympathetically.

"It's fine," Christine said.

"And here's a bowl of limes. Enjoy your meals."

Christine wiped the lime's peel with a napkin, then slid it over the side of her cup.

Jessica started again. "You have no idea what I had to go through to get this set up, not to mention getting the time off work. And I'm not going alone."

"Then take someone else."

"I'm not taking someone else. I did this for *you.*"

"I don't want to go to Peru."

"How do you know? You've never been there."

"I've never been to hell either and I'm pretty sure I don't want to go there."

"This isn't hell."

"It is to me."

"Give me one good reason not to go."

"I'll give you a million reasons. Spiders."

"Spiders," Jessica repeated.

"Millions of them. Big ones. Spiders big enough to catch birds and eat them."

Jessica looked at her blankly. "Where did you hear this?"

"The Discovery Channel. And there are snakes."

Jessica shook her head. "You're impossible."

"I'm impossible? I didn't ask you to do this."

"You shouldn't have to. Friends look out for each other. You just don't know what's good for you."

She raised her hands. "There you go again. How is languishing in a third-world country good for me?"

"It's better than languishing in Dayton thinking about being dumped."

Christine just stared at her. Suddenly tears welled up in her eyes.

"I'm sorry. That didn't come out right."

Christine couldn't speak and a tear rolled down her cheek. Jessica put her hand on top of Christine's. "I'm really sorry."

Christine dabbed her eyes with her napkin.

"Look, there's an orientation meeting Sunday night. We can go and learn all about it.

Just please don't make your mind up until then."

Christine just looked down for a moment, then took a deep breath. "No promises."

"Okay," Jessica said, "No promises."

CHAPTER

Six

The surest way to minimize your own burdens is to carry someone else's.

✦ PAUL COOK'S DIARY ✦

Jessica was careful not to broach the subject of the expedition until the night of the orientation. After fifteen years of friendship she knew that convincing Christine to do something against her will was a lot like fishing—you gave her enough line so that she thought she was in control, then slowly reeled her in.

Christine had thought about the trip just enough to be sure that she didn't want to go.

The orientation meeting was held at the Dayton City Library. As the two women entered the building, Christine was stopped by a woman on her way out. She was tall and elegant, wearing a pink leather jacket and a ring on every finger.

"Oh, Christine, you're already back from your honeymoon. I'm so sorry we couldn't make it to the wedding. Chuck got called out of town at the last minute. I'm sure it was just beautiful."

Christine answered stoically. "The wedding was called off."

The woman's expression went from shock to pity. "You poor dear. I'm so sorry. Are you okay?"

"I'm okay. Thank you."

The woman hugged her. "You hang in there, sweetie. And tell your mom I'll be calling her." She walked away.

When she was gone, Christine frowned. "I'm sure you will," she said.

"Who was that?" Jessica asked.

"Someone in my mother's book club. I can guess what next month's topic of conversation will be: poor jilted Christine."

"A good reason to get out of Dayton," Jessica said, stopping near a woman shelving books. "Excuse me, could you tell me where the Peru group is meeting?"

The woman looked up over her glasses, then pointed toward a set of doors across the room. "The conference room's over there."

"Thanks."

Across the library, taped to a set of double doors, was a piece of paper inscribed with a marker: PUMA-CONDOR EXPEDITIONS. Inside the room a couple dozen people were already seated. It was an eclectic group evenly divided between men and women, most in their twenties, though some looked young enough to be high school students.

A tall, fresh-faced young man with an athletic build stood at the front of the room rooting through an open briefcase. He wore a felt fedora, which made him look a little like Indiana Jones. He glanced up as the women entered, then walked back to greet them, carrying with him a handful of manila envelopes.

"Good evening, ladies, I'm Jim." He looked them both over, his eyes settling on Jessica.

Jessica smiled coquettishly. "Hi. I'm Jessica and this is Christine."

"Right, Jessica. We talked on the phone. Glad to finally meet you both." He turned to Christine. "Glad you decided to join us."

"I haven't decided," she said.

Jim nodded. "Well, maybe the presentation tonight will help you make up your mind. In the meantime . . ." He shuffled through the envelopes. "Here's your packet, Jessica. And here's yours, Christine. We'll be going through everything in just a minute." He glanced up at the wall clock. "In fact, I better get started. Glad you're here. We're going to have an incredible time." He smiled confidently at Jessica, then walked back to the front of the room.

As they sat down, Jessica said, "He is *gorgeous.* Can you believe it? We're gonna hike through a hot, sweaty jungle with *him.*"

Christine shook her head. "Good. You won't need me then."

"We'll talk after the meeting." Jessica said.

Jim closed his briefcase, then leaned against the edge of the table facing the group.

"We're still missing a few people but we'll go ahead and hope they turn up. *Bienvenidos.* My name is Jim Hammer. I'm the Ohio representative of Puma-Condor Expeditions, and I've been to Peru more than twenty times.

"To begin, I want to make something clear. This is *not* a vacation. I repeat, this is *not* a vacation. If this were a television show, it would be *Survivor,* not *The Love Boat.* If you're expecting a leisure cruise with chocolates on your pillow at night, you're in the wrong place."

There were a few laughs from the group and Jim looked around and smiled.

"In fact, based on my experience, most of you will lose a few pounds."

"Sign me up!" a woman behind Christine shouted. The group again laughed.

"You are signed up, Joan," he said. "However, if you're looking for an adventure that you'll be telling your grandchildren about someday, then you've come to the right place. Is everyone clear on that?"

The group nodded or mumbled their consensus.

"I *like* chocolates on my pillow," Christine whispered.

"Great, then let's start." Jim held an envelope above his head. "You should all have one of these packets. If you look inside, you'll find a yellow sheet like this." He held up a paper in his other hand. "This is a list of things that you *must* do before December second. I suggest that you do not put them off. Especially anything concerning your passport."

"Look, Chris," Jessica said, "lists. You love lists."

"Shut up," she said.

He held up a sheet of paper. "The light blue sheet in your packet is a vaccination form. This is for your own benefit. For a two-week stay the Peruvian government will not require a vaccination form, but we require that you have a current tetanus shot and hepatitis A and B."

A pock-faced student near the front of the room raised his hand. "What about malaria or yellow fever?"

"There are inoculations for both, it's up to you. Actually both of those diseases are quite rare. They won't be a problem in Cuzco or the Andes, where we'll be too high for mosquitoes, but down in Puerto Maldonado and the jungle it's possible. In my twenty-plus trips we've never had a problem, but there's always that chance. I suggest you consult your doctor. I need to warn you though, the medicine for malaria tends to cause symptoms that mimic the disease. Not to mention the lucid dreaming."

"Great. Spiders *and* malaria," Christine said.

He lifted another paper off the table. "This pink sheet is your packing list. We'll be packing light. *Very* light. You can only bring one carry-on bag because we have to use your luggage allowance to bring in supplies for the humanitarian work."

"One carry-on for ten days?" a woman asked indignantly. "Can't we just ship the supplies?"

"Not really. It's difficult getting things into Peru. Officials might confiscate the supplies at customs or try to charge a tariff. Besides, you don't need six pairs of shoes in the jungle. Trust me on this."

"Okay, now take out the three white pages that have been stapled together. This is your itinerary. There have been a few changes from the earlier schedule so be sure to reference only this one. This is your rock-solid itinerary." A small smile crossed his lips. "Unless it changes again. Planning a trip through Peru is like planning an outdoor wedding. You can plan until the cows come home and still have the weather ruin it."

"Or the groom," Christine said softly.

Jessica put her hand on Christine's leg and rubbed it reassuringly.

"You're signed up for a ten-day expedition. We'll be flying out of the Cincinnati airport on the evening of December third and coming home in time for Christmas. How you get to the airport is up to you. I suggest you carpool where possible.

"We'll be flying directly into Lima from Cincinnati. That will put us in Lima around seven-thirty A.M. It will take us about an hour to get through customs and pick up our luggage, so even though you'll be excited, you'll want to sleep on the plane. We will not be leaving the airport. We fly out to Cuzco around noon, so it's not worth the trouble to check into a hotel for just a few hours. The good news is that Lima is only one hour behind us, so your sleep won't be that off. We'll get something to eat at the Lima airport.

"We'll arrive in Cuzco around one. After we've picked up our luggage, we'll take a charter bus to the hotel. You'll all be pretty tired by then so we'll check into our hotel. That evening you'll be on your own. You're welcome to go out and see the city.

"The next day we'll start our first project working at an orphanage called El Girasol, which is Spanish for 'the Sunflower.'" He looked up from his sheet. "You'll notice on your packing list an option to bring some children's clothing and toys. Christmas is coming and so they've asked us to bring

some gifts for the children at the orphanage. Of course this is strictly voluntary. But
if you want to participate, there are some
gift ideas and the children's sizes on the
paper."

He looked back down at the schedule.
"That first day we'll work until late afternoon, then we'll go back to Cuzco for dinner and sightseeing. You'll probably be a
bit sore from working, but the evening is
yours."

"Sunflowers, Chris," Jessica said. "It's a
sign."

"The next two days are also at the Sunflower, but we'll leave early the third day and
take our bus into the Sacred Valley. We'll
spend the night in Urubamba, and the next
day we'll take a train into Aguas Calientes
and Machu Picchu. Machu Picchu is something you'll never forget. We'll spend the
day there, then take the train back to
Cuzco. That evening we'll play. There are
clubs, a night market, even a decent dis-
cotheque for those of you who like to get
down."

"Yeah!" Jessica said louder than she had
planned, and everyone turned and looked
at her.

"I can see where the party will be," Jim said. Jessica laughed. He smiled and looked back down at his sheet. "Okay, early the next morning we'll check out of the hotel and fly to Puerto Maldonado.

"Puerto is a small jungle town. We have a one-day service project at an elementary school; I believe we'll be rebuilding their bathrooms. The next morning we'll take a bus to Laberinto, where we'll board our riverboat for the Amazon. We'll be on the river for about four and a half hours. We'll be stopping on the way at the village of the Amaracayre tribe to deliver some books. You'll love this stop. It will make you feel like an explorer for *National Geographic.* The chief of the tribe wears a bone through his nose.

"We won't stay long because we want to arrive at the lodge before it gets too dark. Trust me, you don't want to hike through the jungle at night." As he looked around, he noticed a few anxious-looking faces and smiled. "Don't worry, we haven't lost anyone yet."

"Exciting, isn't it?" Jessica said.

"Oh, yeah. Very."

"We'll leave our boats at the bank and hike

through the jungle. It's a short hike, about twenty minutes. Canoes will be waiting on the other side at Lake Huitoto. It's another forty minutes by canoe to the Makisapa Lodge. We'll be at the lodge for three days. Believe me, after all your hard work and travel you'll be glad for the rest."

A young man raised his hand. "What do we do at the lodge?"

"Favorite jungle activities include crocodile hunting, bird-watching, piranha fishing and some exploring—but only as a group. It *is* the jungle and there are jaguars and anacondas and a nasty assortment of vipers. In the jungle even the frogs and butterflies are poisonous." He smiled again. "It's a lot of fun."

Christine raised her hand. "Yes? Christine," Jim said.

"Are there spiders?"

"Yep. Big ones. Big enough to catch birds."

A groan went up in the room.

Christine nudged Jessica. Jessica just grinned.

"But I wouldn't worry about them. Like most things in the wild, if you leave them alone, they'll leave you alone." He smiled again. "Unless they're hungry."

Another groan.

"Any more questions?"

A new hand went up. "What's the weather like?"

"Good question. Peru is south of the equator, so we'll be there during their summer. Dress accordingly. However, it's also their rainy season, so bring a poncho or rain jacket. And we'll be pretty high up in the Andes so you'll want to bring a sweatshirt or light jacket."

"With all that extra bag space," Christine said.

"Any more questions?"

No one spoke so Jim said, "Okay, I have a little PowerPoint presentation I put together. I want to show you why we do this. Could someone get the lights?"

He switched on his projector as the lights dimmed. The presentation was a five-minute slide show of previous excursions: There were groups of Americans working side by side with Peruvians building greenhouses and latrines, digging trenches for water lines and painting classrooms. There were pictures of Quechuan natives in their bright, dyed shawls and black top hats, standing in the Andes snow, wearing sandals made from tire treads.

Everyone laughed at a slide of a little boy showing off his new eyeglasses, beaming as proudly as if he'd just won a gold medal.

Another slide showed a group of American women bathing babies. Then there were several slides of small children sleeping in doorways or begging, their eyes dark and expressionless. The presentation was set to music and the emotional effect was potent. When the lights came up, most of those in the room were wiping back tears. Jessica handed Christine a Kleenex.

Jim walked to the front of the room. "That's what it's all about. The chance to find yourself by losing yourself in service to others. I look forward to seeing you all in a couple weeks. You have my number. If you have any questions, please call. Otherwise, I'll see you, on time, at the airport."

As the group rose to leave, Christine, still sniffing, said, "I'll go."

Jessica looked at her. "What?"

I said, "I'll go."

Jessica smiled. "You'll never regret it."

As the room emptied, Jessica stopped to talk to Jim. "It worked," she said, "Christine was blubbering like a baby."

He smiled triumphantly. "The slide show gets them every time."

CHAPTER

Seven

It is always winter somewhere . . .
✦ PAUL COOK'S DIARY ✦

"I'm *so* glad we're getting out of winter," Jessica said. With the Jeep's heater blasting on full it was hard to believe that somewhere in the world it was summer. "Girl, we're coming back with tans."

"Yeah, that's good," Christine said softly.

Jessica frowned and turned away. Christine had grown quiet for most of the drive. Jessica guessed that she was regretting her decision. But Christine had grown melancholy for other reasons. She still hadn't heard from Martin and she doubted that he even knew or cared that she was going.

Jessica parked in the airport's long-term parking lot; the two women gathered their carry-on luggage and shuttled to the terminal. Not far from their entry they found Jim, alone, surrounded by a small mountain of second-hand suitcases, backpacks and large canvas duffel bags. In one hand he held a clipboard, which he lifted as they approached.

Jessica lit up in his presence. "Hey, gorgeous."

He smiled. "I was beginning to wonder if you two had changed your minds."

"No chance of that," Jessica said.

Christine didn't look as excited. Jim said to her, "You're going to be glad you came."

"It's for the children," Christine said. "I keep telling myself that."

"What's all this luggage?" Jessica asked.

"Supplies. We've got hygiene kits, eyeglasses, books, blankets, medicine, everything we'll need."

"Can we help you?" Christine asked.

"No, I'm just waiting for a porter. You need to check in at the counter, then go on down to Terminal B. Be sure to be at gate 42 no later than ten-thirty. We'll board together."

"See ya," Jessica said.

"Hasta luego," Jim replied.

"Hasta what?" Jessica said.

"It means 'see you later,' " Christine said.

✦

Christine had never left the country, and standing in the airport's international terminal amid a Babel of foreign languages, she felt the rising discomfort of culture shock.

They perused the airport stores as they waited. Christine bought a paperback romance and some Dramamine, which she took immediately while Jessica filled her purse with magazines and candy. A half hour later Jim arrived at the gate, and the group congregated around him. He quickly went down the roll.

"We're missing Bryan Davis and Kent Wood. Does anyone know where they went?"

A young woman raised her hand. "They went to get Chinese food in the other terminal."

Jim shook his head and sighed. *"¡Aye! caramba.* Listen up, everyone. It's very important that we stay together—*especially* when we arrive in Peru. Everyone please board, do not wait for me. I'll go look for them."

Christine and Jessica boarded with the rest of the group. Their seats were in the rear compartment of the 737, Jessica in the window seat with Christine in the middle. In the aisle seat was a tiny gray-haired Peruvian woman.

Christine looked down at her watch. "What do we do if Jim doesn't make it?"

"We'll cross that bridge when it collapses," she said. "Wait to worry."

Just a few minutes after the plane's scheduled departure, Jim came walking down the aisle trailing two young men with sheepish looks.

As soon as the plane left the ground, Jessica pulled out her iPod, put in her ear buds, propped a pillow against the window, then lay back with her eyes closed. Christine leafed through one of Jessica's magazines until the Dramamine finally kicked in and she fell asleep against Jessica's shoulder. An hour later she was awoken by the Peruvian woman, who was shaking her shoulder and speaking to her in Spanish. It took a minute for Christine to figure out what she wanted. The flight attendants were serving a meal and the woman thought Christine should know about it. Christine thanked her, then closed her eyes. It took her nearly an hour to fall back asleep.

Three and a half hours later the pilot came on the speaker announcing their descent into Lima's Jorge Chávez airport. The announcement was repeated in Spanish and the Peruvian passengers applauded. Twenty minutes later they clapped again when the plane touched down. The passengers disembarked and were herded to the Immigration counters. From the jetway Christine could feel the warmth and humidity of the Peruvian air.

Inside Immigration, Jim corralled the group, his clipboard in hand. The stress of shepherding such a large group was already evident on his face. "Each of you must pick up two of our bags of supplies and carry them through customs. They are clearly marked with one of these bright orange stickers with our Puma-Condor logo. It doesn't matter which bags you grab, as long as you have two of them apiece. Outside of customs there are two men who will take the bags from you and recheck them onto our next flight. Once they have your luggage, just wait inside the terminal. We only have a few hours before our next flight, so do not wander off. *Do not leave the airport,*" he said firmly, glancing meaningfully at the two boys who had delayed the flight. He walked through his group handing everyone immigration declaration cards. As he got to Christine, she asked, "Having fun?"

"It's like herding cats."

"Get any sleep?" Jessica asked.

"I never sleep on these trips. How about you two?"

"I slept like a log," Jessica said.

"Not enough," Christine said.

"Well, you can catch up in Cuzco. By the way, this is a good time to exchange money. The exchange rate in the airport is better than at the hotels."

"How much should we change?"

"Maybe fifty dollars. You won't need much for now."

As Jim watched over the group's stragglers, Jessica and Christine passed through Immigration, pulled four suitcases from the carousel and lugged them through Customs. As promised, two Peruvian men, both young and wearing white tank tops, Levi's and sneakers, stood outside the terminal with a large baggage cart and holding a sign that read PUMA-CONDOR EXPEDITIONS. They left their luggage with the men, then went inside the terminal. They exchanged some money, then wandered around while they waited for the rest of the group to arrive.

When Jim came, he led them to another gate, where they boarded a smaller plane. They touched down in Cuzco around one in the afternoon.

Even before the plane's hatch opened, Christine could feel the effects of the altitude; her head ached and it felt as if her sinuses were going to explode. The temperature was unseasonably cool for Cuzco—much cooler than in Lima, and Christine wrapped her arms around herself as they walked outside to the airport's parking lot.

She stopped to look around. The Cuzco airport was considerably smaller than the Lima international, but the ratio of foreigners to natives was higher. As the heart of the Incan civilization, Cuzco attracted a steady flow of foreign tourists.

In the middle of the parking lot was a large concrete obelisk capped with a bronze bust of the airport's namesake. Modern billboards surrounded the airport with laptop and cell-phone advertisements, all in Spanish. At one end of the airport was a soccer field and at the other, near the bus-loading zone, were a row of small wooden stalls with Peruvian handicrafts. While Jessica went to peruse the shops, Christine sat down on a curb and watched their luggage being loaded into the bus's belly. Her light-headedness increased, and she rested her head in her hand. Jim walked up behind her and sat on the curb next to her. "How's it going?"

"Okay."

"Still tired?"

"I have a headache."

"Probably altitude sickness. We're eleven thousand feet up." After a moment he said, "I'll get you something for it." He stood back up and walked across the lot to a woman wearing a white top hat and bright Quechuan attire. He handed her a coin, and she handed him a small plastic bag filled with dark green leaves. He brought it over to Christine.

"Here."

"What is it?" she asked, examining the leaves.

"Coca leaves."

"Coca? Like cocaine?"

"Same leaf. But it's for tea. It will help with altitude sickness. You can get some hot water at the hotel."

Christine looked at the leaves warily.

"Don't worry, you won't fail your company

drug testing." He walked back to the bus and went inside to talk to the driver.

Just then Jessica walked up wearing a colorful shawl. She looked at the bag in Christine's hands. "What's that? Cocaine?"

"It's tea," Christine said.

"I want to try some."

"I'll share."

She held up her arms and spun around, whirling the shawl. "What do you think?"

"It's pretty."

"It was only fifty soles."

Jim emerged from the bus. "Let's go," he shouted.

✦

A half hour later the bus sided up to the curb in front of the Vilandre Hotel. The group crowded the small lobby. Christine lay on a couch, feeling tired and sick, while the hotel staff began handing out room keys. Jessica and Christine were assigned a room on the third floor. The hotel only had one elevator, so they climbed the stairs.

Jessica opened their door but stopped in the threshold. "Prepare yourself."

"For what?"

"Serious u-g-l-y."

The room was of average hotel room size, austere and dated. The drapes were tan and sun-faded, and the carpet, mauve and balding, was far past its prime if it ever had one. The room's floorboards looked to be of light oak and were scuffed and chipped. There were two twin beds with dark umber quilts, threadbare in places. Between the beds was a simple wooden nightstand.

Christine looked around. "Well, I wasn't expecting the Four Seasons." She stepped inside, set her bags on the bed and opened them. She took out her few clothes and hung them in the closet; then threw her pillow on top of the bedspread. From an inside pocket she took out a bracelet, crouched down and wrapped it around the leg of the bed.

"What's *that?*" Jessica asked.

"They said to bring flea collars."

Jessica stared at the band. "That doesn't look like a flea collar." She took a step closer.

"It was ugly. I hot-glued rhinestones on it." She pulled out three more and fastened them around the remaining legs of the bed.

Jessica burst out laughing until she fell on

her back on the opposite bed. Christine's face tightened. "Don't mock me."

When Jessica finally gained her composure, she wiped tears from her eyes and said, "I'm sorry. You're one of a kind. You're the only girl I know who would mop a dirt floor."

"Glad you find me so amusing." Christine said stiffly. She sat on the corner of the bed and lay back. The mattress was hard and musty.

Jessica sighed loudly, then went to the window and parted the curtains. The rooftops below them were mostly terra-cotta tile with stucco or concrete walls. Clotheslines stretched from building to building like great webs.

"Can you believe we're really here?" Jessica asked.

Christine screamed.

Jessica spun around. "What?"

Christine pointed toward the corner of the room. "There's something up there."

Jessica looked up. A small olive drab–colored lizard clung to the wall. She exhaled with relief. "Man! I thought it was a tarantula or something. It's only a gecko." Jessica walked up to it for a closer look. "They're good luck."

"I can't sleep in a room with lizards crawling around it."

"Can't or won't?"

"Pick one."

"They won't hurt you. Besides, they eat spiders."

"That's comforting."

"Don't be such a wimp."

"It's for the children," Christine said, lying back in the bed. Jessica sat down on the other bed. The springs squeaked beneath her.

"I'm going out to see the city. Want to come?"

"I need sleep. When will you be back?"

"I don't know. Jim invited us all to dinner."

"When?"

"Five."

She glanced at her watch. It was almost two.

"Where are we meeting?"

"The restaurant is in the Plaza. I'll write the address down for you." She got up and scribbled the restaurant's name and address on the back of her airline ticket. "I'm sure they'll be others from the group downstairs when it's time to go. Just come with them."

"All right," Christine said, rolling over, "I'll meet you there."

Jessica stopped in the doorway. "Five o'clock."

"Five o'clock."

"Need a wake-up call?"

"No."

"Maybe you should wear a flea collar around your neck. It might protect you from the gecko."

"Go away."

Jessica grinned. "See ya."

The door shut. Christine rolled over and, clutching her pillow, fell asleep.

CHAPTER

Eight

As much as I have schemed and planned to the contrary, the most central experiences of my life have all been accidents.

✦ PAUL COOK'S DIARY ✦

When Christine woke, the room's curtains glowed dim orange. She immediately looked to where the lizard had been and it was still there, which relieved her on two counts—first, she knew where it was, and second, anything that lethargic couldn't be much of a threat.

She glanced at her watch. It was already ten minutes past five o'clock. She brushed her hair, grabbed her purse, then rushed downstairs hoping to still catch someone from the group. The lobby was vacant except for a middle-aged clerk and a cleaning lady who was spraying plants from a plastic water bottle. She went to the registration counter where the clerk was writing. "Excuse me, sir."

He looked up and smiled. "Yes, *Señorita.*"

"Is this restaurant far from here?" She handed him the address.

He glanced at the ticket then back up. "It

is far to walk. But by taxi it is not far. It is in
the Plaza."

"How much should it cost?"

"It should be just two soles."

"Two *soles*?"

"Yes. Do you have soles?"

"I have these."

She took out a handful of coins and began
to look through them.

"It is this one," the clerk said, pulling a
silver coin from the pile. "Two of them. And
you should take this." He handed her the
hotel's card. "In case you be lost."

"Thank you," she said, stowing the money
and card in her pocket. "Where is the best
place to find a taxi?"

"In the road, *Señorita.*"

She wasn't sure if he was making fun
of her, but he looked sincere so she just
thanked him, returned her wallet to her
purse and walked out of the hotel.

Outside, the air was moist and warm and
filled with the sound of traffic: the rumbling
of older cars, the whining of small motorcycles and the incessant honking of both. A
few feet from the door a young man was
beating a rug against a lamppost.

Christine was immediately set upon by

street vendors hawking their wares. She stopped to look over their offerings. There were small toy llama dolls, sweaters and hats of alpaca wool, and silver and turquoise jewelry on long black velvet-covered trays.

She crouched over a tray and lifted a small pair of sterling earrings. Someone bumped into her. She turned to see a small, tangle-haired boy pulling his hand from her purse. He had her wallet.

"Hey . . ."

The boy darted off. Just then a man stepped from the crowd and grabbed the boy around the waist, lifting him from the ground. He carried the child over to her. When he was near, he said to the boy, *"Devuélveselo a la señorita." Return it to the woman.*

The boy's eyes darted nervously between the man and Christine. Then he timidly surrendered his catch. *"Gracias,"* the man said. He gently pried the wallet from the boy's hands and held it out to her. She put her wallet back in her purse.

"Muy bien. Ahora vete," the man said to the boy. He set the boy back down on the

pavement and the child disappeared like a fish released into a stream.

Christine stared at the stranger. He had long, coffee-colored hair that fell almost to his shoulders beneath a worn, tan leather hat. A leather thong hung around his neck, disappearing into the V of his shirt. His eyes were blue and piercing and his skin was almost the color of the hat, dark from the sun. He had a slightly boyish face yet was rugged-looking, his chin and jaw covered with the start of a new beard. She guessed him to be American or European or maybe Australian, but he did not look out of place. Looking at him, she felt suddenly awkward. "Do you speak English?" she asked.

"*Sí, Señorita.*" The roughness of his face vanished in a pleasant smile. "Are you okay?" The accent was American.

"Yes. Thank you."

"You're welcome."

She stared at him, not sure what else to say but wanting to say more. There was an energy about this man that intrigued her. She asked, "Why did you let him go?"

"Peru has a strict catch-and-release policy with street children," he said. She realized that he was joking and she smiled. He likewise smiled. "Can I help you get some-where?"

"I was just about to hail a cab."

"Allow me." He stepped to the curb and held his arm out to the oncoming traffic. A small car immediately pulled over.

Christine stepped to the car. "Thank you."

"*¿A dónde va?*" the driver asked.

"Where are you going?" the American asked her.

She held out the ticket. "This place. It's a restaurant." He looked at the address and said to the driver, *"La señorita va al restau-rante Inca Wall en la Plaza de Armas."* He turned back to her. "You must be in one of Jim Hammer's groups."

"You know Jim?"

"I know him well. He loves that restaurant. Try the *cuy.*"

"*Cuy?*"

"It's a local delicacy."

"Thank you. I will."

He opened the car's door for her. After she had climbed in, he said to the driver, *"Señor, el restaurante está al norte de la Plaza de Armas. Gracias."* He turned to her. "He knows where to go."

"Thank you," she said again.

"It's nothing," he said. *"Hasta luego."* He shut the door behind her, then walked away as the taxi surged forward, merging into the traffic. Christine was somewhat dazed by the whole experience, and she glanced back once more to see him but he was gone. *Hasta luego.* Would she see him later?

The cab jostled through the traffic and she sat back in the seat. There were no seatbelts, which, from the look of the car, didn't surprise her. The tears in the vinyl seats were taped together with duct tape. Rosary beads dangled and swayed from the driver's mirror. She noticed the driver glance in the mirror at her and she looked away. It frightened her a little; she felt vulnerable.

A few moments later the cab arrived in the Plaza, stopping before a long row of buildings, Spanish colonial in design.

"That was fast," she said. She leaned forward, holding out the address. "Could you tell me where this is?"

The driver looked down at her paper, then pointed to a small red door in the stucco-faced frontage. *"Está allí,"* he said.

"Gracias," she said, *"¿Cuánto?"*

"Dos soles."

She handed him two coins.

"Gracias, Señorita."

Christine stepped out of the taxi onto the black cobblestone street.

The Plaza de Armas was the center of the historic district of Cuzco and looked much more European than she had expected. The dominating feature of the square was the Cathedral, a large, seventeenth-century Baroque structure, domed, and with two large bell towers. In Incan times the square was called Huacaypata—Warrior Square—and it was here that Pizarro had proclaimed his conquest of Cuzco and the Incan civilization. The Cathedral was a monument to their victory, built on the stone foundation of the palace of the Incan king.

In the center of the plaza was a large central square, its cobblestone walkway in the shape of a Latin cross. On the north end of the square was a green fountain with a swan motif. Christine thought that it looked like an oversized grail, its fluted bowls spilling water into the pool below where satyr-faced mermen sprayed water from their horns.

The perimeter of the Plaza was embellished with stone archways, the *portales* of the colorful shops of local artisans and restaurateurs.

Almost as quickly as the cab pulled away from the curb, Christine was surrounded by a group of children, dirty-faced, barefooted, their clothes dirty and ragged. They came at her aggressively and in competition with each other, their hands thrust out to her, some with their wares and some just open-palmed. Christine looked at them sympathetically but gripped her purse tightly.

"Pretty lady, postcards for sale, just one sol. Cheap," a girl said, waving the postcards in front of her. Another child dropped to her feet with a dirty cloth. "Shoe shine, *Señorita.* I shine your shoes."

"Chocolate, sublime," a younger boy said, his eyes white with cataracts, "yummy, *chocolate."*

One bright-faced boy of six or seven said, "George Bush, Bill Clinton, Abraham Lincoln, yes, yes, yes." He held up one thumb and his other hand was out for a donation.

Christine took from her purse a handful of money and gave each child a sol. She walked to the restaurant, still followed by the children, who knew an easy mark when they saw one. They continued to beg until a man standing at the restaurant's entrance lifted his hand and shouted at them and they ran away.

The man opened the door for her and she stepped inside. The restaurant was cool and dark, with terra-cotta floor tiles and stucco walls. The back wall was painted with an Inca-inspired mural. In the center of the restaurant was a rotisserie spit where roasting meat dropped juice into a hissing fire, filling the room with its aroma. When her eyes adjusted to the dim lighting, she could see a large group occupying several tables near the back of the restaurant. Jessica was sitting next to Jim and wearing his hat. As she walked toward the group, someone shouted, "There she is."

Her arrival was met with clapping and cheers and a few groans.

"You made it," Jessica said.

Christine looked at the others. "What's this about?" she asked.

"We had a pool going that you wouldn't find us."

"Gee, thanks," she said, sitting down. She turned and said to the table behind her, "I hope you all lost your money."

Everyone laughed.

"What took you so long?" Jessica asked.

"I slept in."

"Should have gotten that wake-up call," Jessica scolded.

"No," Jim said, "She needed the sleep. Best thing for altitude sickness. How are you feeling?"

"I was feeling great. Up until I got pickpocketed."

"Pickpocketed?" Jessica said.

Jim shook his head and groaned. "How much did you lose?"

"My wallet, for a minute. I got it back. Some American just came out of nowhere and grabbed the kid and made him give it back to me." Christine said to Jim, "He knew you."

"He knew me?"

Christine nodded. "He asked if I was with your group."

"What did he look like?"

"He was kind of tall, with long brown hair—kind of rugged-looking."

"Sounds dreamy," Jessica said.

"Paul Cook," Jim said. "He runs the orphanage we're going to tomorrow. You must have been near the hotel, he was dropping some things off for me."

"I can't wait to meet him," Jessica said, and Jim looked at her.

Just then a waitress appeared carrying several large platters. On one of them was some kind of rodent that had been cooked whole. It looked more like it had been prepared by a taxidermist than a chef. She set it in front of Jim.

"What is *that?*" Jessica asked.

"I'm going to be sick," Christine said.

"I'd be more inclined to bury it than eat it," someone said.

Jim smiled, clearly enjoying the shock his meal produced. "It's fried guinea pig. The Peruvians call it *cuy.*"

"*Cuy?*" Christine asked.

"Yeah. Heard of it?"

"Your friend Paul told me to try it."

Jim grinned. "Yeah, that was Paul."

The waitress set a platter in front of Jessica. There was a fried banana and a baked chicken breast with yellow rice. "Here, Chris, there's enough for both of us."

"I'm starving," she said. "I could eat anything." She glanced at Jim's platter. "Almost . . ."

They ate at a leisurely pace, and when they had finished eating, they moved out of the restaurant into the plaza. It was dark by that time and evening brought to the square a festival atmosphere. A Peruvian folk band, dressed in the brightly dyed weaves of the traditional Quechuan costume, played in the center of the plaza for the donations tourists would throw them. The storekeepers had moved tables filled with merchandise out to the covered walkways, and the square was reborn as a night market, alive with the sound of commerce, music and crowds.

Jessica and Jim had paired off, leaving Christine feeling a little awkward, and she soon wandered off on her own. There were lovers everywhere and where she had tried to push aside thoughts of Martin, they came back stronger now, like an itch delayed. Heaviness settled in her chest as she meandered between the labyrinth of tables and racks of clothing.

Christine's mother collected bells, and Christine found a small sterling bell with a llama figurine on top to add to her collection. She bought it for thirty soles. The woman wrapped it in newspaper and Christine stowed it in her pocket.

At another store she rooted through a

table of clothes and found a black alpaca vest and a matching man's hat. She thought Martin would like so she bought them for him as much out of habit as hope.

She spotted Jessica and Jim sitting on the small concrete ledge around the fountain, and when she had finished her shopping, she walked back to them. They didn't see her approach.

"Hey, guys."

They both looked over. "Where'd you go?" Jessica asked.

"Just shopping."

Jessica looked down at the sack she carried. "What did you buy?"

"Stuff. Clothes."

"Show me," Jessica said.

Christine suddenly felt foolish for buying something for Martin. "I'll show you later. I'm going back to the hotel."

"So soon?" Jim asked. "The night's young."

"Younger than I feel," she said. "I'm a little tired."

"You know the way back?" Jim asked.

"The desk clerk gave me a card," Christine said.

"Don't wait up," Jessica said.

Christine walked to the street and hailed a cab. Back in the room she looked for the gecko, which was still in the same place, and she now wondered if it was even alive. She stowed the bag with Martin's alpaca vest and hat under her bed. She didn't want Jessica to see it, as she knew she would scold her for buying them. Still, she scolded herself. Why did she hang on? Martin hadn't even sent her an e-mail since the day he broke off the wedding.

She knew why. Desperation breeds hope. A counselor had once told her she had abandonment issues. *No kidding,* she thought. Her own father had left her, first through divorce, then, just a year ago, through death. Now, Martin had left her as well. Could she trust any man to stick around? She turned off the light, then got in bed, pulling the covers up to her chin.

In the darkness she thought of the gecko. She wondered if it was exclusively a wall-dweller or if it ever came on to the beds. Christine pushed the thought from her mind. She closed her eyes and rolled over in bed, hugging the pillow. Her mind briefly wandered through the day's happenings. *What would tomorrow bring?* Then she thought of the man who had saved her wallet. Paul. She wondered what he was doing down here and if she'd see him tomorrow at the orphanage. And on the threshold of slumber she hoped that she would.

CHAPTER

Nine

Today I overheard an American
teenager comparing her deprivation
to that of our children, because her
parents would only buy her a used
car. There are none so impoverished
as those who do not acknowledge
the abundance of their lives.

✦ PAUL COOK'S DIARY ✦

Jessica had already gone downstairs for breakfast when Christine came out of the shower. She toweled off, then pulled on her Levi's. They were the loosest they'd been for nearly a decade.

At least the engagement wasn't a total waste, Christine thought. She finished dressing, grabbed her backpack, then went downstairs to join Jessica.

The ground floor was an open, windowless space with pink plaster walls and travel posters of Cuzco tourist attractions. Jessica was sitting in the corner of the room under a poster of a herd of llamas. She was with two of the people from the group, an older woman with a broad face sporting thick, tortoiseshell glasses and a man, short and plump, with a red face and a pleasant smile.

Jessica waved. "Over here."

Christine walked to the table.

"Buenos días," the woman said. "I'm Joan Morton."

"Hello, Joan."

The man extended his hand. "And I'm Mason," he said with a southern accent. "Mason Affleck from Birmingham."

"My pleasure. I'm Christine."

"For the record," Joan said, "I was betting on you last night."

"Thank you. I'm sure it's more than Jessica could say."

Jessica grinned. "Sorry, honey, I know you too well."

"Thanks, babe." Christine looked over their plates. "So what's good?"

"The French toast looks weird but it's good," Jessica said.

"Try the prickly pear," Joan said.

"Is it good?"

"No, but you'll have something to talk about when you get home."

"What's that you're drinking?" Christine asked Jessica.

"I don't know. The sign said GUANABANA, whatever that means."

"And?"

"It's okay."

Christine walked over to the buffet tables.

She picked through the entrées and came back with an apple, a banana and orange juice.

"I see you're not feeling adventurous," Jessica said.

"Not really."

"You feelin' any better?" Mason asked. "Jessica said you had the altitude sickness."

"I did. But I feel a lot better now. I guess I just needed a good night's rest."

"I still have kind of a buzz myself," Joan said.

"What time *did* you get back last night?" Christine asked Jessica.

"Late. After midnight."

"What were you doing?"

"Just talking. I think we were the last ones in the square."

"Speaking of which," Christine said, looking around, "where is everybody?"

"Probably boarding the bus," Jessica said. She checked her watch and groaned. "We're late. We've got to go."

Christine downed her juice, then put the fruit in her backpack. All three of them hurried out.

Jim was standing outside the bus waiting.

"Here you are. I thought you'd gone AWOL."

"No, someone kept me up too late," Jessica said.

"Who kept who up?" he rejoined.

"Sorry we're late," Christine said.

"We're all right," Jim said, climbing on behind them.

The bus door shut as they found seats. Jim nodded to the driver, and they started off.

As they left Cuzco, Jim said, "Let's talk about today's project. We're headed to a town about thirty minutes south of here called Lucre. We'll be working at an old hacienda converted to an orphanage. It's called the Sunflower.

"The orphanage was founded about six years ago by a Peruvian policeman by the name of Alcides Romero. Alcides had become frustrated with how the police handled Cuzco's street children. Unable to arrest them, they basically ignored them, leaving them to starve in the streets.

"Alcides decided to do something. He knew of this abandoned hacienda and with his comandante's support he talked the state bureaucrats into donating it to the police. Then he took half his salary and paid for food to keep the children here. We learned about what he was doing a few years ago and have been helping ever since. For just a few dollars a month we can keep a child fed, clothed and educated."

The bus climbed a dusty road past plaster huts. As they came around a turn, the broad stone and adobe walls of the hacienda stretched out before them.

Once the home of a wealthy eighteenth-century landowner, even in its decline it was clear that the building had been magnificent.

The ground behind the hacienda sloped upward into shallow foothills covered in lush vegetation and large cacti that looked like overgrown aloe vera plants. As the Americans wound their way through the narrow dirt streets, the townspeople, crouched in doorways or walking, watched them pass while cats scurried up trees and dogs ran barking after them.

The bus crept down a steep, gravel slope, stopping at the side of the hacienda, twenty yards east of the rising foothills.

Jim led the group off the bus and down a small path into the hacienda's rectangular courtyard. On one end was a row of windows and on the other was a high wall with several openings for bells.

A short Peruvian man wearing a dirty Puma-Condor T-shirt rushed out to meet them. *"Hermano,"* he said, embracing Jim.

"Hola, Jaime," Jim said, *"¿Qué tal?"*

"Muy bien," he replied enthusiastically. He looked around at the group and extended his hands in the air. *"¡Bienvenidos!"* he shouted.

"He says 'welcome,' " Jim said. "All right, everyone gather up."

The group congregated around the rock wall of a fountain.

"Everything we do is to help the orphanage become more self-sufficient. We've been asked to help them build a greenhouse. We also need a couple volunteers to paint the schoolroom."

Jessica's hand shot up. "We'll do it."

Jim glanced about to see if there were any more takers. None offered. "Okay, Jessica and Christine, you're hired. Jaime here will show you to the room. The rest of you follow me."

Jim led the group through the portico to the hacienda's backyard, leaving Christine and Jessica in the center of the courtyard with Jaime.

"What was that about?" Christine asked.

"Building a greenhouse didn't sound like too much fun."

Jaime looked them over then said, "Okay, *vamos.*"

They followed him to a dim room at the end of a tiled corridor. The room was cavernous and high ceilinged, lit by a single open window. In the center of the room was a metal scaffolding surrounded by sealed cans of paint, an aluminum tray and several paint rollers.

"We paint," he announced, his words echoing in the room.

"Certainly needs it," Christine said.

Jessica looked around. "Probably a century or two since it was painted last." She walked to the center of the room, and stretched out her arms. "Show us thy bidding, Master Jaime."

Jaime looked at her quizzically, then stooped down and pried the lid off the can of paint with a screwdriver. The pale yellow paint was separated. He took the can and set it down next to Jessica and the scaffolding.

"Do you have something to stir the paint?" Jessica asked.

Jaime didn't answer.

"Stir . . . paint," she said, moving her hand in a circular motion.

"Ah," Jaime nodded, *"Mezclar."* He walked out of the room. He returned carrying a short crooked branch. He handed it to Jessica, then went to the opposite side of the room to repair a splintered doorjamb.

Jessica brushed the dirt from the stick, then began to stir the yellow into a deeper gold tone.

"Where are all the children?" Christine asked.

Jaime blinked at her.

"The children . . ." she said slowly. "Chill-dren."

"Ah," he said. *"Niños."*

"Sí."

"Los niños están en la escuela. The school."

"I hope Jim comes back," Jessica said. She tilted the paint can toward Christine. "You think that's good enough?"

"Probably."

"Ask him if they have a drop cloth."

"Yeah, right," Christine said.

They poured the paint into an aluminum tray, then dipped their rollers into it.

"What do we do with the cracks in the wall?" Christine asked, "Maybe they have spackle."

Jessica looked around. "Just paint over them."

"Jaime," Christine said.

He turned. *"Señorita?"*

She pointed to a small fracture in the wall. "Do we paint over the cracks?"

He nodded demonstratively moving his hand back and forth. "Yes. Paint," he said.

"Told you," Jessica said. She rested her hands on her hips. "As if he understood."

"Sure he did."

"Jaime."

He turned again. *"Señorita?"*

She pointed to Jessica. "Should I paint Jessica?"

He nodded. "Yes. Paint."

Jessica started laughing. "Touché."

They started on the south wall. Christine painted the lower section, stretching as high as she could reach with her roller, while Jessica stood on the scaffolding, reaching to the ceiling.

It took them about forty minutes to complete the first wall. Then they dragged the scaffolding over to the next wall. As they picked up their rollers Christine noticed a small boy standing near the door, partially hidden in the shadows. He had coffee-colored skin, large brown eyes and eyelashes long enough to make her jealous.

Christine whispered loudly, "Jessica, look."

Jessica glanced over. When she saw the child, a smile broke across her face. "Have you ever seen anything so cute in your life?"

The boy just gazed at them.

Jaime noticed that they had stopped working and looked over at the boy.

"¿Por qué no estás en la escuela?" *How come you're not in school?*

"Estamos en recreo," he replied. *It's recess.*

"How old do you think he is?" Christine asked.

"He's about the size of my nephew and he's six."

Jessica set down her brush and climbed down from the scaffolding. She stepped toward him, then squatted down to his height. "Where did you come from, little guy?"

He didn't answer. His eyes darted back and forth between the two of them.

"He's gorgeous. Say something in Spanish, Chris. Ask him his name."

Christine stepped up to him. *"¿Cómo . . . te . . . llamas?"*

He looked at them suspiciously.

"¿Tu nombre?"

"My name is Pablo," he said in perfect - English. "I'll be eight years old tomorrow. It's my birthday. I'm just small for my age."

"You speak *really* good English," Jessica said.

"So do you," he replied.

Jessica laughed. "Where'd you learn English so well?"

"Dr. Cook."

"¿Cuándo llega el doctor Cook?" Jaime asked.

"Ya viene." Pablo translated for them. "He wants to know when Dr. Cook will be here. I told him Dr. Cook is coming."

"Who's Dr. Cook?" Jessica asked.

"He's the boss," Pablo said as a man entered the room. Christine immediately recognized him as the one who had rescued her purse. He smiled. "Hello again."

"Thank you again."

"You're welcome." He extended his hand. "I'm Paul Cook."

"I'm Christine."

"My pleasure, Christine."

Jessica stepped forward. "I'm Jessica."

"Hi. Thank you for helping us." He looked down at the boy. "I see you've met Pablo."

"Cute kid," Jessica said.

"He's a handful," Paul returned. He looked around the room. "It's looking much better."

"One wall down, three to go."

"Que pasa, calabaza," Jaime said.

"Nada, nada, limonada," Paul replied. He turned to the women. "Is Jaime being good to you?"

"He's great. We just don't speak much."

Paul smiled. "Be careful, he understands more than he lets on." He walked to the wall, inspecting their work. "When you're done, this room will be used as a classroom."

"Jaime said the kids all went somewhere else to school."

"Right now they do. But it's not the best situation. Most of them are far behind their classmates. It's embarrassing for the teenagers to be in with the first-graders."

"Can I help them paint?" Pablo asked.

Paul looked at the women. "Is that okay with you?"

"Sure," Jessica said.

"All right," he said to Pablo, "But you have to work hard." He looked back at the women. "I'll see you a little later." He glanced once more at Christine, then walked out. Jaime followed him out of the room, speaking and gesticulating as they walked.

"He's *gorgeous,*" Jessica said.

"You say that a lot," Pablo said.

Jessica grinned. "All right, Pablo, let's put you to work." They walked over to the scaffolding. "Have you painted before?"

"I like to paint pictures."

"This is a little different. Actually it's a lot different. You can use my roller. You dip it in the paint like this. Then roll it off a little in the pan so it doesn't drip. Then you roll it on the wall."

She helped guide his movement. "I can do it myself," he said.

"Good. Because we've got a lot to do."

Jessica picked up another roller, then climbed back up the scaffolding. Pablo settled next to Christine to work. After a few minutes Christine said, "Tell us about yourself, Pablo."

"What do you want to know?"

"Tell us about your life."

His brow furrowed. "My life is very tragical."

"Tragical?"

He nodded. "Very."

"Don't you mean 'tragic'?" Jessica said.

He shook his head. "No, tragical."

"Why is it tragical?" Christine asked.

"You're going to make me talk about it?"

Christine smiled. "You don't have to talk about it. We'll talk about something happy. Tomorrow's your birthday?"

"Yes."

"You'll be eight?"

"Yes. We're having a party. A big one. We made a piñata."

"Sounds fun. Can I come?"

"You'll have to ask Dr. Cook. He's the boss."

"We'll get you a birthday present anyway," Christine said.

"Thanks."

"How long have you lived here?" Jessica asked.

"Long, long time."

This sounded funny coming from an almost-eight-year-old boy. "Where are you from?" Christine asked.

At this he hesitated. "I don't know." He looked down and went back to his painting.

✦

They had nearly completed the third wall when they heard the clang of a bell.

"Time for lunch," Pablo said, and he immediately set his roller on the ground and ran out of the room.

Christine smiled. "Guess he was hungry." She went to the door and looked out. Their group had returned to the courtyard. They were standing in small lines to pick up their box lunches or already seated to eat.

They poured the paint from the trays back into the can, sealed it then went out. On one side of the courtyard a water fight raged between the high school students, who were filling buckets from a hand pump and dousing each other. The Peruvian workers watched in amusement.

Jessica got two box lunches while Christine went for their drinks. They sat down together on the stone wall next to the fountain where Pablo and several of the Peruvians had gathered.

"Thanks for your help, Pablo," Christine said.

"It's nothing."

The sun was high in the sky and Jessica leaned back to take it in. "Isn't this weather incredible?"

"Everyone will think we've been hitting the tanning beds," Christine said. She looked down at the box lunch. "So what's for *almuerzo?*"

"Huh?"

"Lunch," Christine said.

Jessica rooted through her box. "A hard yellow roll with a fatty piece of ham and a slab of yellow cheese. A banana. Sweet-potato chips. A piece of chocolate. We're definitely losing weight. What are we drinking?"

"Strawberry yogurt," Christine said, handing her a small carton.

Jim stopped by. "How's the painting going, ladies?"

"You should come see for yourself," Jessica said. She unpeeled a banana, then pulled at its strings. "How about you guys?"

"We're making progress. It's definitely a three-day job."

"Come eat with us," Christine said.

"Thanks, but the driver just told me he's having trouble with the bus, so I better take care of that."

"Yeah, we'd like to go home tonight," Jessica said.

"I'll get you home." He turned to Pablo, who was sitting quietly eating his sandwich. "Hey, Pablo. Staying out of trouble?"

"No."

"He's been helping us," Christine said.

"Pablo always helps. He's a good worker."

"Thanks," Pablo said.

"I better run. Chao," Jim said as he walked off.

One of the Peruvian men sitting near them had a bright yellow and red macaw sitting on his shoulder. It would occasionally squawk, and the man would hand it a piece of bread. The bird would take the morsel in its talon, lift it to its beak, then throw its head back and eat.

"That is such a pretty bird," Christine said. "Look at its feathers." She reached out to touch it. "Hello, pretty girl. Hello, pretty girl."

"He'll bite your finger," Pablo said.

She jerked back her hand. "Are you kidding?"

Pablo said to the man holding the bird, *"Carlos. Muéstrale tu dedo."*

Without looking at them, he raised a scarred finger.

"Thanks for the warning," Christine said.

Just then, on the other side of the courtyard, Paul emerged from a room, picked up one of the box lunches, then sat alone on the stairs opposite them. Both women watched him.

"Wouldn't throw him out of bed for eating crackers," Jessica said.

"Quit ogling," Christine said.

Jessica said, "Let's go talk to him."

Christine glanced at him again. He met her gaze and she quickly turned away.

"Okay."

Taking their lunches with them, they crossed the courtyard. Paul looked up as they neared.

"Mind if we join you?"

He smiled, "Of course not." He slid over to the side of the stair. Jessica sat closest to him while Christine sat three steps below.

"How's the painting coming?"

"It's coming," Jessica said. "How long has this place been an orphanage?"

"About six years."

"How long have you been here?"

His forehead wrinkled with thought. "Maybe four years."

"You don't know?"

He shook his head, "I guess the country's rubbing off on me."

"How's that?" Christine asked.

"Time's different down here. Back in the states I planned my day in fifteen-minute increments. Here, months go by without so much as a nod."

"Sounds nice," Jessica said.

"It kind of is," he replied.

Christine asked, "Where do the children here come from?"

"Mostly from the police. They pick them up off the street."

"How many children do you have?"

"Right now we have twelve boys."

"No girls?" Jessica asked.

"One."

"Why only one?"

"They're harder to find. The girls don't usually stay on the street as long as the boys."

"Why is that?"

He hesitated. "They're sold into prostitution."

Christine shook her head. "Is something being done about it?"

"The government is trying to strengthen the laws. We're trying to bring in more of them. But we're probably going to have to get a place for just the girls. We had a half-dozen girls here at one time, but it didn't work out."

"Why?"

"They kept selling themselves to the boys."

"Selling themselves?"

"For a *sol.*"

"A sol?" Jessica said. "Isn't that like thirty cents?"

"Everything's cheap here," Paul said grimly. "So, where are you ladies from?"

"Dayton," Jessica said.

"Both of you?" he asked, looking at Christine.

Christine nodded.

"Where are you from?" Jessica asked.

"Minnesota. Mostly."

The women had finished eating. Paul finished his sandwich, then unwrapped the chocolate.

"If you'd like, I'll introduce you to the boys."

"We'd love that," Christine said.

They all rose, and Paul led them along the corridor to the end of the porch where it opened to a large, plain dining room. The room was fragrant from the meal underway, and a large bowl of rice steamed in the middle of a long, rectangular wooden table surrounded by eleven boys. A lanky Peruvian man with thick eyebrows and eyes like two briquettes of coal stood next to a glowing hot plate on the other side of the room stirring a pot of greens. He glanced up at Paul but didn't say anything.

"Buenas tardes," Paul said.

The boys all turned from the food.

"Oye, Paul."

"Todavía vamos a tener la fiesta?" Are we still having our party?

"Por supuesto. Mañana," Paul said. *Of course. Tomorrow.*

He turned back to the women. "This is the family," he said proudly. Starting at the head of the table and moving counterclockwise, he named each boy. "That's René, Carlos,

Washington, Gordon, Samuel, Ronal, Oscar, Jorge, Joe, Deyvis, and Juan Carlos. And that's Richard, our cook. He's new here."

"Does your help live here too?" Jessica asked.

"Only Richard and Jaime." He turned to the boys. *"¿Qué tal si le cantamos una canción?"*

The boys all stood and Paul said, *"Uno, dos, tres . . ."* The boys began to sing. The women applauded when they finished.

"What did it mean?" Christine asked.

"It's a song I wrote for them about El Girasol. It says, 'My shirt might be dirty, my hair's a mess, but it's the boy inside that matters.' "

He waved to the boys. *"Chao, guapos."*

The boys returned with a chorus of good-byes for Paul and the women.

Outside the room, Jessica said, "Can you tell me where the bathrooms are?"

He pointed toward a small opening in the courtyard. "Right over there. You need to walk through and out. Want me to show you?"

"I can find it."

"They're unisex, so I'd recommend locking the door. The guys just barge in."

"Thanks for the warning." She ran off leaving Paul and Christine alone.

"I didn't see the girl," Christine said.

"Roxana doesn't like to eat with the boys. They're a little too rowdy for her. I usually take her lunch to her room." Paul turned toward her and his eyes seemed to settle on her as if finally taking her in. Being alone with him suddenly made her feel a little shy.

"Would you like to meet her?"

"I would."

He led her across the courtyard and up a dark stairwell to an upstairs dormitory containing three bunk beds. Sitting alone on the lower bed of the nearest bunk was a little girl, barefoot and wearing a thin red cotton dress. Remnants of her lunch—an unfinished bowl of rice and a banana peel—sat next to her on the mattress. She was holding a book in her lap but was looking up at them as they entered the room. She had delicate features with dark brown almond-shaped eyes. A large scar ran down the left side of her face.

"*Hola,*" Christine said. The girl didn't respond.

"Roxana is deaf and mute," Paul said.

Christine looked at him quizzically. "Deaf?"

"Yeah."

" . . . But she looked like she was waiting for us when we entered."

"She felt our vibrations."

Paul knelt down on one knee next to her and began to sign.

She answered him, then looked up at Christine, and her hands moved in a fury of motion. The conversation continued for nearly a minute.

"What is she saying?" Christine asked.

"She asked me who the pretty white woman was. I spelled out your name for her and she said that she likes your name. She wants you to know her name is Roxana."

Christine walked up to her. *"Hola,* Roxana."

The little girl turned to Paul and signed again.

"What is she saying now?"

"She says you are beautiful like the women on TV and that she wishes she looked like you."

Christine smiled. "Tell her that I think she's beautiful and I wish that I had beautiful black hair like hers."

Paul signed this. A smile broke across her face and she looked away shyly, unconsciously pulling a strand of hair down over her scar.

Paul kissed her on the cheek, then signed their goodbye. As they walked out of the room, Christine suddenly started to cry. She stepped outside the door and covered her eyes with her hand.

Paul gently touched her arm.

"Are you okay?"

She nodded. Paul reached into his pocket and brought out a napkin and handed it to her. She wiped her eyes. "What happened to her? How'd she get that scar?"

"We don't know. The police found her wandering along a street outside Lucre."

"Who would abandon a deaf child in the street?"

"Children are abandoned every day, Christine. You don't know why. Her parents might be dead. Or maybe they just couldn't feed her."

"I feel so stupid. I've been feeling so sorry for myself."

Paul looked at her sympathetically. "Being with these children has a way of putting all kinds of things in perspective."

Paul noticed Jessica wandering around the courtyard looking for them.

"We're up here," he shouted.

Jessica looked up, shielding her eyes from the sun. "How do I get up?"

"We're coming down," Christine said.

When they reached the courtyard, Jessica noticed Christine's red eyes. "What's wrong?"

"Nothing." Christine said. "Let's go back to work."

"Where's our little helper?" Jessica asked.

"I made him go back to school," Paul said. "I better get off myself. I'll see you tomorrow?"

"Tomorrow," Jessica said.

"Bye," Christine said.

✦

Paul walked to the front gate and the women went back to their painting. They finished about three hours later and were cleaning up when the bell rang again. They walked outside, their clothes and hair spattered with paint. Jim was standing in the middle of the courtyard surrounded by the group.

"There's good news and bad news, folks. The bad news is that our bus broke down.

The good news is that we got a new one. So if you left anything on the first bus, be sure to get it now or you'll probably never see it again."

The group climbed the hill to where they had entered the orphanage. Fifty yards away several men had pulled the side panels off the bus and were working on its engine. A new bus idled a few yards from it. As they walked to the bus, Christine asked Jessica, "Did you see Paul?"

"No. Not since lunch."

"I wanted to say goodbye."

"He'll be here tomorrow. Did you leave anything on the other bus?"

"No."

"Good. Then let's grab a seat up front."

When everyone had boarded, Jim sat down in the seat across from the women.

"What do you want to do tonight?" Jessica asked Christine.

"Get out of these clothes."

"Then what?"

"Shower. Read. Sleep. And we need to get Pablo his birthday present."

"Do you really think it's his birthday?" Jessica asked.

"Does it matter?"

"Not really. Maybe we can get something near the hotel. Hey, Sledge."

He leaned over the aisle. "Yeah, Jess?"

"Sledge?" Christine said.

"It's a nickname," Jessica said. "As in 'hammer.' Where can we get a birthday present for Pablo?"

"They have toys at the handicraft mall across the street from the hotel."

"What do you think he'd want?"

Jim thought about it for a moment. "Maybe a toy truck. Something he can share with the other boys."

"You look tired," Jessica said to him.

"I am. Some of those posts we set were more than two hundred pounds."

"You're such a manly man. Move over, I'll give you a shoulder rub."

Jim slid toward the window, and Jessica crossed the aisle to his seat and began kneading his shoulders and neck. A little more than a half hour later, the bus stopped at the hotel. As they climbed off the bus, Jim asked, "What are you gals doing tonight?"

"Christine wants to read. What do you have in mind?"

"I should take you to see the ruins of Sac-sayhuaman."

"What's that?" Jessica asked.

"It's a stone fortress built by the Inca. It's only ten minutes from the Plaza."

"What do you think, Chris? Want to join us?"

Christine could tell by the way Jessica asked that she wanted to be alone with Jim. "No, you two go."

"All right," Jessica said. "But I'll need a few minutes to freshen up."

"Meet in the lobby in ten minutes?" Jim asked.

"Ten minutes."

The women went up to their room. Christine pulled off her shoes and lay across the bed while Jessica went into the bathroom and washed up. When the water stopped, Jessica shouted, "You sure you're okay being alone?"

"I've got my gecko."

Jessica emerged from the bathroom, drying her hands on a towel. "What did you say?"

"I said I'm fine."

"Then I'll see you tonight. By the way, Jim says there's an Internet café across the

street in case you want to check your
e-mails. *Ciao, bella.*"

"Bye."

After Jessica left, Christine picked up her
book but couldn't get into it and put it back
down.

After a while she went out and found the
Internet café. A man led her to a computer
and she logged onto her account. While she
waited for it to load, she was suddenly filled
with anticipation. *Had Martin e-mailed her?
How would she respond?* The exercise was
moot. He hadn't. There was the usual spam
and one e-mail from her mother asking how
she was.

She wrote back to her mother in great detail about the last few days and their work in
the orphanage. When she had finished, she
left the café and went to the handicraft mall.
There were scores of booths inside and
she quickly came across one with children's
toys. She found a large yellow plastic dump
truck, a small spool of yellow ribbon and a
set of pink plastic hair combs with a matching hand mirror. She purchased the gifts,
then went back to her room and drew a hot
bath.

She sat in the tub for nearly a half hour,

scrubbing the paint flecks from her arms until her skin was pink. Then, adding more hot water, she slid down into the bath until it reached her chin. She closed her eyes and relaxed. When the water began to cool, she climbed out and went to bed. The last thoughts on her mind were of Paul, Pablo and a little girl with a scar across her face.

CHAPTER

Ten

Today is Pablo's birthday—or at least his birthday fiesta—as we have no idea when he was born or even where. But it doesn't matter. We commemorate the day he came into our lives, and what more is a birthday celebration than this?

✦ PAUL COOK'S DIARY ✦

The next morning the bus arrived at El Girasol a half hour earlier than the previous day.
Christine left the bus carrying the toy truck,
ribbon, mirror and hair combs.

"Did you check your e-mail?" Jessica
asked.

"My mom wrote."

"Nothing from Martian?"

"No."

Jessica sighed and turned away. "What
are we doing today?" she asked Jim as they
descended the hill into the hacienda.

"Most of the group will be putting wire
netting on the greenhouse. But I'll be in-
stalling electric lights in the boy's dorm. You
guys want to help?"

"You two go ahead," Christine said. "I'll
work on the greenhouse." They walked a little further. "So how were the ruins?"

Jessica winked at Jim.

"We didn't quite make it," Jim said, looking a little guilty. "We're going tonight."

"No we're not," Jessica said, "We're having our fiesta. We're celebrating our last night in Cuzco."

"Oh, right."

The group entered the courtyard and gathered around the well. Jaime was again waiting for them. Christine glanced about to see if Paul was there. He soon emerged and crossed the courtyard and joined Jaime to address the group.

"Welcome back. My name is Paul Cook. I'm the director of El Girasol. I have to say I'm pretty impressed with your industry: you got the greenhouse framed and the schoolroom painted in one day. Today we're going to tie the wire netting on the greenhouse and hopefully get the plastic on. The greenhouse is something we've looked forward to for several years. Right now the boys produce about a fourth of their own food. This greenhouse will enable us to garden year-round and become even more self-sufficient. Jaime will be directing today's work. Thank you for coming. I hope it's a good experience for you. We'll see you at lunch."

As the group dispersed, Christine went to Paul with the presents.

"Good morning," he said.

"Good morning." She held out the truck. "I brought this for Pablo—for his birthday."

He looked bemused. "How did you know?" Then he grinned. "Never mind. He'll be president of this country someday."

She handed him the gifts.

"He'll love the truck. But I don't think he'll care much for the ribbon or the hair combs."

She smiled. "Those are for Roxana."

"I guessed."

"We tried to find you yesterday before we left. We wanted to thank you for the tour."

"I had to go into town." He looked around as if he had just suddenly realized that the group was gone. "I better get out there. Are you helping us on the greenhouse today?"

"Yes."

"Want to help me?"

She hid her pleasure at the assignment. "Sure."

"Good." He looked down at the truck. "I'll put these away. I'll be right back."

Paul disappeared through one of the doors and was back almost as quickly. They

walked together to the back of the hacienda. From the patio the valley was laid
out before them in a lush quilt of green and
amber vegetation. The back property was
mostly fields, and the tender green bayo-
nets of corn and indigo peered above the
stone and adobe walls that surrounded the
property.

On the southern half of the yard the group
was congregated around the wooden frame
of a large greenhouse nearly seventy-five
feet in length and half that wide. Two large
rolls of plastic and several bales of wire lay
on the ground. They were already at work
with wire cutters and hammers, standing on
ladders or planks as they stretched the wire
across the frame. Christine thought there
was something pleasing about seeing the
Peruvians and Americans working side by
side.

"What are they doing?"

"They're making a metal net. It's like the
spring web beneath a mattress. First we
stretch the wire from one end to the other,
then we tie it side to side. When we're done,
we'll put the plastic on it and then repeat the
process on the outside."

"All the greenhouses I've seen were made with glass."

"The plastic sheeting works just as well. And it costs a lot less."

"What do you want me to do?"

"Tying the net is a two-person job. One of us carries the wire, the other ties."

He hefted a large spool of wire onto his shoulder and carried it over to one end of the framework, where a vacant ladder tilted against a supporting beam. "You're not afraid of heights, are you?"

"No."

"All right, then climb on up."

Christine climbed the ladder and Paul handed her a hammer and nail. "First pound a nail in the cross beam, then wrap the wire around it." She obeyed. "Now come down." She climbed down and Paul took the hammer from her, then moved the ladder a few feet. She climbed back up. "Now what?"

"We start wrapping the wire around itself."

"What do you mean?"

"I'll show you." He climbed the ladder behind her, his body sliding up against hers. The warmth and feel of his body filled her with happiness, and only then did she realize how much she missed being held and touched. She wondered if it felt good to him as well, as he seemed perfectly comfortable; he put his arms around her and tied the wire in a loop and pulled it back toward the next pole. "I'll show you a little trick. If you twist it like this, you don't have to pull so hard. Got it?"

Her thoughts were more on him than the task, and she suddenly realized that he was awaiting her response.

"Sure, I can do that," she said. It took her a few tries to get it right. "Like this?"

"Perfect. Now on to the next one."

They climbed back down, and Paul moved the ladder. As he did, the pendant he wore fell out of his shirt. It was a small toy soldier. He quickly pushed it back inside. Christine climbed back up the ladder. "I'm getting the hang of this."

"Good," he said with a grin. "You only have a thousand more to do."

She laughed. "I wanted to tell you yesterday how great I thought you were with the children."

He looked pleased with her comment. "Thanks."

"They really love you. You can see it in their eyes. It's almost like they're your own."

"They *are* mine."

Christine smiled. "Tell me about them."

He wound wire as he spoke. "René is eleven. Both of his parents were killed when he was small, probably by the Shining Path guerrillas. He lived with some adults who put him into a child labor camp to make bricks. He escaped and three years ago was found sleeping in the street.

"Carlos is also eleven. He doesn't know where he was born or the name of his parents. He was found wandering the streets of Cuzco. Ever since we got our cow last summer, he's been our dairyman and very proud of that. He's very dependable. You never have to tell him his duties.

"Washington's real name is Monterroso. He's twelve years old. He has some recollection of his mother but doesn't remember what happened to her or why he's not with her. He has horrible night terrors. And he sings very sad songs."

Christine tied off the wire and climbed down. Paul moved the ladder. She climbed back up.

"Gordon knows he has a father somewhere but doesn't remember where to find him. He was found begging just outside Cuzco.

"Samuel is thirteen. He's from Puerto Maldonado. He was brought here by his family to find work but was abandoned after his arrival.

"Joe comes from a large family. He wasn't wanted and was forced out into the streets by his own parents. He's a sweet boy. He's very helpful and he sometimes leaves little treasures for me."

She climbed down from the ladder. "What kind of treasures?"

"Pretty stones. Once he left me a cookie."

Paul dragged the ladder to the next post. He set the wire on the ground and worked out a knot.

"Go on," she urged.

"Let's see. Oscar is sixteen. He's older than the other boys, but was beaten so severely by his mother that he suffered brain damage. He has the mental capacity of a six-year-old.

"Jorge is nine. He knows where his mother is, but she also lives on the streets and has no way to provide for him.

"Ronal was abandoned as a child. When he was five he was sold as a prostitute to foreign men. He ran away and was brought here. He keeps to himself and rarely speaks.

"Deyvis is fifteen. He's the most rebellious of the group. He also has remarkable integrity. He won't eat until every other boy has been fed. At the age of seven he started a gang in Cuzco to protect the smaller boys from abuse and starvation.

"Then there's little Roxana. She's very shy and stays away from the boys most of the time because they tease her. I'm teaching her to read. And of course there's Pablo. He's my little buddy. We came to El Girasol about the same time. In fact, he arrived just two days after I settled in."

"He idolizes you."

"I shouldn't have favorites here, I love them all, but I think if I ever went back to the States, I'd try to adopt him."

"If you ever went back?"

"If," he repeated.

"How often do groups like ours come down?"

"Maybe a dozen a year. Mostly in the summer months." Paul turned to her. "What is it that you do back home?"

"I'm a dental hygienist."

"Those skills would come in handy down

here." He looked over at her. "I noticed that Jim and Jessica are getting along well."

"You think?"

He smiled. "How long have you two been friends?"

"Forever. Since we were kids."

"What does Jessica do back home?"

"Pretty much whatever she wants. Right now she's working at a public relations firm. Her dad's a U.S. congressman, so she never has trouble getting work."

"Whose idea was it to come to Peru?"

"Jess's."

"But you liked the idea?"

"Not really. Jessica's . . ."—she searched for the right word—"strong-willed."

Paul nodded.

"Speaking of which, she decided that we're throwing a party tonight. We're celebrating our last night in Cuzco. Would you like to come?"

"Thanks, but we have our own party going on here for Pablo. The boys have been planning it for a month now."

"What are you doing for your party?"

"I've been saving a cake mix. And the boys made a piñata."

"May I come?"

Paul looked at her. "Are you serious?"

"I think it sounds fun. Besides, you can't throw a party for a dozen boys by yourself."

"What about Jessica's party?"

"I doubt Jessica would even notice if I wasn't there."

He thought for a moment. "I could drive you back to Cuzco after the kids go to bed. It would be pretty late."

"I can do late."

"Then you're invited."

"Great," she said, and they went back to their wiring.

CHAPTER

Eleven

Tonight I sat under the stars with Christine. I am not sure which was more potent: what she said, how she looked, or how I felt in her presence.

✦ PAUL COOK'S DIARY ✦

The group had completed the roof and two side walls when they broke for lunch. Christine saved a place in the shade while Paul picked up their box lunches. The contents of the box were the same as the day before. "Where's a McDonald's when you need one?" she said. Christine lifted the ham out of the sandwich and placed it back in the box.

Jim and Jessica emerged from a stairwell, picked up their lunches and came over to sit by them. As she approached, Jessica looked at Paul, then gave Christine a curious glance and sat down next to her. Jim sat next to Paul.

"I got the boys' dorm wired," Jim said to Paul. "They have lights now."

"Thanks. The boys will be thrilled."

Jessica leaned into Christine and asked softly, "What have you two been up to?"

"Stretching wire."

" . . . and?"

"And *what?*" Christine asked.

"You look . . . comfortable."

Christine shook her head. "You should talk. Tell Sledge your lipstick becomes him."

Jessica's head swiveled to look at Jim. "I didn't even notice. Do you think anyone suspects something's going on?"

"Jess, everyone *knows* something's going on."

A look of surprise crossed her face. "Really?"

"You two are about as obvious as a bad toupee."

Jessica's forehead furrowed. "That's bad. He's not supposed to fraternize with clients. It's company policy. He could get fired."

"It's a little late to start worrying."

She briefly looked concerned, then relaxed. *"C'est la vie.* What about you two?"

"I've just been helping him like you've been helping Jim." She took a drink of the yogurt. "Well, maybe not quite. Which reminds me, I'm going to help at Pablo's birthday party tonight."

"What about *our* party?"

Christine unwrapped her chocolate. "You and Jim won't notice that I'm not there."

"Of course we will."

"Jess . . ."

Jessica tried another tack. "How will you get back to Cuzco?"

"Paul offered to drive me."

"Whatever," Jessica said.

When they finished eating, Paul and Christine resumed their work on the greenhouse. Within a few hours the group had finished the metal netting and they pulled the plastic over the top of the frame. Then the process began again, sandwiching the plastic between two metal nets.

✦

As the group got ready to leave, Paul and Christine went to the hacienda's kitchen. Richard had already been there and the room smelled of baking pizza. Paul looked inside the oven. "Almost done." He went to a cupboard and took out the cake mix and began reading the box.

"I can make the cake," Christine said.

"All right." He handed her the box.

"Betty Crocker, you're a long way from home." She looked at Paul. "We need vegetable oil and eggs."

"Huevos y aceite vegetal." Paul brought her a bowl of eggs, a bottle of oil, a ceramic bowl and a wooden spoon for mixing. The vegetable oil was in a slim amber glass bottle and the brown eggs still had hay and mud stuck to them. She bit her lip as she examined them.

"They don't get fresher than that," Paul said.

"I'm used to a more *sterile* world," Christine said as she washed the eggs.

"Don't forget to use the high-altitude recipe."

"Oh, right." She was surprised that Paul had thought of this and she hadn't. She looked at the box. "Stir one tablespoon flour into the mix. This says thirty-five hundred to sixty-five hundred feet. Do you think that's enough? We're practically in space here."

"You can add a little extra flour." As she started to crack the eggs into a bowl, Roxana appeared in the doorway. She knocked on the door's threshold to get their attention.

Christine smiled when she saw her. "Come here, sweetie," she said, motioning her toward her. Roxana walked up to her.

Christine cracked the last of the eggs,

then poured in water and oil. Then she put the spoon in Roxana's hands. "Can you stir?" Roxana just stared at her and Christine helped guide the spoon into the bowl and began stirring. After a moment she let go and Roxana continued stirring on her own.

When the ingredients were completely mixed in, Christine lifted the spoon. *"Gracias.* Now you can lick it." Roxana started to put the spoon back in the bowl, but Christine stopped her. "No. Lick it." She turned to Paul. "How do you say 'lick'?"

"Lamer," Paul said, watching with interest.

"Lamer," Christine said. She took the spoon and pretended to lick it, then handed it back to her. Roxana began to lick the spoon, timidly at first, but with growing intensity as chocolate covered her lips and chin.

Richard walked into the room. He glanced at the three of them, then went to the oven and took out the pizza.

"Do you have a cake pan?" Christine asked.

"Of course." Paul spoke to Richard, and he retrieved a shallow aluminum pan along with a cloth. "You can use the rag to grease the pan," Paul said. "It's clean."

Christine poured oil onto the cloth and greased the sides and bottom of the pan then floured it. Then she poured in the batter. "All set. You preheated the oven to three hundred fifty degrees?" she asked.

"It should be about right."

"Three hundred fifty degrees?"

He hid a smile. "It's a wood burning oven, Christine. It doesn't have a dial."

"So how do you tell the temperature?"

"You put your hand inside and count how many seconds you can leave it in there."

"Are you serious?"

He nodded. "Cake is three to four seconds."

"I'll let you handle the cake while I get Roxana ready for the party."

Paul looked at Roxana without comprehesion. " 'Ready'?"

"You know, *ready.* Like wash up, braid her hair. I take it you don't do a lot of that."

"Not really."

"Not really or not at all?"

"Really not at all."

"She's a girl, Paul," she gently scolded. "Would you tell her what I want to do?"

Paul stepped in front of her and signed. Roxana smiled, and she turned and looked at Christine, her face bright with excitement.

"Where are the things I brought for her?"

"I'll get them."

A moment later he returned with the combs, mirror and ribbon. Christine took the items in one hand and Roxana's hand in the other and led her up to her room.

Paul placed his hand in the oven to test the heat, then put the cake in.

Christine sat Roxana on her bed, then sat down behind her. "First, let's see what else you have to wear." She looked around the room. There was a single chest near the door. She opened it.

The chest was filled with clothing, mostly used, brought down by groups from America. She dug through the trunk; finally selecting a pink and white sleeveless dress. She lifted it out, eyed Roxana for size, then brought it over.

Roxana took off her jeans and T-shirt, and Christine pulled the dress on over her head. It was slightly large for her skinny body. Then Christine sat her back on the bed. Roxana sat perfectly still as Christine carefully braided her hair leaving a single lock that partially concealed the scar that ran from her temple to her jaw. She took out the yellow ribbon and neatly tied bows around the end of each braid. They stood out in her black hair like yellow butterflies on a bed of coal.

There was a cloth in the washbowl, and Christine scrubbed the cake mix and dirt from Roxana's face until her skin glowed. She took a small makeup kit from her fanny pack and lightly spread sparkling gloss across Roxana's lips. Then she opened a small vial of perfume and let Roxana smell it. Roxana looked up and smiled. Christine dabbed the scent on Roxana's neck, then did the same to herself.

She handed Roxana the mirror. When Roxana saw herself, her face lit with joy. She cautiously touched each of the ribbons, then smiled at Christine.

"You're a real beauty," Christine said.

Christine then went to work on her own hair and makeup while Roxana watched with fascination. Christine applied a darker shade of gloss to her lips, accentuating their fullness. Then she opened a compact and carefully brushed on blush and a thick coat of mascara. She stowed the makeup back in her pack, then took Roxana's hand. "Let's see what the boys think now."

Paul stared at them as they entered the kitchen.

"So? How do we look?"

"Wow."

"We're girls. We clean up well," Christine said, then added happily, "Quit staring at me, and look at Roxana."

"She looks like a girl."

"Exactly," Christine said triumphantly.

Paul signed to her and she signed back.

"She says she's beautiful like you now."

Christine smiled. "How's the cake?"

"Still baking," Paul said. "It shouldn't be too much longer."

While she was gone, Paul had gathered the ingredients to make chocolate frosting, and Christine put it together. It turned out to be especially good using the richer Peruvian cocoa. Fifteen minutes later they took the cake from the oven. It was a little lopsided and Christine laughed.

"We're used to that," Paul said. "That's what the frosting's for."

Just then Jessica walked into the kitchen.

"Smells good in here," she said. She looked at Christine. "Look at you, girl!"

"Just thought I'd clean up a bit."

"We're going. You sure you don't want to join us?"

"I'm fine."

Jessica kissed Christine's check. "Okay, we'll miss you. Gotta go. Jim says it's 'Hammer time.' " She walked out of the room.

As the group left, the boys began to file in and take their places around the table. They all looked at Roxana as if she were a stranger.

Pablo was the first to speak. "She looks like a girl," he said.

"She *is* a girl," Christine replied.

Deyvis said a prayer over the food, then Roxana and the boys stood in line to get their plates. They filed past Richard, who served up the pizza and toasted garlic bread. Paul and Christine were the last to be served.

Christine stared at the pizza. "What kind of meat is that? It looks like tuna."

"It is tuna," Paul said. "I think America's the only country that doesn't put tuna on their pizza." Christina took a piece and sat down next to Paul and Roxana to eat.

As they were finishing their meal, Paul retrieved the piñata, a crude papier-mâché creation in the shape of a llama and adorned with brightly colored crepe paper streamers. The boys cheered when they saw it and followed Paul out the door to the central corridor. Paul wrapped one end of the twine around the llama's head, then threw the other end over a rafter and hauled it up.

As the birthday boy, Pablo was given the string so that he could move the piñata up and down.

Paul handed the bat to Gordon, but he refused it. The boys all shouted to Paul, and though Christine didn't understand them, she knew from their gestures that whatever they wanted concerned her.

"The boys want you to go first," Paul told her.

She looked at their eager faces. "How sweet," she said.

"Not really," Paul said, slightly grinning, "They just want to make fun of you."

"We'll see about *that*. Where's the blind-fold?"

Paul tied the handkerchief around her eyes. He took her by the shoulders and guided her toward the piñata, then handed her the bat. She clutched it tightly with both hands.

"All right, Babe Ruth, let me clear out before you start swinging." Paul stepped back then said, "Okay, go for it."

Pablo yanked the string and the piñata jumped. She swung five times and missed with each swing and the boys laughed harder with each attempt. Finally she pulled off the blindfold. "Okay, enough humiliation. Roxana's turn."

Christine led her up to the piñata, then tied the blindfold around her eyes. As soon as the little girl had the bat, she began swinging. Pablo didn't pull the string but let her connect, which did little but produce a light thud.

"*¡Muévela, Pablo!*" *Move it, Pablo!*

"*¡Más rápido!*" *Faster!*

"*No,*" Pablo said.

"*A Pablo le gusta Roxana,*" *Pablo loves Roxana,* Joe shouted, and the other boys quickly joined in.

"*¡Cállense, tontos!*" Pablo shouted back, then added in English, "Stupid heads!"

"*Basta,*" Paul said. The boys fell silent.

Roxana's bat struck the piñata several more times but again without effect.

"Okay. Now getting the bat from her is the tricky part," Paul said. After she swung, Paul reached in and grabbed the top of the bat. Then he slid off her blindfold. Christine stepped over and lifted her in her arms. "Good job, sweetie."

Roxana cuddled into her. It took only two swings before Ronal connected, sending candy flying everywhere. The boys fell to the ground, gathering up the candy. Christine set Roxana down.

"Roxana, go," Christine said. "Get some candy." She tried to get her to move, but Roxana just clutched her leg, keeping her distance from the boys' melee. Christine crouched down to help her, but the candy was mostly gone by then. She looked up at Paul for help. "Paul, she didn't get any."

"Don't worry. She will."

When the candy was all collected, the boys put it in a single pile. *"¿Quince?"* Deyvis asked Paul. *Fifteen?*

"No. Trece es suficiente." *Thirteen's enough.*

The boys divided the candy evenly into thirteen piles. Christine watched in amazement. "You didn't even tell them to share."

"These boys would as soon cut off their

own hand as take something the others didn't get."

"We could learn from them."

"I do every day," Paul said. He turned back to the boys. *"¿Quién quiere torta?"* *Who wants cake?*

The boys cheered and ran off.

"Come on, Roxana," Christine said. Roxana had never surrendered her hand and Christine led her to the dining room. When they arrived, the boys were already seated around the table. Pablo sat at the head. Paul struck a match and lit the candles on the cake.

"All right, Pablo," Christine said. "Blow them out."

He looked over the cake. "There are too many candles. I'm only eight."

"It's an American custom," she said. "One candle to grow on."

"Good. I need to grow," Pablo said.

"Cantemos," Paul said. *Let's sing.*

The boys sang happy birthday to Pablo, first in English, then in Spanish. Then Paul cut the cake and put it on plates, which Christine handed out.

Paul gave him a new sweater, a case of watercolors and a thick pad of paper to paint on. Pablo was ecstatic with the gifts, thanking him in both languages. Then Christine gave Pablo the truck and all the boys looked at it enviously. "Wow," he said. *"Un camión.* Cool!" Pablo hugged her. "Thank you, Miss Christine."

"You're welcome."

Christine looked over at Paul and saw his eyes gleam with happiness for Pablo's joy. She realized that Paul didn't love Pablo *like* a son; he felt the boy *was* his son. She wondered if he had named him after himself.

✦

When the cake was gone, all the boys went outside to play, leaving Paul, Christine and Roxana alone in the kitchen. Paul made coca tea, poured two cups and brought them over to the table. Roxana sat next to Christine, her cheek flattened against the table while Christine tickled her back.

"I should have asked if you like coca tea," Paul said. "I can make something else if you don't."

"No, it's fine. It helps with the altitude."

"Are you still feeling it?"

"A little. It's like a constant buzzing."

He sat down across from her. "It's murder when you have a cold. Sugar?"

"Please. A lot."

Paul scooped a heaping teaspoon into her cup, stirred it, then left the spoon. He sat down across from her. "An Italian visitor once told me that coca tea tastes like a horse smells."

She laughed. "It tastes like alfalfa."

Paul took another sip. "I've never thought of that but you're right. I could make coffee instead."

"No, alfalfa's fine. What time do the boys go to bed?"

"Usually around nine. But I told them they could stay up tonight until ten. We're probably about there now."

She finished her tea. "Want me to take the boys up?"

"No. I just need to tell them it's bedtime. But I'm sure Roxana wouldn't mind if you put her to bed."

"I'd love to."

The sun had fallen, leaving the courtyard dark except for a single floodlight that created long dramatic shadows. Paul called to the boys, while Christine took Roxana's hand and led her to her room. Once inside,

Roxana lifted off her dress, then folded it and placed it inside the wooden chest. She took out a large nightshirt, pulled it on and went to her bed. Christine turned down the sheets and helped Roxana climb under them.

Christine lingered at the side of the bed, looking into the little girl's face. Roxana gazed back at her.

The boys' dorm was just two doors down, and the boys ran wildly past Roxana's room, chasing Pablo and his new truck. They were so loud and boisterous that Christine wondered how Roxana could sleep with such noise, then she smiled at her own foolishness.

"I wish I could read you a story," Christine said. She pulled the hair back from Roxana's face. Then she gently touched the scar. "What did they do to you, little one?"

Roxana reached up and touched Christine's lips. Then she signed something.

Christine smiled sadly. "I don't know what you're saying, honey."

Almost as if understanding her, Roxana repeated the motion, this time more slowly. Christine nodded. "I'll ask Paul what that means. Goodnight," she said. She leaned forward and kissed her forehead, then pulled the covers up to her chin. At the door she turned off the light and looked back. Even in the darkness she could see that Roxana was looking at her. She reluctantly turned and walked back to the kitchen. Paul was washing the last of the dishes.

"Need some help?"

"I'm almost done. How did it go?"

"She's adorable." Christine sat down at the table "What does this mean?" She did her best to replicate Roxana's motion.

"She was saying 'I love you.' "

Christine sighed happily. "I'm falling in love with her," she said. Paul looked over but said nothing. He toweled off his hands. "You're probably ready to get back to Cuzco."

"I wouldn't mind talking some more. If you're not too tired."

He smiled. "I'm not tired at all. Would you like to go for a walk?"

"I'd love to."

"I know the perfect place."

They left the kitchen and walked down behind the hacienda into the night, past the greenhouse up the foothill south of El Girasol. As the path grew steeper, Paul took her hand and led her nearly thirty yards up the incline to where a large rock cropping made a flat ledge. Christine was breathing heavily. Paul wiped the dust from the rock, then helped her up on the stone. She sat with her feet dangling over the side. Paul scooted over next to her.

The moon illuminated the valley before them, and the black water of the sacred river shimmered like an earthbound galaxy. Cicadas serenaded them from their hiding places like an orchestra concealed in its pit.

"It's beautiful," Christine said. "Do you come here often?"

"From time to time. Usually when I want to get away from the boys."

She smiled at that. She leaned back on her elbows and looked up at the night sky. "The stars are so clear. Where's the Big Dipper?"

"Wrong hemisphere. Down here we have the Southern Cross."

"I've never really thought that the stars down here would be different than the ones at home. Where's the Southern Cross?"

He leaned next to her, pointing toward the western sky. "See those four stars? The group there with the really bright star?"

"Yes."

"That's the Southern Cross. The brightest of those stars, at the foot of the cross, is Acrux. It's really two stars orbiting around each other." Paul was quiet a moment, then said,

The lovely planet, love's own quickener,
Right-hand I turned, and, setting me to spy
That alien pole, beheld four stars, the same
The first men saw, and since, no living eye;
It seemed the heavens exulted in their
    flame—
O widowed world beneath the northern
    pole,
Forever famished of the sight of them!

Christine sighed with pleasure. "Did you write that?"

"It's Dante. Many scholars believe he was writing about the Southern Cross, except he never saw it. Florence, Italy, is too far north. Still, it's peculiar that he speaks of the widowed world beneath the Northern Light. At one time the Southern Cross was visible from Jerusalem, but, due to the earth's precession, now it can't be seen. They say the last time it was visible from Jerusalem was the same century Christ was crucified."

"How do you know all this?"

"I read a lot," he said. He looked out. "For centuries mariners and sojourners used the Southern Cross to guide their journeys. People have always looked to the stars for direction. Some believe they determine their destiny."

"Do you think they do?"

"I don't know. My last stars didn't do me much good. I came down here and things changed. So maybe there is something to them."

"*I* need some new stars," Christine said.

Paul looked back out over the valley. "The Incas believed that the sacred valley was a reflection of the constellations. You'll see what I mean when you go there tomorrow."

The mention of her departure made her sad. She looked ahead, lightly kicking her feet. "Why do you call your orphanage the Sunflower?"

"It was the name of the hacienda. I suppose it was probably built on a field of sunflowers. We keep the name because I like the metaphor of looking to light. What we do here is about hope."

"I've always loved sunflowers, my whole wed—" she stopped herself. "I just like them."

Paul noticed the slip but didn't pursue it. "Was Jessica upset that you didn't go back tonight?"

"A little. But she'll get over it. She really just wanted me to cover for her. She was worried that people might suspect that she and Jim were a pair—as if everyone doesn't already know."

"I hope Jessica doesn't get her hopes up. Jim's a player. He has a girl on every tour."

"Then they're perfect for each other," Christine said. "Jessica's a male magnet. Men just can't keep away from her. She's just so beautiful and so much fun."

"Like you."

"I'm not as beautiful as she is. And I'm *definitely* not as fun."

"I think you're more beautiful than Jessica. And you were *definitely* fun tonight. The boys thought so too."

"I'm not fun. I'm picky and compulsive and . . ." she stopped.

"And?"

"Afraid."

A breeze wafted between and around

them as if carrying off her words. She looked down over the dark, moonlit fields that ruffled with the wind.

"What are you afraid of?"

"Life, I guess. I think what I'm most afraid of is being alone."

"You and the rest of the world," he said. He looked over at her. "Did something happen to you to make you feel this way?"

"My parents divorced when I was little. I know it happens all the time. But my father eventually just erased me from his life. He had a new family and to him I was just part of a mistake. He died a year ago. By that time we had completely lost touch."

"I'm sorry," Paul said.

Christine stared out at the hacienda.

"I haven't told you why Jessica wanted me to come to Peru." He looked at her. "She was trying to get me out of Dayton."

"What's in Dayton?"

"A lot of pain, mostly." She nervously brushed her hair back from her face. "Last October I was supposed to get married. A week before the wedding my fiancé decided that he wasn't ready and called it off." Her eyes welled up with tears. "I'm sorry. I don't know why I'm telling you all this."

"It helps to talk."

She found comfort in his tone. "Today was the first time since Martin walked out that I haven't thought about him." She frowned. "At least until now."

"Your fiancé's name is Martin?"

She nodded. "Martin Lyn Christensen. I was going to be Christine Christensen. Kind of a bad name, don't you think?"

He shrugged. "At least it's easy to remember."

"Just try saying it three times fast."

Paul tried and failed, and they both laughed. It felt good to laugh, Christine thought, especially about something that previously had only brought her pain. After a moment she said, "So, Dr. Cook, what brought you here?"

"To El Girasol?"

"To Peru."

He looked out into the darkness as if he were contemplating the question for the first time. "I came to surf."

She looked into his face to see if he was serious. "Really?"

He laughed. "No." He turned away and said nothing else. After a moment he looked back over. "Why do you think I came?"

"I was thinking it was probably the Butch Cassidy thing. You got tired of robbing banks in the U.S. so you came down here because you heard it was easier."

He smiled at this but still didn't answer her question. A sudden gust of wind whistled down the mountain.

"You're not going to tell me, are you?"

He shook his head. "No."

"That's not fair. I shared *my* painful secret."

"Proof again that life isn't fair."

"At least tell me why you wear a toy soldier around your neck?"

Paul seemed surprised that she had noticed it. "It's a reminder."

"Of what?"

He smiled. "Of something I'd like to forget."

"You're so . . . *mysterious.*"

"Is that bad?"

"No, it's kind of appealing." She looked down, threading her fingers together in her lap. "We're going to Machu Picchu tomorrow. Then we're flying out to Puerto Maldonado. We're going to stay at a jungle lodge."

"Makisapa Lodge," he said.

"Have you been there?"

"Many times. Sometimes I help Puma-Condor if they're short on help."

"Are there a lot of spiders?"

"I doubt you'll see any. Well, maybe a few." He paused. "Actually they're all over the place."

Christine dropped her head in her hand. "Great."

"You're afraid of spiders?"

"Terrified. Especially the big hairy ones."

"I was bitten by one of those big hairy ones once. A Peruvian pink toe. Beautiful creature, really. It was crawling on my arm and I tried to lift it off. It got both fangs into me."

"Okay, I'm going to have a nervous breakdown. Tell me you're kidding."

"I'd be lying."

"What did it feel like?"

"It hurt."

"No kidding. I want details."

"It was like being stuck with two thumb-tacks. My hand swelled up and turned purple. But it didn't hurt for much more than a day."

"Is it true that there are spiders big enough to catch birds?"

The question amused him. "Why are you doing this to yourself?"

"It's my obsessive controlling side. I've got to know."

"The Venezuelan Goliath bird eater. I've only seen one of them. It hissed at me."

"The spider *hissed?*"

"Some of them do that. But it gets better. A year ago I met this British explorer in Cuzco. He was a spider expert. He was investigating claims about a spider they call *la araña de pollo*—the chicken spider. Eyewitnesses claimed to have seen a spider so big it actually kills chickens and carries them off."

"I'm definitely going to have a breakdown," Christine said. "I don't want to talk about this anymore."

"You started it."

"Well, I'm stopping it now."

He was quiet for a moment, then suddenly started laughing to himself.

"What?"

"I really shouldn't tell you."

"Now you have to."

"Tomorrow night you're staying in a town called Urubamba. *Urubamba* means Land of Spiders."

"This just keeps getting better. So what does *makisapa* mean—lodge of Giant Spiders?"

Paul laughed. "You're not that far off. A makisapa is a Brazilian *spider* monkey."

"A spider monkey. Now I know you're making this up."

"I'm not that clever." He smiled reassuringly, then put his arm around her, pulling her in close. "Don't worry, you'll be okay."

Neither spoke for a few minutes, but it was a comfortable silence. Christine pushed thoughts of spiders from her mind and thought about the man with his arm around her instead.

"Do you miss America?" Christine asked.

"Most of it."

"What do you miss most?"

"My family. My parents and sister."

"When was the last time you saw them?"

"Three years ago. My mother had just been diagnosed with ALS. Lou Gehrig's disease."

"I'm sorry."

"So am I. My sister moved back to help my dad take care of her. I feel guilty about not being there. But I can't just leave these boys." He breathed out deeply. "Sometimes

I miss America more than I can say. And it's not really the big things. You have no idea how nice it is just to speak English with you."

"It's nice talking to you, whatever the language," Christine said. She looked down at the hacienda. A single light flickered from the kitchen. She pulled her hair back over her ears. Then she leaned back on her arms and looked back at him. "So how do you do it?"

"Do what?"

"Leave everything behind. You're a doctor; you must have had a pretty good life in America."

Paul looked suddenly thoughtful. " 'The secret of success in this life is to realize that the crisis on our planet is much larger than just deciding what to do with your own life. The only work that will ultimately bring any good to any of us is the work of contributing to the healing of the world.' "

"That was profound."

Paul rubbed his chin. *"That* was Marianne Williamson. I wish I really were that noble. But I'm no Mother Teresa. Sometimes I wonder what I'm doing here. I still fantasize about the 'good life' Of course my idea of the good life is different now. Luxury is an air-conditioned room, a TV with a clear signal and a shower with more than five minutes of hot water. But then I think, *what is my comfort compared to the lives of these children?*

"And there are millions where they came from. Kids sniffing glue to take away the pain of an empty stomach. Kids sold into slavery. There are actually tour groups that bring American men down here to have sex with children. You read about these things, and you can either try to do something about it or just wince and turn the page to the crossword puzzle. Too many are turning the page. Not so much because they don't care but because it's not on their doorstep. And most of us don't venture that far from our routines."

"You're making me feel guilty."

"That's probably not a bad thing," he said. "But that's not my intent. I'm as guilty as anyone. I didn't come down here to help children. It just happened to land on my doorstep."

"When you came down to surf . . ."

"To rob banks," he said, laughing a little.

"We're talking too much about me. Tell me something about Christine."

"What would you like to know?"

"Something . . . revealing."

"My failed engagement and childhood abandonment weren't revealing enough?"

"No, that was pretty revealing. But I was thinking something lighter. Like what's your favorite movie of all time?"

"My favorite movie. Old or new?"

"Either."

"I should probably say something that makes me seem hip like *Citizen Kane* or *The Godfather,* but honestly I'd have to say *Cinema Paradiso.*"

"A love story," Paul said. "That *is* revealing."

"Not just *any* love story. One of the greatest love stories of all time. Have you seen it?"

He nodded. "I have. So was Alfredo right? Does the fire of love always end in ashes?"

She thought about it. "Probably," she said sadly. She looked to see his reaction. "What do you think?"

"I think passion ends in ashes: But it's just as well. Passion should give way to better things."

"Like what?"

"Real love. The way my father is with my mother."

"How is that?"

"Do you know anything about ALS?"

"Not much."

"Amyotrophic lateral sclerosis," Paul said, sounding like the doctor he was. "It's a disease that causes the degeneration of the nerve cells in the brain and spinal cord. Eventually the body just shuts down.

"The average life span of someone with ALS is three to five years. My mother's almost completely paralyzed now. She can no longer speak or write. She's a prisoner of her own body. The only thing she can move is the forefinger on her right hand. At night she taps her finger against the bedpost when she hurts. My father wakes up and gives her her pain medicine. He hasn't slept through the night for years. He's always with her." He looked into Christine's eyes. "He's given up everything he loves for what he loves most. Her."

"That's beautiful," Christine said softly.

"I asked him how he did it, how he could give up so much for her. What he said taught me more about God and Jesus and life than a thousand sermons ever could."

"What did he say?"

Christine could hear the emotion in Paul's voice. "He said love is stronger than pain."

She looked down and said nothing.

After a while Paul said, "It's late. I better get you back."

"Thank you for letting me stay for Pablo's party. I really enjoyed it."

"It was my pleasure." He slid forward off the rock and turned back, took her hand and helped her down. She landed in front of him, stumbling a little on the incline. He caught her by the waist.

"Whoops," she said, falling into him. She backed off a little and from just a foot away looked up into his face. In the moonlight his eyes faintly glimmered, and she wondered if she had ever seen such beautiful, clear eyes.

"I have a confession," he said.

She cocked her head. "Yes?"

"The first time I saw you, I thought you were the most beautiful woman I had ever seen. I hoped that I would see you again. Tonight was a wish granted for me."

For a moment she just looked at him. "I

think that is the sweetest thing anyone's ever said to me."

As they stared into each other's eyes, the world around them drew far away. They pressed their lips and their bodies together and for a moment they were lost in each other.

When they parted, Christine was breathless. Her heart pounded fiercely. "Thank you for being so kind to me," she said. "My heart needed some kindness."

"It wasn't hard," Paul said.

He held her hand as they descended the hill, holding it until they were back inside El Girasol's courtyard. Christine thought that his hand felt wonderfully warm and strong.

"My car's around the side. I'll pull it around."

"Wait," she said. "What time is it?"

"Probably one."

"How long will it take to drive to Cuzco and back?"

"A little over an hour."

"That means you won't be back until after two. I don't want to make you do that. I could just sleep here tonight. If you don't mind."

"Not at all. I'll sleep up in the boys' dorm. You can stay in my room."

"I don't want to inconvenience you."

"It's more convenient than driving to Cuzco."

"I'd have to let Jessica know."

"I have Jim's cell-phone number. I'll call him."

They climbed the short set of steps where they had eaten lunch the first day and walked through a door into a broad, high-ceilinged hallway.

There were no lights, though it didn't seem to make a difference to Paul. Christine stayed close to him as he led her deeper into the darkness. They stopped outside a closed door at the end of the corridor. He pushed the door open into utter blackness and walked in and found a cord hanging from the ceiling. A single bulb illuminated the room. "It's not much but it's home."

She looked around. The room was small and windowless, with brown plaster walls.

"The bathroom's right next door. If you need to use it, there's a flashlight on the floor there. It scares the bugs away."

"What?"

"Just kidding," he said. Christine suspected that he wasn't. He took a large, bright orange T-shirt out of a wooden dresser. "You can use this as a nightshirt."

"Thank you. You'll call Jim?"

"Right away."

"Thank you. Goodnight."

"Buenas noches," he replied, and stepped to the door.

"Paul."

"Yes?"

Christine walked to him. She put a hand on his shoulder and leaned forward and kissed him gently on the mouth. They lingered, their noses touching, feeling the warmth of each other's breath. "Thank you," she said softly. "I had a really good time."

"So did I. Sleep well."

He kissed her on the cheek, then quickly stepped outside, shutting the door behind him.

Christine listened to his steps grow faint down the hallway and her heart longed to call him back. When all was silent, she sat on the bed. "What are you doing?" she said aloud. She looked around the room. On the wall, hanging from a nail driven into the plaster wall, was a picture of an elderly couple. She guessed the couple to be Paul's parents. They looked to be in their seventies; a thin, tall man, conservatively dressed in a gray suit with narrow lapels and a broad, ample woman in a simple navy blue sheath. Banana and orange, she thought. The woman was standing, so she guessed that the picture had been taken before the onset of her illness.

Next to the picture was a diploma. Georgetown Medical School.

On the floor, leaning against the wall was a large pile of books. She lifted one briefly and examined it. It was a medical text on ALS. She set it back down then undressed, carefully folding her clothes and setting them on the crate. Then she pulled on Paul's shirt. It was large and fell just above her knees.

She tugged the light cord and the room fell into complete darkness. She climbed into bed and pulled the sheets up to her chin. Though she felt a little anxious about being in this strange place there was something secure about being in Paul's bed and wearing his shirt. She thought of the evening and their kisses and she smiled. She wondered what he was thinking. And then she wondered how she could feel so close to a man she barely knew.

CHAPTER

Twelve

*Feelings can be like wild animals—
we underrate how fierce they are
until we've opened their cages.*

✦ PAUL COOK'S DIARY ✦

Christine woke to the sound of hushed voices and giggles. Six boys stood at the door looking in at her. Suddenly she heard Paul's voice. *"¿Qué están haciendo, mirones? Vamonos."*

The boys scattered as he came near. He peered into her room. Something fluttered in her stomach when she saw him. "Hi," she said.

"Sorry about that," he said, walking into the room. "They've never had a woman stay here before."

"It's okay," she said. She gazed at him as if she'd just woken from a pleasant dream to find it was true. He was carrying a plate with a small bowl balanced on it in one hand and a cup in the other.

"What time is it?"

"It's a little past ten. Your bus just pulled in."

"Ten?" She sat up, lifting the sheet with her. "I slept in."

"They'll be okay without you."

She felt her hair. "I'm a mess, aren't I?"

"No. I mean, you are, but you look cute."

She smiled. "What have you got there?"

"I brought you breakfast. Pancakes. And juice."

"Breakfast in bed."

He walked over with the meal. "In case you're wondering what's in the cup, it's our own version of maple syrup. We melt vanilla and water and sugar together. The straw-berries were grown here."

"Thank you."

He set the plate on the crate next to her and to her surprise he turned to go. "I'll see you outside."

"Wait."

He turned. "Yes?"

"Can you stay?"

He looked at her as if it were a difficult de-cision. "Sure." He came back and sat down on the bed next to her. She put the plate in her lap and began cutting the pancakes in small, precise squares.

"I haven't had breakfast in bed since my

mother brought it to me on my sixteenth birthday."

"Then you're overdue," he replied.

She poured a little of the homemade syrup on the pancakes, then took a bite. "This is good. I didn't know you could make your own syrup."

"Deprivation spawns invention. You should try my guinea pig chili sometime. It's amazing."

"I'll take your word for it." She picked up one of the strawberries and put it up to his mouth. "Here." He took a small bite then she finished it, setting the green velvet stem on her plate.

He watched her eat in silence. For all his kindness she sensed that he'd rather be someplace else.

"Do you need an assistant today? I'm told that I'm pretty good with wire."

He didn't smile. "I need to go into Cuzco. The police have a new boy they want us to take in."

"Would you like me to keep you company?"

He didn't look up right away, and when he did, his expression was strained. "I don't know how long this will take. I don't want to hold up your group."

To her heart it sounded like an excuse and she felt her own defenses rise. "Don't let me keep you."

He glanced down at his watch. "I should probably be on my way."

Christine said coolly, "I think we're leaving around two. Will you be back before then?"

"I should be," he said. He slowly stood. "I better go."

Christine set aside the tray, wondering what she had done to scare him off.

"Well, I hope to see you then," she said. He started to leave then stopped. "Chris . . ."

She looked at him, unwilling to let him see she was hurt. "Yes?"

"Take care of yourself." He walked out, leaving her feeling empty.

She looked down at the food but no longer felt hungry. She put the tray aside and got dressed, then went out to find Jessica.

CHAPTER

Thirteen

*Today I said goodbye to Christine.
As brief as her stay was (and as
painful as our parting was) I still
consider her a gift—like a cool
breeze on a hot day.*

✦ PAUL COOK'S DIARY ✦

By the time Christine emerged from the hacienda, the group was already at work on the greenhouse. The sun was high and bright and the contrast from the darkened room made her cover her eyes as she crossed the courtyard. When Jessica saw her coming, she put down her pliers and made a beeline to her.

"Spare no details."

Christine signed. "There's nothing to tell."

"You spent the night with a gorgeous man and nothing happened?"

"I didn't spend the night with him, I just slept here. It was after one when we finished. I didn't want to make him drive me all the way back to Cuzco." Christine started walking toward the greenhouse.

"What did you do?"

"We had a birthday party for Pablo. We broke a piñata and ate pizza and cake."

Jessica stopped walking. "Until one in the morning?"

"We went for a walk."

"A walk?"

Christine smiled at the memory. "It was nice."

"You just walked."

"And talked."

"About what?"

"Things. His life. Mine."

"Did you tell him about Martin?"

"Yes."

Jessica cringed. "Christine, you're *such* an open book. So where did you sleep?"

"In his room."

Jessica raised an eyebrow.

"I didn't sleep *with* him. Paul slept upstairs with the boys."

"So what is he really like?"

"He's a gentleman."

"You mean he's boring."

Christine sighed in exasperation. "End of conversation."

"I'm not done. So where is he now?"

"He had to go to Cuzco."

"And you didn't go with him?"

"He didn't know if he'd be back in time."

She looked down. "Besides, I think I scared him off."

"I'm sure that telling him about Martin helped."

"I don't think it was that. I was just so"—she hesitated—"eager."

Jessica shook her head. "Chris, *eager* is the kiss of death with men. You know that."

"Well, I guess I'm just an idiot."

"I didn't mean that." She pulled Christine into her. "Sorry, honey."

"Me too." She sighed deeply. "Let's go work."

They broke for lunch an hour later. Christine couldn't stomach the thought of another fatty ham sandwich. Instead she went to the bus and found her suitcase. She found her cache of protein bars and ate one, then changed into fresh clothes. Then she tore a page from her journal and wrote Paul a note.

Dear Paul,
I want to thank you for the last few days. What you do here at the Sunflower is beautiful. I will never forget my time here, the children or especially last night. You helped me in ways you will probably never know.

She lifted her pen, hesitant to write what she really felt. She continued.

If I have said or done something to hurt you, I am truly sorry. You are a very dear man.

I wish you happiness.
Affectionately,
Christine

She folded the note and put it in her pants pocket, then went back to the greenhouse to work.

It was a little after one o'clock that things began to wind up. By half past the hour Jim shouted, "Time to go."

"But we're not done," Mason said.

"The men of the village will finish up," Jim said.

"You said we'd be here until two," Christine said.

"I know, but we really should get on the road. It looks like it might rain, and this afternoon's our only chance to see Ollantaytambo."

Christine's heart sank. The small chance she had of seeing Paul again had just diminished. As Christine and Jessica climbed the back stairs into the courtyard, she glanced around the courtyard for one last look. She said to Jessica, "I need to say goodbye to Roxana."

"You better hurry."

"I'll run." Christine looked in the dining room for Paul, but no one was there except two of the boys, Carlos and Ronal. "*¿Dónde . . . está . . . Paul?*" she asked.

Carlos shrugged.

"*No sé.*" Ronal said, "*Cuzco.*"

"*¿Dónde está Roxana?*" she asked.

They pointed up toward her room.

"*Gracias.*"

Christine ran up the stairs. Roxana was in her room playing with her hair combs and ribbon. When she saw Christine, she immediately stood and walked to her, her hands raised to be picked up. Christine crouched down and held her. Her eyes filled with tears. She hadn't considered how difficult it would be to say goodbye. She wondered how Roxana would react.

"I have to go, sweetheart," she said. The words sounded so final. "Take care of yourself."

She again wrapped her arms around the little girl and held her. It was excruciating but she forced herself to her feet. "I'll never forget you."

Roxana just looked at her, confused. Then her eyes filled with tears and she grabbed Christine's legs. Christine bent over and hugged her again and they were both crying. "Please don't make this harder," she said. She kissed her again, then stood and without looking back walked out. She could hear the bus's engine fire up and she knew they were waiting for her.

She walked to the boys' dorm and found Pablo sitting on the floor filling the back of his new truck with the sticks and rocks that he had carried up from the courtyard.

"Hi."

He looked at her tear-streaked face. "Hi."

"Pablo, do you know where Paul is?"

"He's not back."

Her throat tightened. "Would you give this to him." She handed him the note.

"Sure." He shoved the paper into his pocket.

"You won't forget?"

"Nah. I'll remember."

"Thanks, Pablo. May I have a hug?"

He looked up from the truck. "Sure."

She crouched down next to him, and they hugged. "Be a good boy."

"Okay. Bye."

She turned and walked back down the balcony and down the stairs to the court-yard, fighting the growing impulse to cry. She didn't understand why it hurt so much that Paul wasn't there. She told herself it didn't matter; after all, she really barely knew him. The bus honked and she knew it was for her. She hurried her pace. As she passed the well, someone called to her from the classroom.

"Christine."

Paul stood just inside the doorway. He walked to her. In one hand he carried a camera; in the other he held a sunflower.

"I couldn't find you," she said.

"I'm sorry, I just got back."

"I left a note for you with Pablo. Just in case I didn't see you again."

He looked into her eyes. "What did it say?"

"Thank you. Mostly." She hesitated then said, "May I be honest?"

He nodded.

"Last night was so special for me. I've been wondering all day what I did to scare you off. If I said something to upset you, I'm really sorry. I didn't mean to hurt you."

Paul frowned. "I'm the one who should apologize. I shouldn't have done that to you. Last night was wonderful, maybe *too* wonderful." He shifted awkwardly on the balls of his feet. Then he took a deep breath. "Sometimes it's better to just not know what you're missing." After a moment he smiled. "One thing I know for certain— Martin is a real fool."

Christine smiled as well.

"Did you say goodbye to Roxana?"

She nodded. "Yes."

"Is she all right?"

"She was crying."

"I'll go see her." He handed her the flower. "I picked it on the way back. So you'll remember us."

"Thank you." She looked at it for a moment, twisting its stem so the flower faced her. "I don't think I'm in danger of forgetting."

They stood awkwardly, unsure how to say goodbye.

Jessica had left the bus and was walking toward the hacienda. "C'mon, Chris," she called impatiently.

"May I take a picture?" he asked.

"Of course." She held the sunflower up near her face. "How's this?"

"Perfect." He snapped the picture. "You better go," Paul said. He paused, then he suddenly stepped forward and pressed his lips against hers.

"Christine!" Jessica shouted, "You're holding everyone up."

They parted, and Christine took Paul's hand in both of hers, the sunflower crossed beneath. She lifted his hand to her lips. Paul walked her to the outer wall. Jessica saw them together and stopped. "Sorry," she said, and turned and walked back to the bus.

"If you're ever in Dayton . . ."

"I'll call. I promise."

She sighed deeply.

"You better go," Paul said.

She looked once more into his eyes. *"Adiós,"* she said.

"Adiós."

She turned and walked away, clutching the sunflower. The bus door swung open, and Paul watched her climb onto the bus. The bus's brake released and the leviathan slowly crawled back up the dirt and gravel road. The afternoon sun glared across the bus's windows, turning them golden, and he couldn't see Christine staring at him, her face pressed against the glass. When the bus was out of sight, he went to find Roxana.

CHAPTER

Fourteen

The more I study history the more I realize how little mankind has changed. There are no new scripts, just different actors.

✦ PAUL COOK'S DIARY ✦

Christine sat silently as the bus moved past broad terraced fields south into the Sacred Valley. From time to time Jim would take the bus's microphone and point out landmarks, but Christine was oblivious to them. Her mind was still at El Girasol.

"A sol for your thoughts," Jessica said.

Christine looked out the window. "You'd be wasting your money."

"Are you going to tell me why you're being so quiet?"

She sighed deeply. "No."

"Are you mad at me for neglecting you?"

"No."

"Are you sure?"

"I'm sure."

Christine turned to her. "Then why won't you tell me?"

"Because I don't want to talk about it."

Jessica raised her hands in mock surrender. "All right, all right. Sorry." She had barely let the moment settle when she started up again. "Chris, you've got to move on. Martin hasn't even called since he left. He's not worthy of your pain."

Christine didn't respond, and Jessica suddenly understood.

"It *isn't* Martin." Christine's expression confirmed her suspicion. "That must have been some walk."

Christine turned to her. "I want to see him again."

"Don't tell me you're falling for him . . ." Jessica slowly shook her head. "Chris, what are you thinking? The man has crates for furniture. Where are you going to go with that?"

Christine turned back to the window.

"Don't be mad at me, I'm just being realistic."

Without turning back, Christine said, "And your relationship with Jim is realistic?"

"At least he lives in the same hemisphere." Her voice dropped. "Besides, it's as realistic as any of my relationships."

Jessica leaned closer. "Listen, Chris, I have no illusion that this fling with Jim will last past next week. That's just my twisted way of dealing with things. But you don't do anything halfway. There's nothing good you can take from this."

Christine said nothing.

Jessica persisted. "Just like that you've forgotten Martin?"

"Like you said, he's not worthy of my pain."

"Is Paul?"

She didn't answer right away. "I don't know."

Jessica sat back in her seat. "Well at least you know there are other fish in the sea besides Martin."

Christine closed her eyes and leaned against the window.

An hour later the bus pulled off the main road into a mountain valley. Jim stood up and grabbed the bus's microphone. "Just up ahead here is the village of Ollantay-tambo."

"Ollantaytambo is the last stop of the Sacred Valley. It was one of the last strongholds of the Incas. When Pizarro conquered Cuzco, the Incas retreated here. Pizarro sent his brother after them, but the Incas were ready for them and for the first time the Spaniards were defeated. At least for a while. Pizarro sent a larger force and the

Incas retreated to their final holdout at Vilcabamba.

"The town we're passing through is the
original Incan town. As you can see most of
the ruins are up on the mountain. If you look
across to the neighboring mountain, you will
see what looks like a man's head wearing a
crown.

"There's some controversy among scholars, but some believe that this face was
carved by the Incas and is the great white-
bearded god whom the Incas mistook
Pizarro to be. When we arrive, you're free
to climb to the top of the ruins, but please
keep track of the time. Dinner's at six, and
we need to be back on the bus by a quarter
after five."

After maneuvering between several other
tourist buses, the bus braked to a stop in
the parking lot outside the ruins. From below, the ruins looked like a great stone pyra-
mid built into the side of a mountain.

Jessica stood. "C'mon, Chris, let's go."

The group climbed the terraced hills to
the temple above. At the top of the climb
Christine separated from the group and sat
down on a terrace, her feet hanging over a
six-foot drop to the plateau below. Thin gray

clouds collected above, casting a shadow on the valley and the miniature township below. The air was cool and the wind danced her hair around her shoulders. After a few minutes Jim came and sat down next to her. Christine wondered where Jessica was and if she'd sent him.

"Pretty amazing, aren't they?" he asked. "They estimate that some of these stones up here weigh more than seventeen tons. There's a quarry about seven miles from here, just over those mountains, where they cut the stones for the temple."

"It's remarkable."

"Do you know what built this city?"

"Thousands of slaves?"

"That and one man's love. Ollantaytambo was founded by an Incan general named Ollantay. He was the most powerful of the Incan generals. Ollantay fell in love with the king's daughter. He asked the king if he could marry her, but because he didn't have royal blood, the king turned him down. So he took those who would follow him and he left Cuzco and built this fortress. His plan was to finish building the city, then march back and fight for her. But before the city was complete, the king died and his son took over. His son feared Ollantay and didn't care who married his sister, so rather than go to battle he just let Ollantay take her." He looked out over the valley.

Christine looked up at him. "That's a true story?"

"So I'm told."

"It's pretty romantic." Christine pulled the hair back from her face. "So you think maybe I should build a fortress?"

Jim smiled. "The moral of my little tale is that when love is right, things work out. Not necessarily the way you think they will, but they do work out."

She looked at him and smiled. "Thank you."

"Don't mention it."

"How long have you known Paul?"

"Three, four years."

"Is he really as kind as he seems?"

"Yeah, I think so." After a moment he looked at his watch. "I better start rounding everyone up. I'll see you in a few."

✦

Back on the bus, Jessica asked Christine, "What were you and Jim talking about?" There was a hint of jealousy in her tone.

"He was telling me the story of the ruins."

"Really?"

"Yeah." She suddenly smiled. "You know, Jim's a pretty smart guy."

Jessica looked at her quizzically. "Is he now?"

She nodded.

"You sure you weren't talking about me?"

Christine turned away. "No. Just the ruins."

✦

The bus arrived at the hotel as the Sacred Valley settled into twilight. A guard opened a gate in a long sandstone fence and let them into the hotel's parking lot. A sign on the building read BEST WESTERN INCALAND.

"Look at that," Jessica said, "a Best Western in the middle of nowhere. Hey, Sledge, what's this town called?"

Jim looked over. "Urubamba," he said.

"Do you know what Urubamba means?" Christine asked Jessica.

"No. I can't even pronounce it."

"Paul told me it means Land of Spiders."

"I bet you were thrilled to learn that."

"You know I was."

"Let's hope it's false advertising," she said.

The hotel was a labyrinth of small bungalows surrounded by lush Andean flora. In the center of the resort was an Olympic-sized swimming pool, and to one side of it was a corral with well-groomed llamas. Jessica and Christine stopped to look at the animals, then took their bags to their room.

The two women put away their bags, then Jessica left to eat while Christine stayed behind. She wasn't in the mood for socializing. She took her sunflower out of her pack and looked at it. She wondered if Paul missed her as much as she missed him. She wondered if she would ever see him again. Though it didn't seem likely, she held to Jim's words: *when love is right, things work out.*

She set the sunflower on her nightstand, shut off the light and went to sleep.

CHAPTER

Fifteen

I have tried to settle back into my routine, but it hasn't been easy. I wonder how one woman and three days could so change my world.

✦ PAUL COOK'S DIARY ✦

Christine woke before the alarm. Jessica was lightly snoring in the bed next to her. Christine quietly dressed then walked out of their cabana. It had rained during the night, and the grounds of the resort were wet and puddled. The air was cool and thin, and her head hurt a little, whether from emotion or the altitude she wasn't sure. Still she felt better than she had the day before.

Many of the group had already gathered at the breakfast buffet in a large lodge. There were other tourists groups as well, and more than half the room was speaking Japanese.

Joan and Mason were sitting together and they waved her over.

"How'd y'all sleep?" Mason said, lifting a piece of burnt toast.

"Fine."

"I didn't see you last night," Joan said.

"I was tired. I just went to bed."

Mason began scraping the burnt side of his toast with a butter knife. "Where's that friend of yours?"

"She's still in bed."

"She better not be late today," Joan said, "We've got a train to catch."

"Don't forget to take your bags up front," Mason said. "The bus is going to take them back to Cuzco. We take the train the whole way back."

"You know," Joan said, "it's a shame that Paul didn't come along with us. The two of you made a cute couple."

The comment caught Christine off guard. "Thanks," she said awkwardly. "I better go check on Jess."

Christine picked up some fruit and a couple pastries, wrapped them in a napkin and went back to her room. Jessica was already dressed and packing her bag.

"We need to take our bags up front," Christine said.

"I know. What time is it anyway?"

"Almost eight."

"We've got to go. The train leaves in fifteen minutes."

✦

The train station was on the other side of the resort and the women had to run to make it to the train on time, arriving sweaty and out of breath. The train was small, with only five passenger cars; the railroad track had been built alongside the Urubamba River, cutting south deep into jungles until it reached the town of Aguas Calientes—Hot Waters. As they approached the village the waters grew angrier into class five rapids that churned and spit and heaved with such violence that the river's muddy waters almost appeared to be boiling.

As they neared their destination, Jim stood at the front of the train. "If I may have your attention now, I'm going to tell you a little about Machu Picchu. Known as the lost city, Machu Picchu was one of the most beautiful sacred cities established by the Incas and was populated by a specially chosen lineage of Incan nobility.

"As you've seen in Cuzco, the Spanish conquistadors destroyed most of the Incan religious and political centers. Fortunately for us Machu Picchu was never found by the Spanish.

"In 1911 an American explorer, a Yale professor named Hiram Bingham, aided by locals, discovered the city. He was not looking for Machu Picchu, as no one knew it existed. He was looking for Vilcabamba, the last Incan bastion against the Spaniards.

"The large mountain that towers above the citadel is called Huayna Picchu. It was the watchtower for Machu Picchu. It is open to the public and you are welcome to climb it, though I must warn you it's quite steep and even though some handrails have been installed, it's still quite dangerous. But if you're up to it, it's worth the climb. I've climbed it at least a dozen times myself. The view is spectacular."

The train began to slow.

"The last train leaves Aguas Caliente at four-thirty, which means we need to be leaving the mountain by three-thirty. Missing the train is not an option. We're taking the train all the way back to Cuzco and tomorrow morning we fly to the jungle, so everyone must be at the station by four o'clock. No exceptions.

"After we leave the train, we'll walk to town together and take a shuttle up the mountain. You can come back anytime you want, just be here by four. Any questions?"

Joan raised her hand. "How often do the shuttles run?"

"Every fifteen minutes or so. But later in the day they fill up, so it might take three or four buses to get us all down. Again, don't take any chances. There's a lot of shopping in Aguas Caliente, so you won't be sitting around down there."

The train braked to a stop.

They walked as a group from the train down the tracks past a makeshift village of souvenir shops. Christine stopped to look at a chess set with hand-carved wooden figures pitting the Incas against the Spanish conquistadors. Jessica pointed out a glass terrarium containing a tarantula six inches across.

"We'll shop later," Jim said, herding them along.

"Are we going to climb the mountain?" Jessica asked.

"If you gals are up to it."

"We're up to it," Jessica said.

They boarded a shuttle bus and climbed the winding dirt road a mile up the mountain. When they reached the top Jim purchased tickets for the group and stood at the turnstile as everyone passed through. Jessica and Christine were the last ones through as Jim had promised them a personal tour.

The terraced hills were brilliant green and a path led from the main gate across one of the terraces into the city.

"This is incredible," Christine said.

"Machu Picchu's one of those places everyone should see before they die," Jim said. "Like the great wall of China, or Venice."

"Or Dayton," Jessica said.

All three of them laughed. Jim led them down a narrow stone stairway to a tall semicircular building. The stones were carefully rounded and inside the structure there were trapezoid-shaped niches.

"What was this building used for?" Jessica asked.

"This is the Temple of the Sun. The Incas worshiped the sun, water and Pachamama, Mother Earth. These two windows are perfectly aligned according to the points where the sun rises on the summer and winter solstices.

"One of the guides up here told me that

the sunflower was the symbol of the temple and that Incan priestesses wore head-dresses made of golden sunflowers."

"Christine in a former life," Jessica said.

Christine smiled at this and ran her hand across the smooth, moss-covered wall.

Jim led them down to the next ruin, the Temple of the Condor. The natural stone thrust outward like large wings, and on the ground a bird's head was carved into a sac-rificial stone. A trough was cut in the stone.

Jessica crouched down to touch it. "What's this thing?" she asked.

"It's the condor's head. It's believed that this was used for human sacrifices."

"People were killed here?"

"They think so."

Jessica shuddered. "Let's get out of here."

They climbed around the stones through a dozen more structures, with every wall smooth and perfectly aligned. Halfway through the grounds Jessica and Jim were holding hands, seemingly no longer con-cerned with whether anyone else noticed.

They climbed down the steps of the pyra-mid into the center of the ruins, emerging into a broad, grassy plaza half the size of a football field. On the opposite side of the field was the urban section, a row of symmetrical buildings shadowed by Huayna Picchu.

On the same grass a herd of llamas grazed lazily, seemingly oblivious to the tourists snapping their photographs. "Look, Chris, llamas," Jessica said, running off to see them. Jim cast a sideways glance to Christine, then went after her. Christine followed. When they caught up to Jessica, she was standing next to a baby animal.

"Isn't she cute?" Jessica said, "A baby llama."

"I think it's an alpaca," Jim said.

"Alpaca, llama, they're the same thing."

She leaned down next to the animal and began stroking its neck. "Hi, baby," she cooed

"Be careful," Jim said, "They spit."

"She's not going to spit. She likes me."

The alpaca settled down into the grass, its eyelids closing more with each stroke.

"I've never seen one do that," Jim said.

"It's just like a big dog," Jessica said. "Jim, take a picture."

"I'll take it, "Christine said. She took the

camera from Jessica's backpack. "Jim, you get in there with her."

He put his arm around Jessica and she snapped the shot. "Perfect."

"Chris, take one of me kissing the llama," she said. She puckered up, kissing it on the snout.

Jim rolled his eyes. "You think I'm going to kiss you after you've kissed that thing?"

"You don't have to kiss me," she said.

Jim knew he couldn't win that argument. He looked up at the sun. "If we're going to climb Huayna Picchu, we'd better get started."

They hiked to the south end of the citadel, where a dirt path led sharply down a ravine to the base of the mountain. A sign pointed to Huayna Picchu and a different direction to the Temple of the Moon.

"Everyone *sure* they want to do this?" Jim asked.

"We're sure," Jessica said turning to Christine, "Aren't we?"

"Absolutely," Christine said.

The climb took them about an hour. In some places stones had been cut into stairs or ropes hung as guide lines. Even though the trail was well traveled, it was still treacherous in parts. In a few spots they climbed on all fours.

There was a bottleneck at the top of the mountain where the hikers scaled the final thrust of stone to the pinnacle. When the congestion cleared, Jim climbed up first, then held out his hand and helped both women up. No longer protected by the side of the mountain, the wind was strong and loud and the experience reminded Christine of her childhood, when her parents had taken her to the observation deck of the Empire State Building.

"Welcome to the top of the world," Jim said.

Jessica gasped. "It's breathtaking. Machu Picchu looks like a toy village. How high up are we?"

"Huayna Picchu is about a thousand feet higher than Machu Picchu."

"This is amazing," Christine said. "I'm so glad we came."

"It always makes me a little nervous taking groups up here. Last year I met a Frenchman hiking up. He said that his wife had died here from a fall and every year on the same day he came back and hiked it in her memory."

"That's romantic," Jessica said.

"Not my kind of romantic," Christine said.

✦

They took pictures of each other and basked in the sun for about a half hour until the summit became too congested with arriving hikers and they decided to go. Jim led, followed by Jessica and then Christine. The trip down the mountain was considerably faster. Jim kept them at a cautious pace, but they still made good time, catching up with a group of Chinese tourists who had left the summit ten minutes before them. They were about two-thirds down the mountain when Jessica said, "So, Jim. If I fell, would you risk your life to save me?"

Jim was carefully picking his steps and didn't look back. "What kind of question is that?"

"A girl just needs to know these things. She needs to feel safe."

"If you want to feel safe, watch your step and stay as close to the mountain as you can."

"You mean don't do this . . ." she jumped over a small ridge to the step below just a few yards above him. The lip she landed on was held only by vegetation and tree roots and gave way beneath her feet. "Jim!"

Jim spun around. She was above him, sliding feet forward toward the edge of the trail. Without thought, he lunged toward her, catching her at her hips and tackling her back against the inclined path. When their motion had stopped, she lay on her back and Jim lay across her, his chest flat against her pelvis, his feet hanging over the side of the trail. They were both breathing heavily.

"That was the stupidest thing anyone has ever done," Jim said.

"That was the stupidest thing *I've* ever done," Jessica said meekly. "You saved me."

"You okay?"

"I'm okay. Are you?"

"Yeah," he said, though a thin stream of blood rolled down his arm.

"You're bleeding."

He looked down at it. "It's nothing," he said breathlessly. "Don't do that again."

"I don't plan on it."

Jim rolled to his side and lifted himself with his elbows. "Never a dull moment with you, is there?" Suddenly the thin dirt ledge he kneeled on gave out beneath him and he was gone. Jessica screamed, followed by a shout from one of the Chinese tourists below, and both echoes were met only with silence. Jessica lay back, shaking. "How far did he fall?" she asked.

Christine was also trembling. "I don't know."

"Dear God, please don't let him die," Jessica said, "Please. I'll do anything, God. Anything."

CHAPTER

Sixteen

I received an emergency call to help Jim, who had fallen from Huayna Picchu. On my drive to Aguas Calientes I realized that I would see Christine again. Considering the circumstance, I felt guilty in that pleasure.

✦ PAUL COOK'S DIARY ✦

One of the Chinese men grabbed onto the narrow root of a tree that grew horizontally from the incline and leaned out, his companions holding his jacket. He shouted back to them, *"Wo kan ta."* I see him.

"Ta szle?" Is he dead?

"Wo bujr dau." I don't know.

"Do you see him?" Christine shouted to them.

The man glanced up, then pointed below them to an unseen spot. "He down."

Jessica and Christine scrambled down to a lower ledge and Jessica hung out.

"There he is," she said. Jim lay facedown on a terrace about twenty feet below them.

"Is he moving?"

"No," she said, her voice quavering.

They quickly picked their way down to where Jim lay. His face was buried in the dirt, and he had a large gash on his head and one on his right arm. They were near the bottom quarter of the climb, and the mountain flared out a little as the path doubled back on itself.

"Is he breathing?" Jessica asked.

Christine crouched down next to him. "Yes."

"Should we roll him over?"

"No, don't touch him," Christine said.

Jessica got on her knees and forearms next to him, her thoughts wild with fear and panic. Blood had pooled on the ground beneath him, turning the soil dark and wet. "Jim. Wake up. Please, wake up."

Suddenly he let out a low, anguished groan.

One of the Chinese men came nearer and Jessica waved him away. "Don't touch him! No one touch him." She leaned nearer to him. "Jim, can you hear me?"

He didn't respond, then his eyelids flickered and he said in a voice barely audible, "Yeah."

"Do you think your back's broken?"

"Everything . . . hurts." He turned his face toward them. It was caked with mud and blood.

"Don't move," Christine said.

Jessica was shaking. "Can you move your toes?"

His left foot moved slightly but he grimaced with pain. "My legs hurt."

Jessica extended her trembling hand and gently ran it across the back of his leg, then carefully around the front. She suddenly jerked back. "I can feel the bone. It's sticking out."

Christine moved forward. "Come back here, Jess. Get away from the ledge." She took Jessica's place and ran her hand down and touched the fracture. The bone had pierced the skin and it was wet with blood.

A muscular, sandy-haired man flanked by three teenage boys who had been climbing up the mountain stopped next to them. "How far'd he fall?" the man asked in an Australian accent.

"About thirty feet," Christine said. "We need help."

"Is his neck broken?"

"We don't know," Christine said.

"Let's 'ave a gander," he said kneeling down next to him.

"His leg's broken," Jessica said.

He touched his leg and felt the protruding bone. "Bloody oath." He pulled off his jacket. "I'm a fireman, this is right up my alley."

He glanced at Jessica, "My name's Pete. Is this your hubby?"

"He's my boyfriend."

"No worries. We'll get him down."

The young men stood a few yards back, staring with wide eyes. He said to them. "You guys run down to the post and get us some help. We'll need a stretcher. G'on, quick smart."

The boys took off.

Two of the Chinese men stayed behind while the rest of the group moved on down after the young men.

Jim continued to groan while Jessica held his hand. The Australian pulled out a pocketknife. "I'll have to give his Daks a slice." He cut Jim's pant legs up to his thighs. Jessica grimaced at the sight of the fractured bone protruding from his shin. She began to cry. Pete began lightly pressing on Jim's legs. "Can you feel my fingers, mate?" he asked.

"Yes."

"Does it hurt?"

"Not there."

"Good." He took off his belt, then said to

Jessica, "Young lady, could you lend me your belt?"

Jessica quickly unthreaded her belt and handed it to him, then went back to holding Jim's hand and running her fingers back through his hair. The man said, "Listen, mate, we don't have any flat boards for a splint. So we're gonna tie your legs together with these belts."

" 'Kay."

"I'm gonna move your good leg now. It might pinch a bit." He grasped Jim's right leg and pulled it over to the broken one, then took the belt and slid it beneath and around the leg.

Jim cried out.

"Sorry, mate. How's your back?"

"I don't know."

"Where do you hurt the most?"

"My leg."

"Anyplace else?"

"My head."

"I bet. You've got yourself quite a whack."

While they waited for the boys to return, Joan, Mason and three others from Puma-Condo came upon them. Word had spread down the trail that someone had fallen, but they hadn't expected it to be one of their own. When Mason saw the women, he shouted back to the others, "It's one of ours." They quickened their pace. "Jessica, Christine, what happened?" Mason asked.

"Jim fell."

They crowded nearer.

"Let's give him some space, mates. We don't need anyone else falling here today."

"Jess," Jim said.

"What?" she leaned close. Christine listened in.

"The group . . ." he stopped, grimacing with pain.

"Take it slow, honey."

". . . get the group to Cuzco," he said hoarsely. "They need to catch the train. The tickets . . . in my pack."

Christine asked Mason, "Can you get everyone back to Cuzco?"

He nodded. "Can do."

"We'll stay with Jim. We'll call when we know what's happening."

Christine unzipped Jim's backpack and brought out an envelope containing the train tickets and hotel vouchers, and handed it to Mason. "You better get going."

"How are you getting him down?" Mason asked.

"My kid and his mates went for help," Pete said. "We can carry him down."

"We help," one of the remaining Chinese said.

Mason stood. "Okay. I'll round everyone up. We'll be waiting for word."

They went back down the mountain. Groups of hikers continued to pass them from both directions, rubbernecking as they squeezed by them on the trail. About twenty minutes later the three boys returned, followed by four Peruvian men carrying a stretcher. One of them spoke good English.

"Is his back broken?"

"We don't think so," Jessica said. "He can move his feet."

The Peruvian team unlashed Jim's backpack and pulled it off of him. Christine took it. Then they worked their way around him and lifted Jim onto the stretcher. He screamed when they lifted him. He was strapped tightly down, then the Peruvians, Pete and his boys and the two Chinese surrounded the stretcher, each grabbing where he could. They slowly hiked down, breathing heavily with exertion. Jim grew more alert with each minute. The trail dropped down into a cravasse, then climbed steeply to the trail gate that opened out into Machu Picchu. When they reached the end of the trail, the men were out of breath. They set the stretcher down on a soft patch of grass to rest. Jessica sat on the grass next to Jim. "Are you okay, sweetheart?"

"Do you have any coca leaves?" he asked.

"I have some," Christine said. She was wearing the same jacket she had worn upon their arrival in Cuzco, and she still had the bag of leaves that Jim had bought for her. She brought it out and took out several leaves. "Here."

Jim slowly opened his mouth and began to chew the leaves. After a moment he appeared more relaxed.

"All right, mates," Pete said standing, "Let's finish this."

They again hefted the stretcher and started off, following the lead of one of the Peruvian rescue workers, who pushed aside the gaping tourists as the procession passed.

There was no easy way out of Machu Picchu. They carried Jim across the ruins up a long series of steps to the front gate and out to the bus landing. A pickup truck was waiting for them. There was a foam mattress in the truck's bed and they lay the stretcher on it, securing it down with nylon straps.

"There y'ago, mate," Pete said.

"Thanks," Jim said.

"Thank you so much," Jessica said.

"No worries. Good luck. Hooroo." Pete and his boys walked back up toward the entry gate. The Chinese men also took leave, and Jessica and Christine climbed up into the bed next to Jim. Jessica took his hand.

"Jess," Jim said.

"Yes?"

"Call Paul. I don't want someone here patching me up."

"Okay."

"I have his cell phone," Christine said. She reached into Jim's backpack and took out the phone. She handed it to Jessica.

Jessica leaned into him. "What's the number?"

"Hold down the three."

Jessica pushed the three, then held the phone up to her ear. After several rings someone answered.

"Hello, Paul? This is Jessica. Not good. Jim fell from Huayna Picchu. He's hurt pretty bad. Can you come?"

She put her hand over the mouthpiece. "Where will we be?" she asked Jim.

"The medical post in Aguas."

"The medical post in Aguas. I'll keep my cell phone on. Okay. We'll be waiting for you." She hung up. "He's coming."

"Thanks."

Jessica took Jim's hand again. Christine braced herself against the side of the truck bed as they started down the hill. Occasionally they'd hit a bump or brake too quickly and Jim would groan loudly. The truck moved slowly down the steep climb, and it took them nearly forty minutes to reach the medical post. With each passing moment Jim's pain seemed to increase, and Christine, not knowing what else to do, gave him more coca leaves.

When they arrived at the center, a man and a woman wearing white coats walked out to the truck. With the help of the rescue workers they carried Jim inside.

With the exception of the truck driver and an assistant, the rescue crew had stayed on the mountain, and there was no longer anyone with them who spoke English. Jessica and Christine felt even more helpless.

The medical post was small, old and

lightly equipped. It did have a large, clunky X-ray machine that looked like it might be World War II surplus. The medic examined the bone protruding from Jim's leg and frowned. While the nurse cleaned Jim's abrasions, the man cut off Jim's pants and doused his leg with hydrogen peroxide. He took eleven X-rays and determined the greatest cause of Jim's pain was a dislocated shoulder. He tried to set it and Jim screamed so loudly that Jessica started to cry. He tried several more times without success and each time Jim screamed louder. "They're torturing him," Jessica said. "Where's Paul?"

The next two hours passed with excruciating slowness; by the time Paul arrived, Jessica was near hysterics.

She jumped up when Paul entered the clinic. "Please help him."

"I will." He glanced at Christine then went to the back room where Jim lay on the bed, writhing with pain. He gently touched his shoulder. "I'm here, buddy." The clinic's staff appeared as relieved to see him as Jessica and Christine had. Paul carefully looked over the X-rays, then spoke with the medic while he examined Jim's wounds. It had been more than three hours since Jim had fallen, and the muscles in his back and shoulders had spasmed, making his shoulder nearly impossible to set.

Paul took out a syringe of ketamine from the bag he brought with him and injected his friend in the arm. Jim's eyes closed and his muscles went limp. Paul pushed the shoulder down until it popped loudly back in place. He inserted an IV needle in his forearm and started him on an antibiotic, then examined the suture of the large gash and told the medic that he'd done *muy bien,* which pleased the man immensely.

He walked out of the back room to find the women sitting on a bench. Jessica had her arms wrapped around her body, and Christine was next to her, rubbing her back. They both looked up. "How is he?" Jessica asked.

"We've got to get him to Cuzco as soon as possible. We need a CAT scan to make sure there's no internal bleeding. And he has a compound comminuted fracture."

"What's a compound commi . . ." Jessica asked.

"It means that his leg is broken in multiple fragments. He's going to need an orthopedic surgeon. I called the hospital for a helicopter but there's none available. We're going to have to drive him. Where's the rest of the group?"

"They took the train back to Cuzco."

"Okay, we'll put him in the back of my truck."

Paul gave Jim another shot of ketamine; he wanted to make sure he was knocked out for the whole trip. Three hours later Paul pulled up outside the emergency room of the Cuzco hospital. He honked his horn and a gurney was brought out, accompanied by the E.R. personnel. The gurney and Paul disappeared into the hospital.

The women went inside the lobby to wait. A little after midnight Paul came and sat down next to them, visibly fatigued.

Jessica stood. "How is he?"

"Much better than he should be. He has a concussion. And the leg was pretty bad; they had to pin it together. But he'll be okay until we get him back to the States."

"When is that?"

"He wants to go back with the group."

"Is he awake?"

"He's a little groggy, but he's awake."

"May I see him?" Jessica asked.

"You're the first one he asked for. It's the second door on the left."

She walked down the hall and opened the door. The room was dark and Jim lay on his back, his leg held up in traction. His face and neck were bruised, and his right eye was swollen shut. When Jessica saw him, she began to cry. He turned toward her.

"Hey, Jess," he said, his voice slightly slurred.

She went to his side and took his hand. "I'm so sorry."

"It's not your fault."

"If I hadn't been so stupid. I was just flirting with you."

"No one held a gun to my head." He forced a smile. "Maybe to my heart."

"I've ruined everything. What will the rest of the group do?"

"Paul's going to take you to the jungle."

She shook her head. "I'm not leaving you."

"When will you get another chance? You really . . ."

She put her finger on his lips. "I'm staying." She leaned over and kissed him.

"You win," he said.

"I always do."

CHAPTER

Seventeen

Jim has asked me to lead the group into the jungle. I'd lead them to Everest if I knew Christine was with us.

✤ PAUL COOK'S DIARY ✤

Paul and Christine sat alone in the hospital's tiled hallway. It was past 2 A.M. and most of the overhead fluorescent lights had been turned off, leaving them in shadows. Their hushed voices echoed off the walls.

"How did it happen?" Paul asked.

"We had climbed Huayna Picchu and were most of the way down when Jessica began joking around and slipped. Jim saved her. But then the trail just seemed to collapse beneath him."

"That's why she feels so responsible." He threaded his hands together. "At least no one was killed."

"Thank God for that."

Silence. After a moment Christine asked, "Was Roxana okay after I left?"

"She cried for a while. Then when I told her that you wouldn't be back at all, she cried a lot more. She was pretty taken with you."

"It goes both ways."

"Thank you for the note."

"I wanted to write more, but under the circumstances . . ." She looked down, then said, "I missed you."

"I missed you too." Their eyes locked on each other. "Jim asked if I would lead the group into the jungle. So you're stuck with me for a little while longer."

She didn't try to hide her smile. "So the cloud does have a silver lining."

He smiled too, then looked down at his watch. "We fly out in six hours. I better get you two to the hotel."

"I'd like to see Jim before we go."

"Of course."

They walked to his room. Paul knocked softly on the door, then opened it. Jessica sat on a chair next to the bed, her head on Jim's chest.

"Hi, Jim," Christine said.

"Hey."

"How are you?"

"Alive."

"Alive is good. You look great."

"I look like I just went five rounds with Mike Tyson."

"Okay, you look awful," Christine said. "But you sound good."

He smiled.

"You're a hero, you know. You saved my best friend's life."

He stroked Jessica's hair. "I kind of like her."

"I think you proved it. I'm sorry you can't come with us. Are you going to be okay here alone?"

Jessica looked up. "He won't be. I'm staying with him."

Christine looked at her in surprise. "You're staying?"

"Yes."

"Good," Paul said. "From what I know of Jessica the hospital staff will be on their toes."

Jim smiled at her, then looked back at Paul. "The school in Puerto is expecting us."

"Everything's set," Paul said. "I spoke with the headmaster a few hours ago. Don't worry about a thing."

"Just bring them back alive," Jim said.

"I will." He turned to Jessica. "Take good care of him."

"And you take care of my best friend."

"I promise."

Christine walked over to the bed. She bent over and kissed Jim on the forehead. "Take care, Sledge."

He smiled. "Thanks."

Jessica and Christine hugged. "See you in a few days."

"See you, girlfriend. Take lots of pictures for me."

"I will. Be good."

Jessica laid her head back on Jim's chest as they left the room.

CHAPTER

Eighteen

*Christine's path has again crossed
mine. Fate has a way
of cutting corners.*

✦ PAUL COOK'S DIARY ✦

"Do you know where we're staying?" Christine asked.

"*El hotel Vilandre.* It's the same hotel where we first met."

She smiled. "You sure you didn't set that up? The pickpocket thing . . ."

"If only I were that clever."

The hotel was only a fifteen-minute drive from the hospital. Paul parked in front of the hotel and they went inside.

The lobby was dark, lit only by a single lamp in the entryway. The front counter was vacant. Paul looked around for someone, then finally just took the one key that was sitting on the desk behind the counter. "I guess this is your room," he said, handing her the key.

She checked the room number on the key tag. "This is the same room Jessica and I had before. I hope they brought my bag in. What about your things?"

"Jaime is bringing my bag to the airport. He's going in with us."

As they climbed the darkened stairwell, Paul asked quietly, "It was just the two of you in the room?"

"Actually there were three of us." She smiled proudly. "We have a gecko."

"Does he take up much room?"

"No," she said. "He sleeps on the wall." They stopped in front of her room.

"Could I sleep in your room?"

"Where else would you sleep?"

"Well, there's a couch in the lobby."

"Yeah, right."

She handed him the key. He unlocked the door and opened it. He reached in and flipped on the light, then pulled back the door to let Christine enter first. She sighed with relief when she saw her bag next to the bed.

The room was hot and humid, and Paul went over and turned on the window air conditioner. He looked around. "Where's your gecko?"

Christine looked at the wall and was a little disappointed. "I guess he checked out."

Christine went into the bathroom and undressed. Paul set the room's radio-alarm clock then took off his shirt and lay back on the top of one of the beds.

Christine stuck her head out the bathroom door. "Would you close your eyes?"

"If I must."

"You must." She made sure that he had closed his eyes before she came out in her underwear and climbed in her bed. She reached over and turned out the light between their beds.

"You can open your eyes."

"No reason to anymore," he said.

She laughed.

She heard him unbuckle his belt, pull off his pants, then roll over in the bed. A half hour later she asked in a voice slightly above a whisper, "Are you awake?"

"Yes."

"How come you're not asleep?"

"I'm afraid of geckos."

She started laughing and threw a pillow at him. He caught it and put it under his head.

"Your pillow smells better than mine."

"It's probably baby powder. Now give it back."

"I don't think so."

"I need my pillow."

"You should have thought of that before assaulting me with it."

"Please."

"You can have mine."

"Okay."

He threw his pillow to her. It was warm from his body and it made her happy. "Good night."

"Good night."

"Paul."

"Yes."

"It's good to be with you again."

"You too."

The conversation died into the hum of the air conditioner. She shut her eyes and imagined that he was holding her.

CHAPTER

Nineteen

Last night I had a nightmare. Christine and I were hiking in the jungle when we somehow became separated. She was frightened and I could hear her calling to me. I slashed at the foliage with my machete but I could not get through. There was just too much between us.

✴ PAUL COOK'S DIARY ✴

The radio alarm went off, waking them to the staccato Spanish of the local announcer. The sun shone through the partially drawn curtains, casting one long column of light on the opposite wall. Paul groaned as he rolled over and shut off the alarm. "Someone kill me."

Christine liked the raspy sound of his voice. "Good morning."

"Not until I've had coffee," he said.

"Are you going to shower?"

"No. I'll just get dirty again."

"Then I will." She sat up in bed. "Wait. Close your eyes."

"I'm a doctor, Christine. I've seen more naked bodies than Hugh Hefner."

"You haven't seen mine," she said. He put his hand over his eyes. "All right."

She climbed out of bed, took some clothes from her bag, then hurried into the bathroom. When the door shut, he sat up on the side of the bed, pulling on his jeans, then his socks and shoes. Then he fell back on the bed and closed his eyes.

Ten minutes later the water stopped. Soon after, Christine emerged, wearing a hint of makeup and her hair neatly styled. "I'm ready," she said brightly. Paul rubbed his chin. "Me too," he said, though he looked like he'd been pulled from an interrupted tumble-dry cycle. "We better go."

Paul herded the group together in the lobby. By half past the hour the bus fired up. Christine sat on the front bench, and when the door shut, Paul sat down next to her. She opened her backpack. She had gone to the lower level and gotten them some pastries and fruit. "I brought us breakfast."

"Thank you. It's been a while since anyone brought me breakfast."

She winked at him. "Then *you're* overdue."

He took an apple, wiped it on his shirt and took a bite. As the bus approached the airport, he stood and faced the group.

"First, I'm sure you are all wondering how Jim is. He's going to be okay. He has a concussion and a compound fracture but fortunately nothing worse. He'll be staying in the hospital for the next few days and he plans to fly back home with you. He asked if I would take you into the jungle. This morning we're flying into Puerto Maldonado. We'll arrive around eleven. When we get there, we'll check into our hotel, then go right to work. We only have one day in Puerto and we have a project at an elementary school."

The bus stopped in front of the airport and they carried their things inside the terminal. She heard a shout and Jaime came running toward them, several bags in tow.

Paul was pleased to see him. *"Estoy feliz que podiste venir,"* he said. *Glad you could come.*

"A tu disposicion." At your service.

✦

Although the flight to Puerto Maldonado was only a little more than an hour, it was a study in geographical contrasts. The mountains surrounding Cuzco were snow-covered, rising in majestic peaks, then slowly declining into rocky foothills that fell still further into a vast blanket of rainforest.

From Christine's window she could see a large brown river winding through the terrain like a snake through grass. She put her camera against the window and took a picture of it.

An hour later the plane set down on the asphalt tarmac carved into a thick jungle that encroached on all sides as if trying to reclaim its ground.

The airport terminal looked like an old airplane hangar. There was no control tower, just a windsock hanging limply from a pole. Christine felt like she had stepped into an adventure movie, made all the more real when the plane's door opened and the warm tropical breath of the jungle filled the plane. A mobile passenger stairs pulled up to the plane's rear door; the passengers disembarked and walked across the hot black asphalt to the terminal. Christine looked around. The landscape was lush and green and wild.

The terminal was high-ceilinged, with tin walls and exposed metal rafters. Ceiling fans buzzed twelve feet above them. There was a single baggage carousel.

Paul's bag was the first one out. He opened it, pulled out a felt fedora and put it on.

When everyone had claimed their luggage, they moved outside to the airport parking lot. Two Peruvian men were waiting for them and they appeared surprised and pleased to see Paul; they both embraced him. He spoke with them for a moment, then they walked through the parking lot, rounding up motorcycle tri-wheel taxis until eleven of them had gathered near the terminal exit.

The two men helped guide everyone to the carts and secured their luggage while Paul shouted out instructions to the drivers. The tinny whine of the two-stroke engines rose, and the carts carried them off in one large sortie, like a buzzing squadron of fliers. Christine climbed into the back of the cart with Paul. As they gained speed, she held her head out and closed her eyes. The warm air blew her hair back from her face, accentuating the elegant lines of her features. Paul looked over at her and smiled. "Having fun?"

Her smile grew and she pulled her head back in. "I can't believe I'm in the jungle."

"Tomorrow I'll show you *jungle,*" he said. He pointed up ahead to the left of the road. "See that building up there? When we get back, I'll take you to see a friend of mine.

She rescues injured animals and raises them. She has jaguars, snakes, crocodiles, a tapir and a few animals I guarantee you've never seen before."

"What's a tapir?" she asked.

"It looks a little prehistoric—kind of like an oversized rodent with a big snout. I've seen their tracks in the jungle. They're actually gentle creatures."

She shook her head. "This is so not Dayton."

"No, this isn't Dayton." She leaned back into him and he put his arm around her and pulled her tighter. A few miles later the carts pulled off the main road, and the ride declined into a rutted dirt path that led up the palm-lined road of the Don Carlos Hotel.

CHAPTER

Twenty

I have come to believe that the only true way we can serve God is to serve His children.

✦ PAUL COOK'S DIARY ✦

"Looks like we're roommates now," Christine said to Joan.

"Lucky you. I snore."

"It's okay, so does Jessica."

They carried their luggage up to their room, then hurried back to the hotel lobby as instructed. Paul was leaning against the front counter. When Christine saw him, she came and stood next to him. He said to her, "I count twenty-four. Who are we missing?"

"Did you count me?"

He smiled. "We're all here." He walked to the center of the lobby. "All right, they're waiting for us at the school. We've got a lot to do, but before we start, the children have a little program planned for us. So don't go in until I lead you in."

The carts delivered them to the school, less than a mile away. They gathered outside while Paul went alone inside the gate. A moment later the Peruvian national anthem blared from loudspeakers, and Paul walked back out, waving the group forward. "They're ready," he said.

Only half of the gate was unlocked and they entered single file. The children were lined up on both sides of the walkway and cheered as they entered, throwing confetti at them as if they were returning heroes.

They were led to folding chairs that had been set up on one side of the schoolyard. When they were all seated, the children disappeared into a school building, then came back out bearing a refreshment for each of their honored guests—a green coconut with a straw protruding from a hole drilled in the top.

"Coconut milk?" Christine asked Paul.

He nodded. "It's not as sweet as you might expect. But it's not bad."

She took a sip; it was refreshing. The music stopped and the school's headmistress picked up a microphone. She spoke in Spanish, stopping after each sentence to tilt the microphone toward Paul so he could translate.

"We welcome our American friends . . . Thank you for coming so far to help our little school . . . The boys and girls of San

Juan School hope you have a good stay in our country. And come back soon . . . We will now be pleased to offer you a dance from our country."

Paul added, "These children's costumes and dance represent the three regions of Peru: the sea, the mountains and the jungle."

Three children, a boy and two girls, came and stood before them. The music started and each child danced in turn. When the children finished, the group clapped loudly. Then the other children shouted "Thank you" in English and the teachers led the children back into their rooms.

Paul picked up the microphone. "All right, let's get to work. Our job today is to fix their bathrooms. We need three groups—a roofing group and two painting groups. Jaime will lead the roofing group. Mason will lead the painting and cleanup group for inside the latrine. And Christine will lead the painting group for the building's outside."

Christine looked surprised.

"Is that okay?" Paul asked. "I know you have experience."

"It's fine."

"Great."

Jaime selected seven men and handed them work gloves as the rest of the group assigned themselves to one group or the other.

It was dark when the roof was finally completed. The sun had fallen and the grounds and latrine were lit by the lights outside the school. The workers stood together to have a picture taken of them standing in front of their project.

"When do we eat?" one of the men asked.

"I have a treat for you," Paul said. "American-style pizza. The owner of this restaurant has a brother in Seattle, so the pizza is pretty authentic. At least as far as I remember."

They walked the six blocks to the center of town and the pizza parlor. American music from the eighties played inside the restaurant. A large brick woodburning oven stood in the corner of the restaurant, and a man shoved pizzas into its open mouth.

They were the only foreigners in the place. A young woman led them to a back room where there was a long, rectangular table. As they sat down, Paul said, *"Señorita, tráiganos cuatro pizzas grandes. Una con jamón y piña. Dos con todo y una con sólo queso. Tráiganos también dos litros de agua fría sin gas."* Miss, bring us four large pizzas, One with ham and pineapple, two with everything and one with just cheese. Bring us a couple liters of cold bottled water."

The woman ran off to fill the order. Paul sat back in his chair. Several of the teenagers lay with their heads on the table, exhausted from the day's work. "You guys did great work."

"Thanks."

"Is there an Internet café around here?" Christine asked.

"In the next block. Would you like me to show you?"

"No, I can find it. Just point me in the right direction."

"Out these doors and turn left. Look for the Internet sign."

"Thanks. I'll be right back." Christine walked out into the street. There was a group of young men sitting on motorcycles and scooters, and they all stopped talking to look at her. She felt more flattered than ogled. She crossed the street, and halfway down the block saw the sign with the @ symbol.

The room was filled with cubicles, each

with a computer, running up one side and halfway down the other. Hanging from the ceiling was a TV with poor reception; a soccer game was being broadcast. At the entry was a laminate-topped desk; behind it a young man sat back on a wooden chair, his feet up on the desk as he watched the game. He looked up at Christine.

"*¿Qué pasa? ¿Qué desea?*"

"I need a computer, please."

He nodded, then led her over to a cubicle and logged on. He held up one finger and said slowly, *"Una hora, tres soles."*

"Sí. Gracias," she said.

Christine sat down to the monitor. The words on the screen were in Spanish but the symbols were universal. She pulled up her e-mail. There was something from her mother.

Dear Christine,
I hope you are safe and well and having a good time in Peru. You are in all my prayers. Martin came by the house the other day. Will wonders never cease? He said he was having trouble finding you. You would have liked to have seen his face when I told him that you were in Peru. Needless to say he was

very surprised. He stayed a while and we talked. He apologized several times about breaking off the wedding and he seemed sincerely remorseful. He said he had something very important to speak with you about. He asked if you had a phone number where he could call you. I told him that I didn't think so as I didn't have one. Let me know. Please be safe and call when you can.
Love,
Mom
P.S. BE SAFE!

Two weeks ago she would have been running for the nearest phone. Now she felt distanced from Martin, almost as if the events of the last three months had happened to someone else. The greatest emotion she felt was curiosity. What would bring Martin to her house? Soothing a guilty conscience? Or was there more? She read the e-mail again, this time smiling at her mother's continual concern for her safety. She wrote back:

Dear Mom,
I am safe and well. Jessica and I are having a great time. I forgot to tell you that I found

*a really great bell for your collection. We
have seen many fascinating things and met
some really great people. The highlight of
my trip, so far, was when we worked in an
orphanage. I fell in love with a little deaf girl
named Roxana. I wish you could have seen
her. We are going into the jungle tomorrow.
There's no way to reach me until we're
back. If Martin has something to say to me,
please tell him to e-mail me at this address.*

Even as she typed the words, she was
amazed at her own coolness. Just then Paul
entered. He spotted her in the corner and
walked back, leaning over the cubicle's low
wall. "Hey, beautiful, pizza's ready."

She looked up, and seeing him at that moment felt right. Whatever she now felt about
Martin, she was certain that Paul had something to do with it. His friendship had made
her strong.

"Thank you. I'm almost done. I just need
another minute."

"I'll go pay."

Christine finished the e-mail, then clicked
SEND. She walked to the front of the building. Paul was reading from a newspaper

tacked to the wall. He turned to her. "News from home?"

"From my mom."

"Anything important?"

She looked at him and smiled. "Not really." She took his hand. "Let's go eat. I'm starving."

CHAPTER

Twenty-One

It's always fascinating to watch the Americans meet the Amaracayre— they are so amused with the tribe's peculiarities that they fail to see that the Amaracayre are equally amused by theirs. One teenage girl thought it odd that the chief had a bone through his nose and didn't notice that he was just as fascinated by the metal posts in her nose, tongue and ears.

✦ PAUL COOK'S DIARY ✦

They woke the next morning to a steady drizzle of rain that turned the foliage an even more vibrant green. Christine and Joan lugged their bags down to the lobby. They each grabbed a carton of juice, a sweet roll and banana and boarded the bus. Paul was already on board and Christine and Joan sat down next to him.

"Good morning, Dr. Cook," Christine said.

"Morning. How did you sleep?"

Christine smiled. "I had *good* dreams."

The bus started up. Paul stood and counted heads then turned to the driver. *"Vámonos."*

As the bus turned onto the open road, Paul stood. "Okay, campers. Today the adventure begins. It will take us all day to get to the lodge. We'll be making a short stop at the village of the Amaracayre tribe to drop off some books and medicine. So keep your cameras handy."

The first eighteen miles to Laberinto were on paved streets, then the bus turned onto red dirt roads past large fields of sugarcane and sorghum. The red clay soon turned to mud, slowing their journey.

It was nearly an hour before they reached the town. Chickens and dogs ran free in the muddy streets, and the people watched the bus navigate past small shops and an open fish market down a slope to the riverbank. When they reached the waterfront, the driver set the brake and shut off the engine. Paul stood, clinging to a rail. "Those on the left side of the bus can see our boat. Take your bags off the bus and leave them on the shore next to the boarding plank. Our guides will pack your luggage on the boat. If anyone needs to use the bathroom, there's a public restroom fifty yards up the road. It's pretty dodgy, but it's all there is. I recommend that you avail yourself since we'll be on the boats for the next four to five hours. There's a charge for the bathroom, half a *sol*. See you at the boat."

They all took their bags to the boat, then headed up the road to the restrooms. The lavatories were constructed of cinder block, with tile walls and concrete floors that were constantly wet as they were sprayed down every few hours. For half a *sol* each, they were given entrance and a small package of tissue paper. The building was crowded and dirty and the toilet was just a hole in the floor. Christine gagged as she entered the stall, and Joan shouted from the stall next to her, "Somebody just kill me."

When Christine returned, Paul was loading the last of the luggage onto the boat.

"You weren't exaggerating about how awful it is," she said.

He smiled wryly. "You should have seen it before they remodeled."

The wooden boat was nearly sixty feet long, with dull red paint peeling from its hull. Two long seats with foam rubber cushions ran along the sides of the boat with a three-foot space between them to move forward and aft. The seats were sheltered beneath a faded green-and-white canvas canopy; the bow of the boat had been filled to capacity with backpacks and luggage. It started to rain again; a plastic tarp was thrown over the luggage and plastic sheeting was unrolled from the canopy, covering the open sides of the boat.

With everyone on board, one of the guides untied the thick rope from shore and pushed out, jumping at the last minute onto the bow.

"Our guides are Marcos and Gilberto," said Paul. "They are both real jungle men and you'll be glad they're with us."

The men went about their work without acknowledging Paul's introduction.

The boat had an outboard motor with a propeller extended about eight feet out on the end of a long pole so the driver could lift it from the water if necessary. The Madre de Dios was filled with debris and a fixed prop could easily be damaged. Gilberto throttled the engine to full and they headed upriver into the jungle. Marcos put on a plastic poncho and sat on the front of the boat looking over the bow for debris and giving hand signals to Gilberto in back.

Christine sat near Paul at the front of the boat. The river widened and the trees rose in height to more than a hundred feet. Paul rearranged some of the bags, then lay back on them, pulling his fedora down over his eyes. Christine dragged her hand over the side of

the boat, the cool green water gliding between her fingers. Marcos looked over at
her. *"No, Señorita,"* he said, *"no ponga la
mano en el río."*

"What did he say?" she asked Paul.

"He wants you to take your hand out of
the water," Paul said, then casually added,
"probably because of the piranhas." Christine jerked her hand out. Marcos laughed
and Paul's mouth rose in a smile beneath
the hat's brim.

The rain turned to a mist. Christine lay
back against her pack and closed her eyes.
The lapping of the water against the stern
was comforting.

An hour and a half into the ride, Marcos
whistled to Gilberto and pointed portside
to a small cove. Gilberto steered the boat
toward the shore and cut back on the engine.

Christine looked up. "Are we already
there?" she asked.

Paul lifted his hat and looked around. He
stood up, looking down the hull of the boat.
"Listen up, everyone. This is the village of
the Amaracayre. You are welcome to get off
the boat, but there are a couple things you
should know. The chief will likely be the first

one to greet us. Do not take his photograph or videotape him without his permission. He will let you take his picture, but he will expect you to tip him. It is customary to pay him five to ten *soles* a picture. Also, some of the tribe members might offer to sell you beads. They are not expensive and make very cool souvenirs. Most of them have teeth or claws on them, usually from wild boars or parrots. Do not purchase from them until someone has purchased from the chief. It's how things work here. The chief is considered very holy and what he says is law."

The boat struck the shore and Marcos jumped off, pulling the boat up on the muddy bank. The boat came to rest beneath an overhang of tree limbs, which shielded them from the rain.

"By the way," Paul said, "don't be shocked, but the women don't wear shirts. It's not *pornographic,* it's national *geographic.* Most of the Amaracayre are elderly, and like most of these Amazonian tribes, they are dying out. You might have heard the fact that every hour two species become extinct due to deforestation. But it's not just the animals. In the last century ninety Amazon tribes have ceased to exist."

Marcos shouted something to Gilberto and the motor shut off. Paul started up toward the bow. "All right. Let's go."

Marcos tied the rope around a nearby tree, then waded in through the thick mud to give them a hand in climbing off. One by one they leapt from the bow to the marsh-like earth beneath them.

As they disembarked, a short, broad-chested man appeared on the shore. He wore no shoes or shirt, just a simple loin-cloth. He had a small bone through his nose. Paul turned toward the group. "This is the chief."

Christine was the first up the bank, followed by Paul. The chief, who was two inches shorter than Christine, stepped forward and embraced her.

"*Woomenbooey,*" he said.

She turned to Paul, not sure how to respond.

"*Woomenbooey* means 'brother' or 'sister'," Paul said. "It's a term of endearment. Just say it back to him."

"*Woomenbooey,*" Christine said, and the

chief laughed. Then he stepped toward Paul.

"*Marinka!*" he shouted, and embraced him.

"*Woomenbooey,*" Paul said.

The rest of the group filed up the bank and the chief greeted each of them.

"Paul, what did he say to you?" Christine asked.

"He has a nickname for me. He calls me *Marinka.* In their legend there was a tree that grew to Heaven called the *Marinka.* Anyone who climbs the tree is *'Marinka,'* or *'He Who Looks for God.'* "

The village was a collection of small wooden huts built in a semicircle under a tall canopy of trees that kept much of the rain from reaching the ground. There was a fire pit in the center of the village with logs placed around it for sitting. The one feature that looked very much out of place was a large satellite dish.

"They have TV?" Joan asked.

"No. It's for radio. The government set it up for them. They do have communication with the outside world."

"What language do they speak?" Christine asked.

"It's their own dialect. I only understand a few phrases. But missionaries come through here from time to time, and a few years back they taught the chief and a few others some Spanish."

An elderly Amaracayre woman, barely five feet tall and missing most of her teeth, approached Paul jabbering happily. She wore no shirt, but a brown shawl was draped over her shoulders.

"What's she saying?" Christine asked.

"I have no idea," Paul said, leaning over to hug her.

She looked at Christine and said something, then embraced her as well. Then she walked off.

"What's she wearing?" Christine asked.

"It's a shawl made of tree bark."

Christine smiled. "I thought it was wool."

They walked into the center of the village and the tribespeople came out of their huts. They were all barefoot and their toes were bent and calloused. A man held a bead necklace out to Christine. She glanced at Paul and he shook his head. "Not yet." When the chief had greeted everyone, he went to his hut and tied a headpiece made of parrot feathers onto his head. Paul told him it was beautiful and bought it from him for thirty *soles.* Then he brought out several others to sell and the other tribesmen began selling their items as well. Paul walked around helping the group negotiate their purchases.

"Would you ask the chief if I can have a picture with him?" Christine asked. "They'll love this at the dentist's office."

"Sure." Paul spoke to the chief, then gave him a five-*sole* coin. The chief stood next to her while Paul took their picture. Gilberto and Marcos brought up several cardboard boxes from the boat, and Paul presented them to the chief, who squatted down and looked through them as Paul explained to him how the medicine should be used. When Paul finished, they embraced again, then Paul led everyone back to the boat.

When they were all on board, Christine said, "That was unforgettable."

"Makes you see the world a little differently, doesn't it?"

Christine nodded. As they left the cover of the trees, the rain fell on them again. Paul looked up at the sky. "At least the rain won't last."

"You know this?" Christine asked.

"The chief told me. He can predict the weather. Gilberto told me that in the last twelve years that he's known him he's never been wrong."

"How does he do that?"

"The chief is a holy man. Every few months he walks to a special place where he communes with spirits. You noticed that the chief was waiting for us at the shore. He told Gilberto that the spirits told him we'd be here today at that hour."

"Do you believe that?"

"I believe a lot of things I didn't before I came down here. Besides, I have no reason not to. The Amaracayre don't lie. It's not part of their culture."

Gilberto guided the boat back to the middle of the river and they continued to journey deeper into the Amazon.

CHAPTER

Twenty-Two

"Lions, tigers and bears, oh my!"
✳ PAUL COOK'S DIARY ✳

Not long after their departure from the Amaracayre, the rain stopped and the plastic sheeting was rolled up from the sides of the boat and strapped to the canopy. Three hours later the boat veered from the middle of the river to the east shore, edging up to a small embankment with stairs cut into the dirt. Several Peruvian men walked down as the boat approached, carrying a large cardboard box.

"This is where we leave the river," Paul shouted back, moving toward the boat's bow. "We have a short hike through the jungle. On the other side is Lake Huitoto. From there it's forty-five minutes to Makisapa Lodge."

The men reached the boat and pulled it tight to the shore, securing it with ropes. The cardboard box was lifted over the side of the boat and Paul opened it. It was full of rubber boots.

"Listen up. It's the rainy season, so the trail's submerged in places. We're going to have to wear galoshes. Go ahead and put them on."

The boots were passed down in pairs. Christine slipped off her shoes and slid her foot inside a boot. She quickly pulled it out. "I think something's inside this one," she said. She turned the boot upside down and cockroaches erupted from the boot in a thick stream. She screamed and dropped it, and the bugs disappeared in the boat's grated flooring. Paul tried not to laugh but could not stop himself.

"It's not funny," she said, trying to sound mad.

"I know," he said, still laughing. "I'm sorry."

"I'm not putting those on."

"Here," Paul said, lifting her boots. He first shook them, stuck his hand inside, then handed them back to her. "There you go. Just be glad it wasn't a tarantula."

"Is that supposed to make me feel better?" she asked as she pulled them on.

Everyone found their bags and carried them up the bank. At the top of the ridge was a clearing with a shack perched on stilts. A dozen chickens roamed the grounds pecking at insects.

Gilberto began walking toward the forest and everyone followed. He stopped where the forest became denser and shadow fell over the trail. Paul came and stood next to him. "Okay, campers, this is where we hike through. Remember, this is the real thing. Stay alert. Don't change places. Keep together. We keep two machetes in front and one in back."

"Why two in front?" Mason asked.

"Because sometimes the first hiker only wakes the animal," Paul replied.

Several in the group chuckled nervously.

"Follow your guides, keep to their footsteps. There are jaguar, puma, vipers, constrictors, wild boars and quicksand, among other ways to ruin your day. So be smart. I promised Jim I'd bring you back alive." Paul took out his machete; then seeing how frightened everyone looked, he said, "Lions, tigers and bears, oh my!"

Everyone laughed.

"Okay, campers, *Vamos.*"

Jaime and Gilberto led off, Marcos fell in to the middle, while Paul waited for the back of the line to pass him so he could bring up the rear. Christine stopped next to him. "I'm sticking with you."

The path was well enough trodden that it was not difficult to follow, though it was mostly mud. In many places logs and thick roots fell or grew over the path, and it was crossed by an occasional streamlet. At one point the water was more than two feet deep and water spilled into the top of their boots. The thatch canopy above them grew thicker until it blocked most of the light.

"Cuidado con las anacondas," Gilberto shouted back. *"A ellas les gusta este tipo de agua."*

"Watch out for anaconda," Paul said. "They love water like this."

Christine said nothing but looked more anxious. Paul held out his machete. "Just stay close."

The deeper into the forest they went, the less talking there was, the chatter replaced by the sounds of their steps and of unseen things moving in the foliage around them. At one point Paul stopped and crouched down next to a tree. "Look at this." He ran his hand across four large gashes in the tree. "This is new. A jaguar was cleaning his claws."

Christine glanced around. "Should we be nervous?"

Paul stood. "No. Jaguars usually attack solitary things."

After about forty minutes the trail began to slope down slightly as the lake came into view. The trail ended in a steep embankment and below them were several canoes bobbing in the muddy green water.

As Gilberto descended the incline, there was a sudden splash as a startled crocodile fled into the water.

"What was that?" Christine asked.

"Nothing," Paul said.

Gilberto gingerly stepped to the back of one canoe, then motioned for everyone to follow his lead. One by one they carefully filed into the boats, sitting on wooden planks two across. Christine sat near the front. A large spider suddenly ran across her leg and then Joan's. Both women shrieked.

"They're harmless," Paul said calmly.

When everyone had boarded, the oars were distributed among them and they paddled off toward the southern end of the lake. The sun fell to the tree-rimmed horizon and the last spears of light sparkled in the water like liquid gold, then vanished, leaving the rippling water dark and menacing. Twilight was brief and the light faded quickly. The two boats stayed close together, moving forward against the dim silhouette of the trees. Nearly an hour later a faint electric light could be seen in the distance.

"Makisapa," Marcos said.

"We're here," Paul said.

As they approached the camp, the muffled sound of an electric generator grew louder. The first canoe slid up to the dock and Jaime climbed out and tied the boat to a mooring. Suddenly a man wearing a white shirt and Levi's appeared on the shore. Paul shouted out to him and the man walked down the dock's wood planks. A monkey was wrapped around the top of his head, with its hands around his ears and its tail curled around his neck. "That's Leonidas," Paul said. "And his friend is our camp mascot, a baby makisapa monkey. Its name is Maruha."

"It's so cute," Christine said.

Paul put down his oar and held out his hand to Leonidas, who pulled them in.

"Hermano," Paul said.

"Es un placer volver a verte." *It's good to see you again.*

"*Es un gusto volver a verte. ¿Está lista la cena?*" It's good to see you too. Is dinner ready?

"*Sí.*"

✦

When everyone was on the dock, they gathered their bags and walked to where a steep dirt stair had been cut into the side of the mountain. Gilberto and Leonidas led the group, holding their flashlights to light their steps. Lizards scampered up the dirt walls, and dark shadows jumped around the trees leading up the path. At the top of the rise the ground leveled off and they could see the whole of the camp. Oil lamps burned to light the path and several thatched-roof bungalows were visible.

Paul led them to the *comedor,* the largest of the structures, and the camp's central gathering place. They went inside. The *comedor* had a kitchen and a spacious dining area. The tables were thick rounds sawed from a tree trunk and sanded smooth. The roof was thatched and the windows were open but covered with thick screens.

The room smelled of tomato sauce and garlic.

"I'm sure you're all hungry," Paul said, "so get something to eat, then we'll assign bungalows and go over a few rules."

Leonidas's wife, Rosana, was the camp's cook. She had laid out two great pots of cooked spaghetti, and a large saucepan of spaghetti sauce. There was a basket of garlic bread and two whole watermelons, with cold spring water to drink.

The group lined up at the table, filling their plates to capacity. When everyone was seated and eating, Paul addressed the group.

"First, there's plenty of food. So don't be shy about seconds."

"How about thirds," Mason shouted. Everyone laughed.

" . . . or thirds. Welcome to Makisapa Lodge. Our stay is short but we're going to have a lot of fun. For your own safety there are some rules you need to abide by." Paul lifted a laminated sheet of paper. "Rule number one. Do not play with or tease any snake. If you find one near the lodge, let one of the staff know about it immediately. Be smart. The Amazon snakes tend to be more aggressive than snakes in North America, and most of them are venomous."

"What do you mean by tease?" one of the teenage boys asked.

"Don't try to catch or poke them or throw things at them."

"Yeah, I was going to do that," Joan said.

"Rule number two. If you leave the lodge area, do not go out alone and always have at least one machete with your group. You can get one from any of the staff. I repeat, never go out alone into the jungle. Especially at night. The vegetation is thick and it's easy to get disoriented. You could get lost just thirty feet away from camp. And there are things out there you really don't want to meet."

A teenage girl raised her hand. "Do dangerous animals ever come into camp?"

"Sometimes. Earlier in the year Gilberto had a puma walk through the middle of camp. Fortunately they didn't have any groups here at the time. In the unlikely event that you encounter a jaguar or puma, back off slowly but maintain eye contact with a dominant stare. Whatever you do, *do not* run. It triggers the chase instinct in them. And trust me, you can't outrun one."

He again looked at the list. "Rule number three. We'd prefer that you not swim in the lake. There are crocodiles along most of the shores. There are also piranhas, electric eels, leeches and anacondas. You've all filled out your liability release forms, so it's your choice. But consider yourself warned. We'd like to have you come back with us, preferably in one piece.

"Rule number four. If you want to fish for piranhas, we have lead-coated fishing line, but have one of the staff remove the fish. Piranhas can bite even after they're dead.

"Anything else?" He looked at the monkey on Jaime's head, "Oh, yeah, rule number five, no monkeys allowed in the bungalows. They have a knack for destroying whatever they touch. Especially Maruha here; she loves to eat books. Any questions?"

Joan raised her hand. "Are we going to get out of here alive?"

"They haven't lost anyone yet. But re-member, this isn't a theme park, it's really a jungle out there. Err on the side of caution. You'll notice that, unlike El Girasol, every-thing here is enclosed. Primarily for your own safety. You'll hear all sorts of noises at night, mostly birds and insects, but larger animals as well. We are intruders in an active ecosystem and potentially a part of the food chain.

"This time of the year you need to be especially wary of the fleas and mosquitoes. One night I got more than one hundred and seventy bites. So in addition to your mosquito netting, be sure to use repellent and flea collars. If you forgot to bring repellent we have extra."

Another hand went up. "What are we doing tomorrow?"

"Whatever you want. There's an island right across from us that we'll row out to in the morning and hike through. Mostly we'll just relax. After working as hard as you have, I know most of you could use a little R and R. We have a saying here: *there are no clocks in the jungle.* We eat when we're hungry, sleep when we're tired and the *comedor* is always open.

"Okay, one more thing. Jim sent you a treat." He reached behind the counter and brought out two brightly colored boxes. "Hostess Ding Dongs. One for each of you"

A loud cheer went up.

Paul handed one of the boxes to Gilberto,

and they threw out a foil-wrapped cake to each person.

"Your bungalow assignments are on this sheet," Paul said, holding a clipboard above his head. "When you finish eating, get your things and get settled in for the night. The generator goes off in two hours. If you have any questions, I'll be here in the *comedor.*"

Christine brought Paul a slice of watermelon.

"Thank you."

"It's very sweet," she said, sitting next to him. "I love watermelon."

"Me too." Paul took a bite, wiping the corners of his mouth.

"What bungalow am I in?" Christine asked.

"You and Joan are in Guacamayo," Paul said. "Turn right outside and follow the path to the second building."

"And where are you?"

"I'm on the other side of the camp in *Vampiro.*"

She stood. "Would you like to come by for a visit?"

"Actually, I had other plans for you. I need to meet with the staff, then I'll be over."

Christine smiled. "I'll be waiting."

CHAPTER
Twenty-Three

I took Christine out to the lake, hunting crocodiles by moonlight. She returned to camp exhilarated by the experience. We never feel more alive than when our existence is uncertain.

✦ PAUL COOK'S DIARY ✦

The Makisapa Lodge consisted of nine bungalows connected by a network of paths lit by tiki lamps. The buildings looked as Christine had imagined them, constructed from dark hardwood cut from the surrounding jungle. They each had a thatched-palm roof, a front porch and a large screen window. Inside the huts there were three beds each with a mosquito net tied in a massive knot and suspended from the ceiling above it. There were two electric lights—one in the middle of the room, the other in the bathroom. The bathroom had a curtain instead of a door, a shower, and a porcelain toilet and sink. There was only one temperature of water and that was whatever the jungle provided. The shower's drain emptied beneath the hut. The room was clean but smelled of petroleum oil.

"What's a *guacamayo?*" Joan asked. "Sounds like a chip dip."

Christine grinned. "I think it's a parrot."

Joan untied her mosquito netting, letting it drape down over the bed. "Ever slept under a mosquito net?"

"No," Christine said. "I've never even been camping."

"What do you think that smell is?"

"Maybe it's jungle wood." Christine leaned against the windowsill and looked out. The teenagers were in the middle of the compound aiming flashlights at monkeys hanging in the trees.

"It's hard to believe it's winter at home," Christine said.

"I'm not missing it. I hope there's a raging blizzard." Joan sat on her bed. "So what's the deal with you and Paul?"

The question surprised her. "What do you mean?"

"I've seen the way the two of you look at each other. It's not a whirlwind like Jessica and Jim, it's just kind of . . . sweet. Besides, he's a fine-looking man. If I were twenty years younger and twenty pounds lighter . . ."

Christine sat back on her bed, eager to change the subject. "I wonder how Jessica and Jim are doing."

"We're lucky that boy's still alive." She squinted. "What's that on your arm?"

Christine lifted her arm. "Oh, I got some mosquito bites. There were a million of them in Puerto."

"You better use more repellent."

There was a knock on their door.

"Come in," Christine said.

Paul stepped in. He was wearing his fedora, and a camera hung around his neck. "Evening, ladies. Is everything okay with your bungalow?"

"Fabulous," Joan said. "Except for the smell. What is that?"

"The wood's treated with motor oil. It discourages the termites. There are more than ninety-one species of termites out here."

"Fascinating," Joan said facetiously.

"Sorry. I'm really a jungle geek. Anyway, it also protects the wood during the rainy season, and it helps to keep the mosquitoes away, so triple benefit. You'll get used to it."

"I kind of like the smell," Christine said. Joan just looked at her.

"So would you gals like to join me? I'm taking a group out crocodile hunting."

"At night?" Joan asked.

"It's the best time to catch them."

"And vice versa," Joan said. "I'll pass."

"I'll go," Christine said.

Paul looked at her with surprise. "Really?"

"I trust you. You wouldn't take me if it weren't safe, would you?"

"Reasonably safe," he said.

"When are we going?"

"Right now."

She stood up. "Let's go."

They walked out and Paul called to the teenagers. "We're going." Five of them joined in, as well as Gilberto, who was sitting on the steps of the *comedor* feeding watermelon rind to the macaws. Paul pulled his machete from the bare stump he had stuck it into and carried it as they hiked back down the incline to the dock. As everyone walked out to the canoe, Christine stopped. "We're going out in a boat?"

Paul turned and looked at her quizzically. "Of course. How else would we catch a crocodile?"

She looked out over the ink-black lake. "Can't we just do it from here?"

Paul laughed. "No."

"You expect me to go out in a boat over piranha-infested waters hunting crocodiles?"

"What happened to 'trust'?"

She took a deep breath, then walked toward the boat, shaking her head. "I hate you."

Paul grinned. He took her hand, helped her into the second seat of the boat and handed her a paddle. Then he climbed in front of her. As they paddled toward the opposite shore, the jungle noise seemed to increase. The low guttural moans of the red-throated Koto monkeys echoed across the lake followed by a deeper bellow that came from the blackness somewhere ahead of them.

"What was that?" Christine asked.

"Crocodile," Paul said. "Probably Elvis."

"You name them?"

"Just Elvis. He's the granddad out here. He's about sixteen feet long."

"What exactly am I doing out here?"

Paul dug in with his paddle. "You're having fun. You just don't know it yet."

Something suddenly swooped down through the boat, and Melissa, the girl behind Christine screamed. "What was that?"

"*Vampiros,*" Paul said calmly. "Just vampire bats. They eat the mosquitoes."

"Oh good, it's *just* vampire bats," Melissa said sarcastically.

The boat glided silently over the black water, and the dark shore opposite them slowly came into view. Trees hung over the water, and monkeys and birds scurried up them as the canoe approached.

"Don't get too close to the trees," Paul said. "Vipers sometimes hang in them."

Everyone quickly stopped paddling. Paul panned his flashlight across the water in front of the bank. He immediately found two amber eyes glowing as brightly as roadside reflectors. "There's a croc."

Christine stared. "Look how bright its eyes are."

"They're like cat eyes. Only more reflective." He changed the direction of the beam. "There's another. It's a little one."

"How can you tell how big it is?"

"By how far apart the eyes are." He turned around, speaking in a hushed voice, "Paddle toward it. I'm going to try to catch it."

"With what?" Christine asked.

"My hands."

"Are you insane?"

"We do it all the time." Paul hung over the side, as the boat slid up to the crocodile. The reptile started to sink in the water and Paul reached in past his elbow to grab it.

Suddenly his arm jerked and he dropped to his shoulder in the water. He shouted, "It's got me! It's got me!"

Christine screamed, and Paul fell back in the boat laughing, water dripping from his arm. "Just kidding."

"You are *so* stupid," she said and hit his back.

"Gilberto, vamos a tratar de nuevo." Let's *try another one.*

While Paul looked around with his flashlight, the rest of the group paddled. Gilberto sat in the back of the boat, using his oar as a rudder and keeping the boat moving perpendicular to the shore. It wasn't two minutes before they found a new set of eyes. "There's one," Paul said. "He's a bit bigger. Everyone stop rowing. *Gilberto, acércame."* *Bring me closer.*

Gilberto took long, steady strokes and they glided close enough for Paul to reach in. This time he snatched the crocodile by the neck. It thrashed its tail wildly until he pulled it from the water and it froze, stunned by its new environment.

"Give me some light," Paul said.

Four flashlight beams illuminated the animal. "Gnarly," someone said.

The crocodile was nearly three feet in length. Its eyes were yellow and catlike, its teeth visible around its closed snout, red from the meal they had interrupted. Paul held it up. "Notice that it's missing most of its toes. When they're little, the piranhas eat them."

"Oh my gosh, oh my gosh, oh my gosh," Christine said. "I can't believe you just did that."

"Here," he said, holding it out toward her, "You hold it."

She backed away. "Get it away from me."

"I want to take a picture of you with it. You can do it, Christine."

"You're serious."

"As malaria."

She stared at the creature and couldn't believe what came from her mouth. "How do I do it?"

"First, get closer." She leaned forward.

"It's like holding a snake. As long as you keep a hand behind its head, it can't bite you. Move your hand up behind mine and when you feel you're ready, I'll slide my hand out and you grab it. Use your other hand to hold its tail."

"I can't believe I'm doing this." She grabbed its tail. "It's slimy."

"He's a reptile. Okay, move your hand up. Are you ready?"

"No, no, no, not yet," she said nervously. She slid her hand up its ridged back beneath Paul's. The animal suddenly jerked and Paul clamped down harder. "He's getting restless, we need to hurry. On the count of three. One. Two. Go."

Paul released his grip as Christine moved her hand up and clamped down on the crocodile's neck. The animal didn't move and Paul pulled away. "You did it."

Her face animated with excitement. "I'm holding a crocodile! Quick, get a picture of me. Jessica will never believe it."

Paul lifted his camera and took the picture.

"What do I do now?"

"Let it go."

"How?"

"Just drop it back in the lake."

She held the crocodile over the side and released it. It splashed in the water, whipped its tail and disappeared.

"Who's next?" Paul asked. All of the teenagers wanted to hold a crocodile, and Paul panned his flashlight across the shore until he found a marsh with no fewer than a dozen sets of eyes. "One for each of you." As they paddled toward the marsh, he said to Christine, "I was thinking that for a crocodile this must seem like an alien abduction: a bright light comes out of nowhere, suddenly paralyzing you, you're lifted into the air while strange, soft creatures look you over, then suddenly you're dropped back into the water. I bet that little guy will be telling that story back at the marsh for the rest of his life."

Christine laughed.

In all, they pulled out five crocodiles, the largest about forty inches from nose to tail. Around midnight they paddled back to the camp. They hiked the trail together and the teenagers ran back to their bungalows to share their stories. Gilberto went to the *comedor* while Paul walked Christine back to her bungalow. They climbed the porch and stopped at the door. Joan was asleep inside and they could hear her snoring.

"Want to talk?" Christine asked.

"Sure."

They sat down together on the porch stairs.

"I'm proud of you," Paul said. "You were really brave tonight."

"That's why you took me out, isn't it?"

"If you can go out at midnight on piranha-infested waters, surrounded by vampire bats, and hold a crocodile, there's nothing you need to be afraid of."

She smiled. "I can't believe I did that. You make me brave."

"No, you already were. You just didn't know it."

"Don't you ever get scared?"

"Of course I do."

"Of what? What's the most frightening thing that's happened to you since you came to Peru?"

He thought about it for a moment. "That would be my brush with an anaconda."

Christine leaned forward. "This sounds good. Go on."

"It was about three years ago. I was in the jungle looking for this tree root that Gilberto told me cured kidney infections. The tree was close to our camp, so I didn't bother to take my machete. I walked right into an anaconda. I'm not sure how big it was since it was coiled, but I'm sure that it was easily more than twenty feet long." Paul held his hands about eighteen inches apart. "It was at least this wide."

Christine's mouth slightly opened. "How terrifying."

"A little. Anacondas raise themselves to look their prey in the eyes. It was actually taller than I am. You'd think you could easily outrun something that big, but you can't. But seeing how I didn't have many options, I started running and it came after me. Then I had a stroke of brilliance. I slipped off my backpack. The snake immediately struck it and coiled around it. By the time it realized my pack wasn't edible, I was back at camp."

The story left Christine gaping. "I don't know how you live here. I could never do it."

She saw something flicker in his eyes and sensed that he was saddened by what she'd said.

"Actually, I've seen worse in America," Paul said darkly. "I did my residency at George Washington University Hospital in D.C. One day we had seven people admitted to E.R. with machete wounds. Some guy went crazy at a bus stop and started hacking innocent bystanders. Another time a man was brought in unconscious from a stab wound to the heart. I cut open his chest and directly shocked his heart while my nurse tried to insert a catheter into the wound. Blood was spraying everywhere. In the middle of this he woke up, and there I am, literally holding his heart in my hands and he's looking at me, wondering what's going on. Some of the things I've seen in America make the jungle seem civilized."

The light in the *comedor* switched off and Paul looked at the glowing hands of his watch. "On that bright note, I better let you get to bed. Do you need anything?"

"No. Thank you for tonight."

"You're welcome." He leaned forward and they kissed. "See you in the morning."

"What are we doing?"

"We're going on a nature walk. I promise we'll find you some spiders."

"Thanks."

He stepped down from the porch and Christine watched him disappear in the blackness. Then she went inside and climbed under her mosquito netting to sleep.

CHAPTER

Twenty-Four

*The jungle absorbs all things in it.
Wood rots and earth melts and all
dissolves in an unending cycle of
life, death and life again. To be in
the jungle is to be a part of it.*

✷ PAUL COOK'S DIARY ✷

Rosana's pancakes weren't quite Denny's but no one was complaining; it was the most normal breakfast they'd had since they arrived in Peru. Christine sat at a table with Mason and Joan, telling them about her nighttime adventure.

Paul entered the *comedor* wearing a Makisapa T-shirt. Maruha the monkey sat on his head, her long arms draped over him like a hunting cap. Paul walked over to their table and they all looked up. "Good morning."

"Morning," Paul said.

"Do you know you have a monkey on your head?" Joan asked.

"I do. Do you know you have a crocodile hunter in your midst?" He turned to Joan as he cut his pancakes. "We'll make it three by tonight."

"In your dreams. So what, besides crocodile hunting, is on today's agenda?"

"This morning we're going on a nature

walk. Over the summer Leonidas and Gilberto cut a trail through the jungle."

"What time are we leaving?" Christine asked.

"As soon as everyone finishes." He shoved a bite into his mouth.

"Do we need anything?" Mason asked.

"Repellent, sunscreen, and your camera."

A half hour later the group was gathered below at the dock. It was a beautiful day and the first time they could see the lake clearly and the opposite shore. The group divided into two and they filled the boats and began paddling off south of camp where the lake turned in a half crescent.

When they were away from the dock, Paul said, "About six months after they bought the land for the lodge, they discovered giant sea otters in the lake. They're an endangered species, so this land is now a government-protected reserve."

"Have you ever seen them?" Christine asked.

"I've seen them every time I've come, though usually at a distance. But once they came up to the boat. They're very curious."

"How do they live in here with all the crocodiles and piranhas?" Mason asked.

"Actually they're tougher than you'd think. The natives call them *los lobos,* the wolves. They travel in packs and pretty much everything in the lake fears them."

"I hope we see them," Christine said.

A half hour later the first boat pulled into a small clearing on the bank. The second canoe slid up next to it. Everyone moved forward and climbed off the bow of the boat through thick vegetation onto the land. Gilberto and Jaime stayed inside the boats. They would row to the pickup point at the trail's end.

As they moved into the jungle, the sound of chirping grew louder.

"I wonder what kind of birds those are," Christine said to no one in particular.

"No birds, monkeys," Leonidas said, which surprised her because she didn't know he spoke any English. "Come."

He led them twenty yards into the jungle until they came to a small clearing. There were monkeys everywhere. In the uppermost regions of the canopy there were shadows of larger monkeys that appeared to be four to five feet in length.

Paul pointed up. "Those monkeys up there are kotos. They're pretty big. The smaller monkeys are rhesus and capuchin. The smallest are tamarins.

At their arrival the smaller monkeys climbed down for a closer look, swinging from the branches and vines as if exhibiting their acrobatic skills. Several of the monkeys came within an arm's length of Christine.

A hand-sized tamarin climbed out on a bough next to her. Its movements were quick and birdlike.

"Look at her," Christine said. She stepped toward it. "I'm going to feed her." She reached into her shirt pocket and pulled out a granola bar, broke off a piece and held it out. The monkey snatched it from her, then ran up the tree. Christine broke off another piece and held it out to a larger monkey, a black capuchin. Instead of reaching out for it as the tamarin had done, the monkey jumped onto Christine's shoulder. She screamed. "Paul!"

The monkey reached into Christine's front pocket and grabbed the entire granola bar, then jumped back onto a nearby bough.

Paul laughed while Christine raised a hand to her chest. "That scared me."

The capuchin held the bar with its feet,

peeling the paper back like a banana. Two other monkeys descended on the capuchin and they began screeching at each other. Then the capuchin pulled the bar up under one arm and scurried up the branch, chased by the other two.

"The show over," Leonidas said, showing off his English. "We go."

Unlike the trail they'd crossed through to the lake, the path was dry and new and everyone followed Leonidas closely. In several places spiderwebs as thick as fishing line crossed the path. At one point Paul put his hand on Christine's shoulder and helped guide her under a web. When he lifted his hand his handprint was still visible on her wet T-shirt. He looked at her quizzically. "Do you feel okay?"

"Sure. I'm just a little winded."

"You're really sweating."

"Of course. It's hot."

A hundred yards further they came to a large peculiar-looking tree. Its roots rose a meter above the ground, straight up.

"This tree is called a walking palm," Paul said. "It actually moves."

"How?" someone asked.

"When nutrients get scarce in one area, it

grows new roots on one side and abandons the old. It doesn't move fast but it does move."

"This place is Jurassic Park," Mason said.

They continued their hike. Every now and then they would stop and examine the tracks of some animal that had crossed the path. Then Leonidas led them off the trail to a slim, white-barked tree, standing alone like a misplaced quaking aspen.

"This is the tangarana tree," Paul said. "You'll notice nothing is growing around it."

Everyone looked. There was no vegetation for four feet in any direction.

"That's weird," Christine said.

"Las otras plantas le tienen miedo," Leonidas said.

Paul translated. "The other plants are afraid of it."

"Afraid?"

"Yes," Paul said, "for two reasons. First, the tangarana secretes an acid that is deadly to other plants. The other reason is because of the ant that lives in it. The tangarana ant." Paul tapped the tree with the broad side of his machete. A stream of small red and black ants poured out from the base of the tree, climbing up its bark.

"The ant protects the tree. The bite from that ant is about seven times more painful than a wasp's sting."

A teenage boy who was leaning against the tree quickly jumped back.

"And they can jump."

He stepped back further.

"Have you ever been bitten by one?" Joan asked.

"No. But Gilberto was. He said it was *'in-olvidable.' Unforgettable.* This tree has an interesting history. If a woman was found to be unfaithful, the tribe would tie her to the tree and let the ants eat her."

"That's awful," Christine said.

"What about the man?" Joan asked angrily.

"They didn't say," Paul said.

They went back to the trail.

"Why does everything here bite, sting or want to eat you?" Christine asked.

"Not everything," Paul said. "There are things to heal as well. For instance"—he took a few steps to where a tangle of vines grew down from a tree—"this vine is an antitoxin for the guajave viper. Guajave is one of the few vipers that's not brightly colored, so it's hard to see. And, unfortunately, it's not only aggressive, but its venom is highly toxic. If you're bitten, you'd never make it out of the jungle alive."

"Last year Leonidas was bitten by one of them. He found these vines and began chewing them. Then he cut more and brought them back to camp. He boiled them into tea and drank it. As you can see, he lived. Every bad thing in nature has its opposite. There's a tree out here that can cure kidney problems. There are more than two hundred plants proven to be anti-carcinogenic."

As they started off again, Paul looked at Christine. "Are you sure you're feeling okay?"

"No, I don't feel too good."

"What do you feel like?"

"Kind of crummy. Like I'm coming down with the flu."

Paul put his hand on her forehead. "You're a little warm. But it is pretty hot."

"I'm sure it's nothing," she said.

A few minutes later they were paddling back toward the lodge.

CHAPTER

Twenty-Five

Christine is sick. I have found it useful to remain as clinically detached as possible, as the depth of my fear would do neither of us any good.

✦ PAUL COOK'S DIARY ✦

Lunch was a salad made mostly from fruits that no one had seen before and a fish-and-rice concoction made from a large piranha that Marcos had caught that morning.

Paul had gone back to his bungalow for a short nap and came back to the *comedor* to eat lunch. Most of the group had already eaten and a few of the teenagers had set up a Monopoly game on one of the tables. Neither Christine nor Joan was there.

"Hey, Paul," one of the boys said. "Want to play?"

"Have you started?"

"Just about to."

"Sure. I'm the terrier."

"I'm already the dog," a girl said. "You can be the wheelbarrow."

"All right. Let me get my lunch."

Rosana heaped two large paddles of rice on his plate and he joined the teenagers at the table.

Paul had just passed GO when Joan walked into the *comedor.* She walked directly to him. "Paul, Christine's not doing well."

He looked up from the game. "What's wrong?"

"I think she has a fever. She was moaning and saying strange things."

Paul stood. "Hate to do this to you guys, but I've got to go."

As they walked to the bungalow, Paul asked, "Have you given her anything?"

"I gave her some Tylenol. And I put a wet cloth on her forehead."

Inside the room, Christine was lying on her back under the mosquito netting. Her skin was pale and the sides of her face were beaded with perspiration. Paul sat down next to her.

"Hey. What's going on with you?"

"I'm not going, Paul." Her speech was slow and slurred.

"Where aren't you going?"

"I don't want to see any more crocodiles. They scare me."

"You don't have to."

Her chest rose and fell with her labored breathing.

"Joan says you're not feeling well." He pulled up the mosquito netting, tying it above her. Then he lifted the cloth from her forehead and felt the damp skin beneath. "You're hot."

"I feel . . . sunburned."

He turned to Joan. "Go to my room. I'm in Vampiro, it's the second bungalow on the other side of the *comedor.* Next to my bed there's a purple vinyl bag. You can't miss it. Please get it for me."

"Okay." She left. Paul turned back to Christine and gently pulled the hair back from her face.

"How else do you feel?"

She hesitated. "I don't feel . . . *right.*"

"Can you describe it?"

"I feel . . . fuzzy. Like my head's floating."

"Do you have any rashes?"

Pause. "I don't know."

Her head fell to one side and Paul let her rest there. Joan returned, breathing heavily from jogging across the compound. She gave the bag to Paul. He set it on the ground, opened it and took out a thermometer.

"Chris, I'm going to take your temperature. I need to put something in your mouth. Can you open a little for me?"

Her lips slowly parted. He slid the thermometer under her tongue and her mouth shut around it. Joan looked at him anxiously.

He kept time on his watch. After two minutes he pulled the thermometer out and held it up to the window. He frowned. "How long ago did you give her the Tylenol?"

"Maybe a half hour."

"She's at a hundred and three." He returned the thermometer to its case and turned back to her. "Chris, do your joints ache?"

Her voice was weaker. "My eyes hurt."

"How about your joints? Your elbows, shoulders, knees . . ."

"I don't know."

He looked at her quietly for a moment. "Have you had any mosquito bites?"

"She has," Joan said. "We talked about them last night."

"When did she get them?"

"Back in Puerto Maldonado."

"Chris, what shots did you have before you came?"

Her answer came in short puffs. "Tetanus. Hepatitis."

"Did you have a malaria or yellow fever shot?"

"They said we didn't need it."

He slowly exhaled. "I wish they wouldn't tell everyone that."

Joan bit her lip. Paul stood, his hand still on Christine's shoulder. "I'll be right back." He walked outside and signaled Joan to follow him. Her face was tight with concern.

"What does she have?" Joan asked.

"I can't be certain yet, but I'm pretty sure that it's one of three things—malaria, yellow fever or dengue fever. My best guess is dengue fever."

"What's dengue fever?"

"It's another disease carried by mosquitoes. There's been an epidemic around here."

"Is it fatal?"

"It can be. But I'd take it over malaria or yellow fever."

Joan began wringing her hands. "Shouldn't we get her to a hospital?"

"She's not up to the travel. Besides, there's nothing a hospital within a thousand miles of here could do that I can't."

"When will we know what she has for sure?"

"Within the next twenty-four to forty-eight hours. If she really starts complaining of joint pain, we'll know it's dengue. Whatever it is, she's going to be pretty miserable for the next week."

". . . But we're leaving the jungle tomorrow."

"She's not. When was the last time she ate or drank anything?"

"I don't know. Not since we came back this morning."

"We need to keep her hydrated. Go to the *comedor* and get a couple bottles of water. Do you know who Jaime is?"

"The little guy from the orphanage?"

"Right. Find him and tell him I need to talk to him."

"But I don't speak Spanish."

"Just say my name. He'll figure out the rest."

"I'll be right back."

She ran off. Paul went back inside. He reached into his bag and brought out a container of Vaseline. He rubbed some across Christine's parched lips. "I won't let anything happen to you."

Five minutes later Joan returned with the water and Jaime, who looked at Paul anxiously.

"*Jaime. Christine está muy enferma. No puedo salir de la jungla con el grupo. Tu tendrás que llevarlos sin mí.*" Christine's very sick. I won't be able to leave the jungle with the group. You'll have to take them out without me.

He nodded.

"*Necesitas llamar a Jim y decirlelo que ha pasado. Ellos necesitan llamar a la madre de Christine. Díganle que no se preocupe. Después regresa a El Girasol y mira cómo están las cosas. Gilberto y Marcos te llevarán a Puerto.*" You will need to call Jim and tell him what's happened. They need to call Christine's mother. Tell her not to worry. Then go back to El Girasol and keep an eye on things. Gilberto and Marcos will go with you to Puerto.

"*Sí,*" Jaime said, and left the bungalow.

Paul took a pillow from another bed and pushed it under Christine's head. Then he unscrewed the cap from the bottle and placed its rim against her lips. "Christine, you need to drink." Her lips slightly parted and he poured the water in her mouth, occasionally stopping so she could swallow. When half the bottle was gone, he let her head back down.

"Good job." He took the washcloth from her head and poured the cool water onto it. He wrung it out over the floor then put the cloth back over her eyes.

"Paul?"

"Yes?"

"I want my mother."

"I wish she were here," he said.

She didn't speak for a while. "Am I going to die?"

"No. But you're very sick."

"What's wrong with me?"

"I'm not sure yet."

"Please don't leave me."

"I won't."

"Men always leave." A tear ran down the side of her face. "I'm afraid."

"I won't leave you," Paul said. He wiped her tear with his finger. Then he leaned over and kissed her forehead. "I promise."

CHAPTER

Twenty-Six

*A door was slightly opened
in Christine's soul . . .*

✦ PAUL COOK'S DIARY ✦

The jungle was black except where the moonlight pierced the canopy and glistened from the moist surface of vegetation. It was possible to believe that there were spectators just beyond the cleared ground of the compound, hidden but watching, like a theater audience after the lights are dimmed.

It was half past three in the morning and the group had stumbled to the *comedor.* They dropped their bags and sat on the floor against the wall, the teenagers sleeping against each other while others yawned and grumbled about the insanity of a 3 A.M. wake-up. It was the only way they could get out of the jungle and back to Puerto Maldonado in time to make the flight out.

Paul had slept in the room with Christine while Joan had moved to the Vampiro bungalow so she could dress and pack without waking her. When the group had assembled, Jaime woke Paul, and he pulled on his clothes from the day before, slipped on sandals and followed him back to the *comedor.* Paul looked over the group. He thought they resembled a scene from *Dawn of the Dead.*

"I know you're tired, but once you're back on the river, you can sleep. I won't be going back with you. Christine is too sick to travel, so I'll be staying here to take care of her. You're in good hands. Jaime, Marcos and Gilberto will be taking you back. Thanks again for all you've done to help the people down here. I hope to see you all again. Travel well."

With that the group rose to their feet. Paul shook a few hands and everyone gathered their bags and followed Jaime to the boats. Paul followed them down to the dock and saw them off, then returned alone to the bungalow.

He put his hand on Christine's forehead. She was warm, but not enough to warrant concern, so he crawled back under his mosquito netting and fell asleep. He woke two hours later to Christine mumbling. The sun had barely begun to soften the darkness and he could see her moving uncomfortably under the net, her head turning from side to side.

"I need to call." She said. "I've got to call them."

Paul rolled from his bed and went to her side. "Who do you need to call?"

"The caterer."

"It's okay," he said.

"It's *not* okay," she protested, "There won't be enough éclairs."

"I'll call the caterer," Paul said.

"Okay. Okay. You call." She calmed and her breathing slowed. A minute or two later she said, "Martin?"

Paul took her hand.

"Martin. What's wrong with me?"

Paul rubbed his hand along her face. "There's nothing wrong with you."

"Why don't you want me?" She began softly whimpering, and though her eyes were closed, tears seeped up through her eyelids and ran down her face. "Where are you going, Daddy? When are you coming back? Why don't you want me?"

Paul took her hand and held it tightly, and she gripped his with equal force, as if she were falling. Her rambling degenerated into incoherent babble as she fell back asleep. The last words Paul understood were, "Don't leave me."

CHAPTER Twenty-Seven

Each moment with her has carried her deeper into my heart. She is afraid I'll leave her. How could she know that I cannot bear the thought of being without her.

✦ PAUL COOK'S DIARY ✦

Late afternoon of the second day a storm moved in. The monkeys' chatter grew louder under the burgeoning clouds and the jungle fell into shadow. The rain pounded on the bungalow's roof, and water fell from the thatch eaves to the dark red dirt below, running in a million small veins back to the lake. It is the way of the jungle—all water seeks larger water.

Paul never left Christine's side. He watched the storm come and was glad the group had gotten out before it hit. He lit a candle inside the bungalow. The generator had been shut off, as they couldn't risk running out of gas.

He had placed a chair next to Christine's bed and checked her temperature every four hours. It kept steady at around 102 degrees, spiking at times as the acetaminophen wore off. Paul had treated dengue before. Several years earlier, on a humanitarian expedition in the jungle, a child and an old man were brought to him infected with the disease. The child lived; the old man didn't.

Though he worried about Christine, he held himself apart from his fears with a clinical distance. It wouldn't help her to see him afraid.

Rosana brought food for them and cold packs from the refrigerator. She made strong tea from the bark of the cinchona tree.

Christine ate little but Paul made her drink. Dehydration was his greatest fear. As twilight fell on the second day, she spoke his name. For the first time in hours she was coherent.

"How long has it been raining?" she asked.

"A few hours. Do your eyes still hurt?"

She lightly nodded. "And my back hurts. It feels like something is poking in my bones."

Paul was relieved: It confirmed that she had dengue fever. The mortality rate of dengue was considerably lower than that of yellow fever or malaria. "It's the fever. It will go away."

"It hurts."

He gently rubbed her arm. "I know. But it will go away."

It wasn't until the next evening that Christine fully realized that the group had left the lodge. She asked about Jessica.

"She's in Cuzco," Paul said.

"When did she leave?"

"She never came. She stayed with Jim." Paul looked at her sympathetically. "Do you remember?"

"When he fell," she said. It seemed to her like such a long time ago. She breathed in deeply.

"Did Joan leave?"

"She left two days ago with the group."

"Who's still here?"

"Me," Paul said. "And Rosana and Leonidas."

"My mother will be worried."

"Jessica will call your mother."

"She'll be so worried." She closed her eyes again. After a few more minutes she asked, "When can I go home?"

"When you're well enough to make the trip. After the fever breaks."

"Will you be leaving too?"

"Not without you."

"Do you promise?"

"I won't leave you, Christine. I promise."

She squeezed his hand tightly and closed her eyes again.

✦

It rained all that night and the next day. Christine's condition was stable, though a few times her temperature rose higher than 104. Paul would damp her forehead and neck with cool water until her temperature fell. On the fifth day of her illness the rain stopped. Gilberto and Marcos returned with the canoes and the report that the group had made the flight out of Puerto.

Paul ate and slept in the room, reading from a stack of books Rosana had brought him from the *comedor.*

It was the middle of the sixth night when Christine's fever broke. Her teeth chattered and she moaned loud enough to wake Paul; he climbed out of bed and went to her side, laying his hand across her forehead. It was wet and her hair was damp at the roots. Her nightshirt was soaked through.

Paul took a towel from the bathroom and softly patted her face and forehead; then he lifted her nightshirt up over her head and gently dried her body. Her skin pebbled with goosebumps in the cool air. When he finished, he pulled one of his own shirts over her and lifted the blanket to her chest. Then he sat back on the stool next to her bed.

The moon peered through a flat ceiling of clouds and lit the bungalow, illuminating Christine's face in a pale glow. In medical school he had been taught the importance of remaining emotionally detached from a patient, and in this case he had failed utterly. He had been at her side for nearly a week, and the longer he was with her, the closer he felt to her. He looked at her now as if she were a sleeping Juliet laid on her bier.

"You have no idea how beautiful you are," he whispered, "or what you're doing to my heart."

She didn't move and he leaned over her and softly kissed her lips. She showed no reaction but turned her face slightly toward him and sighed. He lay his head next to her body and fell asleep with exhaustion.

CHAPTER

Twenty-Eight

Sleeping Beauty has woken.

✦ PAUL COOK'S DIARY ✦

A sharp ray of light broke through the eastern window and fell across Christine's bed. She raised a hand to cover her face, then her eyelids fluttered and opened. At first she wasn't sure where she was, but the neatly woven lines of thatch above her brought her back.

Paul was asleep, slumped over her bed, the crown of his head pressed against her waist. He was unshaven, his eyes dark-ringed from exhaustion.

Through it all he had never left her side. It was like waking from the murky depths of a bad dream to light and air and next to her was the man who had pulled her up. She had been drawn to Paul the first time she saw him, but now she was overwhelmed by the strength of her feelings.

She was glad that he was so close to her and wished that he were closer. She wanted to feel all of him next to her.

She slowly reached down and touched his hair, gently crushing it between her fingers. Then she touched his stubbled face.

He groaned softly, then raised his head, looking at her.

"Hi," she said.

"Hi," he replied. He could see that her eyes were bright again. "You had me worried."

"I'm sorry."

He reached up and felt her forehead. "How do you feel?"

"Better." The sweet, pungent smell of the wood mixed with that of her body.

"What day is it?"

"Thursday."

"How many days have I been here?"

"Seven."

"Seven," she said aloud as if she had to hear herself say it. "Is it over?"

"Mostly. Your fever broke around three in the morning. But it's still going to be a while before you feel like yourself again."

She looked down at the clothes she wore. She had a slight recollection of Paul undressing her, but she felt no embarrassment, only that she had been cared for. "Where are my clothes?"

"They're over there. They were wet."

She glanced over to the pile of towels and clothing, then back at him. She took his hand. "You never left me, did you?"

"No."

She gripped his hand tighter, lifting it to her cheek. "You never left me."

CHAPTER

Twenty-Nine

We carry around in our heads these pictures of what our lives are supposed to look like, painted by the brush of our intentions. It's the great, deep secret of humanity that in the end none of our lives look the way we thought they would. As much as we wish to believe otherwise, most of life is a reaction to circumstances.

✳. PAUL COOK'S DIARY .✳

By evening Christine felt strong enough to stand on her own. Rosana brought soup and bread to them and she smiled when she saw Christine sitting up.

"La señorita está mejor ahora." The señorita is better now.

"Sí," Paul said. *"Mucho mejor."* Much better.

Paul was glad to see that Christine's appetite had returned. They ate dinner together, then Rosana brought in clean towels. Paul left so she could bathe. Christine showered and washed her hair, then sprinkled talc on her body. It was good to feel human again, she thought, or better, feminine. She cinched the belt of her shorts around her waist and realized that she had lost even more weight.

Paul picked up some playing cards from the *comedor,* and two packages of cookies from his own stash and brought them back to her bungalow. When he returned, she was on her bed, sitting on top of the covers. She eyed the packages he carried with interest. "You have cookies?"

He set the cookies down on the bed and held the deck of cards in one hand, fanning them. *"American* cookies. And cards. Want to play?" Paul asked.

"Sure. What are we going to play?"

"I'll teach you a game called Texas Hold'em."

"Poker?" she asked.

"Yes."

"Sounds fun. What should we bet?"

He smiled at her eagerness. "You're getting ahead of yourself. You should learn how to play first."

"Are you chicken?"

"What do you want to bet?"

"How about your cookies?"

"My cookies?"

"Well, if they're already yours, you won't feel so bad taking them from me."

"Good point."

Paul opened the packages. "Oreos are worth one and ginger snaps worth five."

By nightfall Christine had won the last of the cookies.

"So you're a cardsharp," Paul said.

"There's a lot you don't know about me. Granted, not as much as last week, but I still have a few secrets." She lifted an Oreo, breaking it apart and holding it in front of him. "Want one of *my* cookies?"

"Yes."

"It's going to cost you."

"How much?"

She looked at him coyly. "It's a pretty good cookie. And I doubt you'll find any more this far from civilization."

"What do you want?"

"A date."

"Where would I take you on this date?"

"On a boat ride."

He looked at her with surprise. "You want to go back out on the lake?"

"Just the two of us this time."

He thought about it for a moment. "You feel up to it?"

"I've got to get out of here." She held up the cookie. "Want it?"

"Let's go."

He retrieved his flashlight from the floor, and, taking her arm, they walked across the camp. She was weaker than she realized and the short walk to the incline had winded her. She looked over the steep, uneven steps cut into the dirt and frowned. "I don't think I can walk down that."

Paul stepped down on the earthen ledge below her. "Put your arms around my neck."

"You're going to carry me down?"

"Yes, ma'am."

"I'm heavier than I look."

"I've hiked the Inca trail with packs heavier than you. But you'll have to hold the light for me."

"I can do that." She took the flashlight from him then draped her arms around his neck laying her head against his shoulder. He put his arms under her legs and lifted her, then cautiously started down while she pointed the light at the ground ahead of his feet. At the bottom of the hill he let her down. He was breathing heavily.

"See, I'm heavier than I look."

"No, you're a lightweight."

"We'll see after you carry me back up," she said.

Gilberto had tied the canoes side by side. Paul held Christine's hand as she stepped into the first canoe to get to the outer boat. He untied the rope from the bow, brought the rope inside the canoe and stepped in behind her. Lifting an oar, he began to paddle backward. The canoe slipped quietly from the dock into the black of the lake. The only sound was the continual fall from the waterwheel and the occasional splash of the oar as the jungle shore faded into a black tangle behind her. The water did not frighten her tonight.

When they were halfway across the lake, Paul pulled the oar inside, placing the dripping blade toward the back of the boat. Then he slid the wood back from Christine's seat, laying the plank next to the oar on the seat behind him.

"Lie back," he said.

She laid her head back in his lap, looking up into the clear, starlit sky. The boat rocked gently and the humid, tropical breath of the jungle warmed them.

"It's hard to believe it's almost Christmas," she said. "I don't even know what day it is."

"It's the fifteenth."

"Just ten more shopping days," she said. "What do you do for Christmas?"

"If it wasn't for the children, I'd just skip it."

"Scrooge," she said.

"I have my reasons." He ran his fingers up

the side of her jaw, then through her hair, raking it back across her head. She closed her eyes and exhaled with pleasure.

"Out here it's possible to believe that we're the only two people in this world."

"We are." He was suddenly quiet and for the next few moments he just stroked her hair.

"Why did you come to Peru?" she asked.

Her eyes were still closed and he looked at her for a long time without answering. "For some of the same reasons you did."

"Martin bailed on you too, huh?"

They both laughed.

"You're crazy," he said.

"I must be. I'm in the middle of a piranha-and-crocodile-infested lake in a leaky canoe and I wouldn't be anyplace else."

He pulled her into his chest, and for a moment she was happy with his silence. Then he took a deep breath.

"It started on Christmas Day. I was working as an emergency room doctor. The E.R. was crazy. There were only two doctors on call, and the other doc was trying to save a woman who had a heart attack during labor.

"A child was brought in. He had swallowed something." Paul took the soldier out from his shirt. "This."

Even though she had seen the soldier before, Christine raised her head to look at it. Then she looked up into Paul's face. She noticed that his voice had changed, but as she looked into his eyes, she saw just how much the incident still affected him. She guessed that he was opening a part of himself that few had ever seen.

"I had just started on the boy when a man was brought in. He had just had a heart attack. I did everything I could to save them. But I lost them both." His words slowed. "The boy was only five. The man was in his early forties. He left behind a wife and five children."

Christine reached up and touched his face. "I'm sorry."

"It was the worst day of my life. But it didn't end there."

She looked at him for explanation.

"In most cultures there's a certain acceptance that bad things happen. But in America if something bad happens, then people think that someone's got to pay. The child's mother was convinced that I had killed her son. I wasn't the one who had left my child alone in a room with small ornaments. The man's wife didn't think I had done enough to save her husband. He was forty pounds overweight, had high blood pressure and hadn't seen a doctor in six years. But both blamed me for their tragedies and both families sued me."

"They sued *you?*"

"This kind of thing happens every day. My second year in residency a woman broke into the E.R. and stole several vials of morphine. She gave it to her boyfriend, who overdosed on it. The woman sued the hospital and won.

"It seems that juries are always looking for some scapegoat. And there's always some doctor willing to take payment to tell a jury what you did wrong. In many cases there's not a clear choice. Sometimes you have just seconds to make a decision. You pick right you're a saint; pick wrong you're the devil. And in the end it really comes down to a throw of the dice.

"I knew that no matter how good a doctor I was that the odds would eventually catch up to me. I thought I would be able to handle it. It should have been easy. I'd done everything by the book. The hospital supported me. The E.R. staff stood by me. I won both cases.

"During all this I saw a psychiatrist friend. He told me that, statistically speaking, a doctor going through a malpractice suit has a far greater chance of dying than an inmate on death row."

"From suicide?" Christine asked.

"Suicide, the immune system breaks down or maybe they just don't turn fast enough out of the way of an oncoming semi. The will to live, or lack of, is a powerful thing.

"I had gotten engaged that Thanksgiving. We planned to get married the next June. But things got pretty strained between us. At first we delayed our wedding, hoping things would get back to normal. But there was no normal. I tried to go back to my practice, but I was just going through the motions. I stopped trusting my instincts. It was like being a professional snake handler. It didn't matter how careful you were, you knew that someday you'd be bitten.

"After a while I just couldn't do it anymore. I told my fiancée that I was giving up medicine. I had this naïve assumption that it wouldn't matter, that love would see us through." Paul shook his head. "It didn't. She wanted the doctor and the life of the doctor's wife."

He looked into her eyes. "I guess it's true what they say, 'Men marry women, women marry situations.' "

Christine didn't respond.

"That was pretty much my lowest point. I thought of ending it. You know, those midnight moments when insanity starts making sense. I knew just how to do it, the right cocktail of medications. I wouldn't feel a thing. I'd just disappear. But in the end I couldn't do it.

"Instead I bought a backpack and a one-way ticket to Brazil. I didn't tell anyone where I was going because I didn't know myself. I hiked throughout South America; Ecuador, Paraguay, Columbia. I stayed in hostels or under the stars. I grew my hair long. Somewhere along the road Dr. Cook ceased to exist.

"I hadn't been to Peru yet when someone told me about Machu Picchu. I think I had some desperate, New Age notion that I might find enlightenment in the sacred city. I asked God to show me a path—any path. I took the next train to Peru. I hiked the

Chocaqui, the Incan Trail. I meditated in the Temple of the Moon. But there was no inspiration, no divine guidance. Then, on the train back from Machu Picchu I sat next to a group of teenagers from Houston. They were in Peru for the summer on a Baptist mission. They were talking about this orphanage they'd worked in. I asked them about it. For some reason I couldn't get it off my mind.

"So after we arrived in Cuzco I hitchhiked to Lucre and found El Girasol. I originally intended to stay for just a few days. But working with these children did something to me. I kept telling myself that I would leave next week. I think I did that for about six months. Then one day the police officer running El Girasol received notice that he was being transferred to Lima. There was no one to take his place. It was either take over or send the children back out to the streets.

"That's where I am today. And after all this time I found what I was looking for."

"What's that?"

"Peace." For a moment he was silent. "Or at least I had."

She looked at him quizzically. "What do you mean?"

"Do you remember when you asked me what was the scariest thing I'd encountered since I came to the jungle?"

"As if I could ever forget . . ."

"Well, I was wrong."

"You thought of something more frightening?"

"You."

She sat up and looked at him indignantly. "I'm scarier than a *snake?*"

"The most the snake can do is kill you. And it's a fairly quick thing at that. In less than a week you'll be back in Dayton and I'll be here, unable to forget you for the rest of my life."

She stared at him for a moment. Then she leaned forward into him, pressing her mouth onto his and they lay back together. When they finally parted, she put her head on his chest. She could hear the pounding of his heart.

"Come home with me," she said.

For a long time he didn't answer. "And the children?"

She cuddled into him. The boat gently rocked as they held each other beneath the stars.

CHAPTER

Thirty

Love is never convenient—and rarely painless.

✦ PAUL COOK'S DIARY ✦

Christine woke in her bed a little before noon. Her fever was mostly gone, and she felt only the remaining soreness in her muscles and joints—like a runner the morning after a marathon.

She could hear Paul, Gilberto, and Marcos shouting to each other across the camp and she knew they would be leaving soon. She got up and showered, then dressed in her last set of clean clothing. She was packing her things when Paul joined her, carrying a Tupperware container. She guessed that it wasn't the first time he'd been in that morning.

"How do you feel?" he asked.

"Much better." She walked over and put her arms around him and they kissed. As they parted, she sighed with pleasure. "Last night seems like a dream."

"In a week, this whole experience will seem like a dream." He handed her the Tupperware. "I brought you some breakfast. You're going to need energy."

She sat down on the bed and pried the lid from the container. Inside was a napkin, yogurt, fruit and a cinnamon roll. "Thanks. I'm starving."

"You should be. You haven't eaten for a week."

"The Dengue Diet Plan," she said. "I could sell it." She took a bite of the cinnamon roll. It was no longer warm but still fresh. "This tastes *so* good."

"Rosana does all right."

She took another bite of the roll. "When are we leaving?"

"In the hour. We need to get back to Puerto before dark."

She wiped her finger on the napkin and set the container aside. "And then what?"

"Tomorrow we fly back to Cuzco and meet up with Jim and Jessica. Then you fly on to Lima and home."

"And what about you?"

"I go back to El Girasol."

She stepped back from him. "And that's it? Nice to meet you, I love you, goodbye?"

"Do you have a better ending?"

"Don't you?"

He put his hands in his pockets. "I do. But I couldn't ask you."

"Why?"

"Because you wouldn't stay."

She looked into his eyes. She suddenly understood that he hadn't asked her the night before because he already thought he knew the answer and didn't want to hear it anymore than she wanted to believe it of herself. *Men marry women, women marry situations.* She had no idea what to say. In that brief moment of silence the space between them hardened.

After a while Paul said, "I'll be back to get your bags." The door banged shut behind him. As he walked away, shame rose in her chest, lodging painfully in her throat. She finished packing the rest of her things.

✦

Christine was sitting on the porch when Paul came for her luggage. He said nothing as he threw her bags over his shoulder, and she silently followed him to the edge of the incline above the dock.

"I'll be back to carry you down," he said.

"I can walk by myself," she said coolly.

He looked at her for a moment. "Okay." He started down. She descended the hill after him, using the dirt wall to steady herself. When she reached the bottom after him, Rosana went to her and kissed her, and Christine thanked her for all she had done. Gilberto and Marcos had already boarded the canoe, one in front and the other in back. Christine climbed in first, then Paul, and Leonidas and Rosana waved them off from the dock as the men paddled away from the shore. Christine looked back as Makisapa grew small in the distance. She and Paul did not speak.

They had covered a quarter of the distance across the lake when Marcos pointed across the bow and shouted to Paul.

"Christine, the otters," Paul said.

A hundred yards ahead of them the animals frolicked, their snouts and webbed feet breaking the surface. They veered slightly for a closer glimpse, but the otters were gone by the time they reached the place they had seen them.

They arrived at the jungle path an hour later, and Gilberto handed them their galoshes. Paul took Christine's boots, inserted his hand inside them, then returned them to her.

"They're empty."

"Thanks."

Paul grabbed her bags along with his own. They climbed the bank and started off onto the shadowed trail. The walk was no longer frightening to Christine, and she knew she was not the same woman who had marched into the jungle the week before. She did her best not to slow the men, though she knew she was doing so. Her weariness grew as she walked, and a few times she stopped to catch her breath. Paul told Marcos and Gilberto to go on without them and prepare the boat while he waited for her.

"I'm sorry," Christine said.

"Take your time. You're still weak."

Paul set down the bags and brought out his machete, strapping it across his chest.

It took them nearly an hour to reach the clearing, and Christine was relieved to see the river stretched out before them, broader and faster than she remembered. Marcos and Gilberto were waiting for them, sitting on the grass ridge above the river. Christine took off her boots, and Gilberto helped her down the bank. Gilberto went to the back of the boat and started the motor while Marcos helped Christine in, then climbed in himself. Paul threw his bags on board, untied the boat's moorings, then pushed them out, climbing over the side in the same motion. The outboard motor roared, pushing them out into the current.

Marcos sat on the bow to watch for debris and Paul and Christine lay on the benches across from each other. The wind and spray increased, and without a word Paul brought out a blanket and wrapped Christine in it. The silence between them was unbearable to her. She looked at him, and he looked back without turning away, his eyes clear and sad. She searched them for something; reprieve, forgiveness, love? She wasn't sure. Finally, Christine closed her eyes and tried to sleep. A half hour later she opened her eyes. He was looking at her. "Are you hungry?" she asked.

"I'm okay."

"I have cookies."

He smiled a little and it felt to her like the sun breaking through the clouds. She moved over next to him. "Paul, I'm sorry. I . . ."

"Don't," he said. "I understand."

"But . . . I love you." She looked at him and sighed. "I love you. And we don't have much time left. I don't want to waste any more of it."

He smiled sadly then opened his arms to her. "Come here."

She went to him, and he held her as she tried to believe that the boat ride would never end.

CHAPTER

Thirty-One

We have returned to civilization. I fear the "real" world holds far more peril than the darkest jungle.

✦ PAUL COOK'S DIARY ✦

The jungle gradually changed as the river widened and the trees thinned, then it changed with man's encroachment, the clearings of the lumbermen and ranchers and the ugly slag heaps of the gold-mining camps. From Paul's backpack came an electronic beep.

"I have reception," Paul said. He lifted out the phone. There were twenty-two messages. "Do you want to call Jessica?"

"Not yet."

✦

Paul woke Christine as they arrived at the dock in Laberinto. The waterway was busier than before, and Gilberto skillfully maneuvered their boat to the concrete slip between two other boats filled with green bunches of bananas.

"This is where we say goodbye," Paul

said, standing, hunched beneath the boat's canopy. "Marcos and Gilberto are taking the boat to a dock downriver."

Christine looked at the men fondly. *"Gracias, Marcos. Gracias, Gilberto."*

"De nada," they both returned.

Paul carried his and Christine's things to shore, then returned to help Christine. Marcos and Paul embraced, then Marcos climbed back into the boat. *"Chao, hermano,"* Marcos said, and he pushed them away from the dock. The boat's motor sputtered, then fired, pulling them away from the slot.

"I'm starving," Paul said. "Are you?"

"I could eat a *cuy,"* Christine said.

Paul laughed. They walked up the road a way and stopped at a café. An elderly woman brought them a small loaf of bread, and Paul ordered roasted chicken, yams and orange Fanta. "Are you ready to go home?" he asked.

She nodded. "I miss my mother. And hopefully my boss hasn't replaced me."

"Just think of the stories you'll have to tell at the water cooler," Paul said. "I'll send the picture of you holding the crocodile." He broke off a chunk of bread and took a bite.

"May I call Jessica now?"

"Of course." He pulled the phone out of his pocket. He pushed the numbers then held the phone to his ear. As he waited for it to ring, Christine reached out and took his hand. *"Hola, amigo. ¿Qué pasa?"* He smiled and looked at her. "Yeah, she gave us a scare. But she's fine. A little thinner, but fine. No, she didn't need to lose any weight." Pause. "She wanted to speak with Jessica." He nodded. "No worries. We'll call back."

"May I speak with Jim?" Christine asked.

"Just a minute, Christine wants to talk."

He handed her the phone.

"Jim?"

"Christine! Welcome back from the dead."

She was happy to hear his voice. "Look who's talking? How are you?"

"Takes more than a mountain to stop the Hammer. Of course it doesn't hurt having a doctor around."

She looked at Paul. "I know what you mean. Where's Jessica?"

"She got bored and went shopping."

"Do you know if she called my mother?"

"She did. She's fine, just worried about you."

"How's Jessica?"

"The nurses at the hospital have a name for her. La Loca."

"I'm not surprised," Christine said, laughing. "When will she be back?"

"In a couple hours. She's been dying to talk to you. She has some big news."

"What?"

"She'd kill me if I told you. I'll have her call. Glad you're back, Christine. I look forward to seeing you tomorrow."

"Me too," she said. "Bye."

She hung up and gave the phone back to Paul. "Jim says Jessica has some big news."

"What is it?"

"He wouldn't tell me." She thought about it and smiled. "Maybe they eloped."

The waitress brought their food. When they finished eating, Paul left Christine at the café while he went looking for a taxi. He returned a few minutes later in the backseat of a station wagon. He climbed out and opened the door for Christine. The driver spun the car around in the middle of the road and they started back to Puerto Maldonado.

CHAPTER

Thirty-Two

*Such fickle days of love when pain
and ecstasy share the same hour.*

✦ PAUL COOK'S DIARY ✦

It was nearly dark when the taxi arrived at the Don Carlos Hotel. Paul checked them in at the front counter then carried their bags to their rooms. When he came back, he asked, "How do you feel?"

"Pretty tired."

"Do you want to go to bed?"

"No. It's our last night together."

"Are you hungry?"

"Not really. Maybe we could get a coffee."

"There's a café a few blocks from here."

In the clear jungle skies even a partial moon seemed brilliant, and they held hands as they walked the rutted dirt road. They were both silent for a while.

"What time is our flight tomorrow?"

"I'll have to call the airport. But the flight usually leaves around eight. It's too bad we don't have more time. There were some more things I wanted to show you."

"This trip has already been so much more than I thought it would be."

"I would say so. Dengue fever, falling off mountains . . ."

"Falling in love," she said. "I thought I was coming here to heal my heart. Not to lose it." She looked up at him. "Tell me what to do, Paul."

"I can't do that."

She looked back down and frowned. "I know."

They reached the café and the proprietor led them to a table and lit a candle. Paul ordered two decafs and a bowl of taro chips. The light danced across Paul's face, and as she looked at him, the weight of their impending separation seemed unbearable.

"I don't want this day to end."

Just then Paul's cell phone rang. He looked at the number displayed. "It's Jessica."

"Don't answer it."

Paul looked at her. Then he turned off the phone and put it back in his pocket. The owner returned with their order and put it on the table. Christine took a sip of her coffee, then looked up into Paul's eyes. "Ask me to stay."

He slowly shook his head. "I can't."

"You don't want me to?"

"Of course I do. I just don't think you could be happy here."

Christine frowned. "I don't know if I could be happy here either. But I know for certain that I'd be miserable without you."

Paul looked thoughtfully at the flickering flame, then up into her eyes. "Marry me."

Christine stared at him in astonishment.

He took her hands. "Christine, I've waited my whole life to find someone that I could love like you. You have no idea what you've done to me. I can't breathe when I think of losing you."

Christine looked down at the table. Tears gathered in her eyes. When she looked up again, a smile slowly broke across her face. "Shouldn't you be giving me a ring or something?"

Paul looked at her in surprise. "Are you accepting?"

Her smile grew still wider. "Yes."

His eyes glistened in the candlelight. He took the gold band from his hand. "Will this do for now?"

She held out her hand. "It's perfect."

His hand trembled as he slid the ring on

her finger. It was too large and they both laughed.

"Well, it's almost perfect," she said. "How about I wear it on my thumb for now."

He moved the ring to her thumb, then held her hand. "I promise to do everything I can to make you happy."

She couldn't stop smiling. "You already have, my love."

CHAPTER

Thirty-Three

*Our announcement was about as
well received as a bowl of soup
with a hair in it.*

✦ PAUL COOK'S DIARY ✦

The flight out of Puerto was delayed two hours and they sat in the airport café playing cards and drinking Cokes in the sweltering heat. When they finally boarded, the plane was less than half full. Paul lifted the armrest between their seats, and Christine lay into him. "Did you get hold of Jim?" she asked.

"They'll be at the airport to pick us up."

"I can't wait to find out what Jessica's big news is. What if she and Jim eloped?"

"You think that's it?"

"I can't think of anything else." She smiled. "I can't wait to tell her *our* news."

Paul rubbed his hand across her cheek, pushing her hair back over her ear. "It's been a long time since I've felt this happy," he said.

She took his hand and kissed it. "Then you're overdue."

⋆

As the plane touched down in Cuzco, Christine felt the altitude pressing in on her sinuses. She rubbed her forehead. Paul leaned over and kissed her. "Altitude?"

"Yes. Will I ever get used to it?"

"Eventually."

The plane taxied over to the terminal. They disembarked, holding hands as they walked. Jessica and Jim were waiting for them near the baggage claim. When Jessica saw her, she ran to her.

"Christine!"

"Jess!"

They embraced. Then Jessica stepped back to look at her. "My gosh, you're a twig." She turned to Paul. "And welcome back, handsome."

"Hi, Jessica." They hugged.

Jim hobbled up on crutches. "Welcome back, you two."

Christine hugged him. "How are you?"

"Better than the last time you saw me."

"Glad to see you *vertical*," Paul said.

"Glad to *be* vertical. Thanks for putting me back together. In fact, thanks for everything. I saw the rest of the group before they flew home. They said the jungle was their favorite part of the trip."

"Glad I could help."

Christine leaned into Paul, putting her arm around his waist. "Okay, you two, the suspense is killing me. What's your big news?"

Jessica glanced at Paul. "It can wait."

Christine looked at her quizzically. "It can *wait?* Come on!"

"No, really. It's not that important."

Christine eyed her incredulously. "Then why did you keep calling me?"

"I'll tell you later," Jessica said.

Christine shook her head. "You make me crazy, girl. Well, *we* have big news that won't wait."

Jessica's eyes darted between them. "What?"

"We're engaged."

Jessica looked at her as if awaiting the punch line.

"Well?" Christine asked.

"Congratulations," Jim said, stepping forward. "That's great." He hugged Christine then Paul. "Didn't I tell you that things would work out?"

"Well, you had to fall to make it happen," Christine said.

"You've given meaning to my suffering."

Jessica stepped forward and hugged her. "Congratulations," she said weakly.

"You look like you're in shock," Christine said.

"I am. It's so . . . *unexpected.*"

"You've always told me to be more spontaneous."

"I guess you were saving up for something *really* big." She said to Paul, "So you're coming back to the States."

Christine hesitated. "We're going to live down here."

Jessica looked tortured. "You're moving to Peru?"

"That's the plan."

Jessica stared at her in disbelief. Christine was hurt by Jessica's reaction and the awkwardness between them grew palpable. Jim spoke to break the tension. "Hey, let's get you two back to the hotel." Then he turned to Paul and handed him a key. "I've a few errands to run. You can chill out in my room."

"Thanks," Paul said, still looking at Christine. He wanted to comfort her but knew she needed time with Jessica.

"I almost forgot, Jaime's been trying to reach you. He says it's *muy importante.*"

"I'll call him from the hotel."

As they walked to the parking lot, Jessica led Christine away from the men.

"So you have reservations," Christine said, trying to control her anger.

"That doesn't even touch what I'm feeling. This is *insane.*"

"Insane?" Christine repeated indignantly.

"Leaving everything you know for a man you just met is *insane.* I know I've always told you to think outside the box. But girl, you're thinking outside the solar system."

"Thanks for your support."

Jessica stopped walking. "Chris, there's something else."

Christine looked at her anxiously. "Is it my mom? Is she okay?"

"Your mom's fine."

"Then what is it?"

Jessica glanced over at Jim and Paul. "Let's wait until we get back to the hotel."

CHAPTER

Thirty-Four

If the road to hell is paved with good intentions, today I met the road crew supervisor.

✦ PAUL COOK'S DIARY ✦

Paul was lying on Jim's bed when there was a knock on the door. Without getting up, he said, "Come in."

Jessica entered. She looked even more distressed than before. Paul's stomach tightened.

"Hey, what's up?"

"Got a minute?"

"Sure. Where's Chris?"

"She's back in my room . . . crying."

Paul sat up. "What's wrong?"

Jessica sat down on the corner of the bed. "Chris *really* is in love with you."

"You say that like it's a bad thing."

"In this case, it is."

Her expression turned more intense as she searched for the right words. "Paul, I have nothing but the upmost respect for you. What you do for those children in these conditions is beautiful. But the Christine I know could never live a life like that. The woman owns a carpet rake." She shook her head. "This is my fault. I never should have brought her down here when she's so vulnerable."

"Isn't that why you brought her down?"

She looked at him sympathetically. "You've got to see that she's fallen in love with you on the rebound, right? Rebounds never work out. *Never.* You can't do this to her."

Paul reacted angrily. "I'm not doing anything to her. Christine can make her own decisions. She's not a child."

"When it comes to men, she is." Her voice softened. "Before Martin came along, she dated a guy named Justin. He was a real loser. He'd belittle Christine in public. Stand her up. Cheat on her. He treated her like a doormat. I begged Christine to drop him but she wouldn't. She just can't stand being alone.

"Then one day she decided to stand up for herself. He beat her up. That should have been the end of it, but even then she wouldn't leave. She made up some lame excuse for him. So I told him that if he didn't leave her, my father the congressman would see to it that he did serious jail time. He said

'fine' he 'was just using her anyway.' "
Jessica's voice grew hard. "When it comes
to men, I've always had to look after her."

"Like now?"

"Precisely," she said. "Listen, I'm not
Martin's biggest fan. But aside from chick-
ening out of the wedding, he's been good to
her. Even after he broke her heart, Christine
told me that Martin was everything she
wanted. That's why they were together for
six years. That's a lot of history."

"That's all he is," Paul said curtly. "History."

"Not anymore."

Paul looked at her quizzically.

". . . he's in Lima."

For a moment Paul was speechless.
"Does Christine know?"

"She does now."

He lowered his head into his hands. "So
that was your big news." He looked up.
"What did she say?"

"She didn't know what to say." Jessica
sighed. "He makes her happy, Paul. He's
her happy ending."

Paul's cell phone rang. He ignored it. "So
what am I supposed to do? Just fade into
the sunset?"

Jessica didn't answer.

"I won't do that to her."

"Not *to* her. *For* her."

Paul stood. "I can't believe we're having this conversation."

"I wish we weren't," Jessica said. "I'm so sorry. You're such a great guy. But Christine could never be happy living like you do. And did she mention her mother? They're inseparable. She couldn't possibly live without her mother. She's the only family Christine has. Even if she could leave her, she'd hate herself for it."

Paul's cell phone rang again and this time he shut it off. Jessica knit her fingers together. "I'm sorry, Paul. But if you don't let her go, you'll end up hurting her. I know that's not what you want."

Paul leaned his head against the wall and for several minutes nothing was said. The hotel phone rang. On its thirteenth ring Paul walked over and picked it up.

"*¿Qué?*"

Jessica could hear a voice speaking in Spanish excitedly.

Paul answered in Spanish. *"What do you mean? Did the boys see her? What about*

Richard?" He shook his head. *"All right. I'll be right there."* He hung up the phone.

The pain in his eyes had turned to panic. "What's wrong?" Jessica asked.

"Roxana's gone." He grabbed his bag. "I've got to go." He walked to the door.

"What do I tell Christine?"

He stopped, then looked back at Jessica. His eyes were dark and hard. "Tell her that I wish her and Martin well."

He disappeared behind the closing door. Jessica lay back and put a pillow over her face and cried.

CHAPTER

Thirty-Five

All is chaos.

✦ PAUL COOK'S DIARY ✦

Christine knocked twice, then pushed the door open into Jim's room. Her eyes were red and puffy. She was surprised to see Jessica sitting on the bed.

"Where's Paul?"

Jessica exhaled. "He left."

"Where'd he go?"

"He went back to the orphanage."

"What?"

"He went home, Chris."

"He told you this?"

"Yes."

"Was he angry?"

Jessica wrestled with the truth and what she should say. "He just said to tell you that he went home."

Christine went to the phone and dialed Paul's cell-phone number. There was no answer.

"That's all he said?"

"No." Jessica looked at her sympathetically. "He said he wished you and Martin well."

"You told him that Martin was here?"

"Of course I did." Jessica went to put her arms around Christine, but she pulled away angrily.

"You had no right to do that."

"I was just looking out for you." She walked around to face her. "You told me that all you wanted was a second chance with Martin. He flew all the way from Ohio to Peru to bring you back. Isn't this what you wanted?"

Christine sat down on the bed. "Yes. No." She took a deep breath, then started to cry. "I'm so confused."

"I know, honey." Jessica sat down next to her. "But once you see Martin, everything will be all right. I promise."

CHAPTER
Thirty-Six

Christine's ex-fiancé, Martin, has come for her. Though I am assured that it is all for the best, I cannot feel it. I've heard it said that to love someone is not to desire them but to desire their happiness. If this is true then I must question my love— because I desperately desire her.

✦ PAUL COOK'S DIARY ✦

Jessica and Christine carried their bags down to the lobby. Christine found a place to sit alone while Jessica perused the leather purses for sale at the small gift concession. A few minutes later Jim returned, swinging on his crutches, their plane tickets protruding from his front pocket. He hobbled over to Jessica. "How'd it fly?"

"Like the Hindenburg."

"Where's Paul?"

"He went home."

He looked at her quizzically. "Really? And Christine?"

"She's over there."

Christine was curled up in the corner of the sofa. "Oh no," he said.

"She's pretty upset."

"Will she talk?"

Jessica shrugged. "You can try."

He walked over and sat down on the

couch's arm, leaning his crutches against the wall.

"Hey, you okay?"

"No."

"I can't imagine what you must feel like."

"A fool. An idiot. A traitor. Pick one."

"I'm sorry," he said. He didn't say anything for a moment. "On the other hand, that's pretty great that your fiancé flew all the way down here to see you. I mean, that's good, isn't it?"

She didn't answer for a while. "Yes."

He put his hand on her shoulder. "Don't worry, things will work out. They always do."

"No, not always," Christine said.

"No, not always," he said. He sat quietly for a moment, then checked his watch. "It's time to go. Let's go see how this story ends."

CHAPTER

Thirty-Seven

*For the second time in my life a
child has been lost on my watch.*

✦ PAUL COOK'S DIARY ✦

Paul made the thirty-minute drive to Lucre in under twenty minutes. He spun his car out in the hacienda's gravel driveway and ran into the courtyard yelling for Jaime. Jaime ran out to meet him, his face tight with distress.

"*¿Ya regresó?*" Has she returned?

"*No, Señor.*"

"*Dónde han buscado?*" Where have you looked?

"*Hemos buscado en el pueblo y en el campo.*" We've checked the village and the surrounding fields and hills."

"*¿Y después dónde?*" And then where?

"*¿En qué otro lugar pudiera ella estar? Si ella hubiera estado caminando alguien la habria visto. Pero nadie la ha visto. Alquien la debe haber robado.*" Where else could she be? If she had wandered off, she would have been seen in the village. No one saw her. She must have been taken.

Jaime's last words left him breathless. More than anything he didn't want to believe that someone had taken her. The organized exploitation of children was a cartel generating billions of dollars a year. Worldwide there are more than 2 million children being held in sexual slavery.

That wasn't the only means of exploitation. A few years earlier the Cuzco police had broken a ring of Peruvian kidnappers that was sending street children off to Switzerland and Italy to be killed for their organs.

In either case the chances of her being found were slim. Paul fought back feelings of panic and guilt. She had trusted him to keep her safe and now she was gone.

Paul called the comandante of the Cuzco Police Department to report Roxana's disappearance, praying against hope that she might have already been picked up by the police. She hadn't been. The comandante was a supporter of the orphanage and over the last four years he and Paul had become close friends. He expressed his sincere remorse and promised to look into the matter personally.

Paul went to his room and found several photographs of Roxana and, taking Richard and Jaime with him, he went to the nearby town of Lucre to look for her.

CHAPTER

Thirty-Eight

Absence is to love what wind is to fire—it extinguishes the small and inflames the great.
—Anonymous

✦ PAUL COOK'S DIARY ✦

From the Lima airport Jim hailed them a cab to Larco Mar, a wealthy seaside suburb of Lima. The three of them ate a somber dinner at the Hard Rock Café. Before they finished eating, Christine excused herself and went out alone to think. She walked along the boardwalk to a quiet outlook above the Pacific. She leaned against the rail and watched the waves crash against the rocky coast.

A half hour later Jessica came up behind her.

"You okay?"

Christine didn't answer. Jessica looked out over the sea. "The ocean always looks so angry at night."

Christine continued to look ahead. "How can there be so much wealth here and so much poverty everywhere else?"

Jessica sighed. "Martin just called. He was checking to see if we made it." She turned to Christine. "Are you ready for this?"

"I don't know."

Jessica put her arm around her. "I'm sorry this is so hard. But maybe it's all for the best."

"That's what people say when it couldn't be worse."

"Yeah, you're right," she sniffed. "Do you know that I love you?"

"Yes."

"What do you say we go?"

Christine took her hand. "Okay."

The cab let them off in front of the Swissôtel, the nicest hotel Christine had seen since she'd come to Peru. As the uniformed porters loaded their bags onto a brass lug-gage cart, Christine glanced around the marble-floored entryway.

In the center of the lobby was a large, ornate mahogany table with an enormous crystal vase filled with a spray of fresh flowers.

Jim checked in for the three of them, then handed Jessica a room key. "You're on the seventh floor, room 713. I'm one floor down."

"What room is Martin in?" Christine asked.

"Three eleven."

Jessica looked at her and smiled. "Go get him, honey."

"Good luck," Jim said.

"Thanks." She walked to the elevator, stepped inside and pushed three. Jessica blew her a kiss and Christine forced a smile as the elevator door shut. She got off on the third floor and stopped to look at herself in the hallway mirror. She pulled her hair back, and applied some more lip gloss. Then she walked down the hall to 311.

Christine could hear the television playing inside the room. She looked down at the gold band Paul had given her. She slipped it off, letting it drop into her pants pocket. Then she knocked. The television went silent. She heard footsteps. The brass chain of the lock slid and the door opened. Martin stood before her.

For a moment neither one of them spoke, both of them watching the other for some cue as to how to proceed. Martin acted first. He stepped out into the hall and hugged her.

"It's so good to see you."

Christine leaned into him. "It's good to see you too."

After a moment they released each other and he stepped back. "I've been so worried about you. Come in."

She followed him inside. The room was pristine, everything in its place. His bag was on the luggage rack, his laptop neatly centered on a glass-topped desk.

"This is a little nicer than where we've been staying," she said.

"Not bad for a third-world country," Martin said. "When your mother told me you'd come to Peru, I was more than a little surprised. Of course I figured that Jessica had something to do with it."

"Of course."

"How are you feeling?"

"Much better."

"I can't tell you how worried I was when I found out you were sick. I knew I needed to be here for you."

Christine didn't answer.

He walked over to the table and picked up a bouquet of long-stemmed red roses. "When Jessica said you'd be back today, I went out looking for these. You have no idea how hard it is to find roses in Lima."

She took the flowers. "Thank you." There was an awkward silence.

Martin forced a smile. "Can you believe we're here? Who would have thought we'd end up in Peru, of all places. Look at you. You've gotten so thin. I guess it's no surprise after what you've been through in the last three weeks."

"The last three months. And the dengue was the easy part."

He smiled in embarrassment. "I deserve that."

Christine set the flowers on the bed. "You didn't even call. Do you have any idea how hurt I was? Did you care?"

"Of course I cared. I was just so . . . stupid. And confused."

"So what changed?"

"I guess sometimes you need to lose someone before you realize how much they mean to you."

He reached into his pocket. "I know it's hard for you to trust me. That's why I came all the way down here. Call it my penance." He stepped over to her and touched her arm. "I brought you something." He pulled from his pocket a small velvet jewelry box. His voice lilted. "Do you want to see what's inside?" She nodded. He smiled and opened the box. Inside was her ring, but the diamond had been replaced with a much larger stone. It was now at least two carats.

She looked at the ring but didn't take it. She sighed heavily. "I don't know, Martin."

"Remember how happy you were the first time I gave it to you? You showed it to everyone. Even that weird guy outside the Starbucks."

She smiled then chuckled in remembrance. He reached up and touched her cheek. "That's what I was waiting for, that smile." He took her hand. "For six years things were good between us, weren't they?"

She nodded.

"Then I made a mistake. Granted, it was a big one . . . but in six years?" He looked at her, his eyes pleading. "Give me the chance to make it up to you. We still have everything we dreamed of." He knelt down on one knee, took the ring out of the box and held it out to her. "Give me one more chance. Who could love you like I do?"

As she looked at the beautiful ring she thought of the simple gold band in her pocket. Then she looked over at the roses.

CHAPTER

Thirty-Nine

We spend our lives building higher fences and stronger locks, when the gravest dangers are already inside.

✦ PAUL COOK'S DIARY ✦

Paul, Richard and Jaime walked up and down the streets of Lucre, knocking on doors, walking into shops and stopping everyone they saw. No one had seen Roxana.

At seven o'clock Richard went back to feed the boys while Paul and Jaime continued on until nightfall. Roxana had simply vanished. It was past ten when they returned to the Sunflower. As they pulled down the gravel drive, Paul asked Jaime, "What do the boys know?"

"They know she's gone. They're worried."

Paul's frown deepened. *"I'll talk to them."*

Upon their arrival Paul and Jaime went up to the boys' dorm. Richard had seen them return and he followed them up the stairs. When they entered the room, the boys fell silent. From the men's expressions they knew she hadn't been found.

Paul said in Spanish, *"We haven't found*

her. I can't believe she just disappeared. Someone must have heard something."

"We were asleep," said Deyvis. *"We wouldn't let someone take her."*

"Of course you wouldn't." Paul looked them over and sighed, "Okay, off to bed."

As the boys went to their bunks, only Pablo didn't move. Paul walked over to him. *"Are you afraid?"*

Pablo looked down, then he glanced furtively at Richard but said nothing.

Paul said slowly, "Tell me in English."

Pablo swallowed and continued to stare at the floor. "I heard men talking and I looked down from our window. I saw men and a car."

"Did you see Roxana?"

He shook his head. "I heard a noise. She might have been in the car." Tears began to well up in his eyes. "I didn't know she was gone."

Paul crouched down in front of him. "It's not your fault. Do you know what kind of car it was?"

"It was big."

"Had you seen it before?"

He shook his head.

"Did you recognize the men?"

"One."

Paul clasped both of his shoulders. "Who was it?"

He looked down, afraid to say.

"Whisper it."

Pablo leaned forward. "Richard."

Paul hugged Pablo. *"We'll find her.* Now go to bed."

The three men walked back downstairs. Paul bid Richard goodnight and Richard went to the kitchen to finish preparations for the morning. Paul took Jaime aside. A few moments later Paul walked into the kitchen. He asked in Spanish, *"Where is Roxana?"*

Richard looked at him quizzically. *"No se, Señor Cook. We spent the night looking for her and you ask me this?"*

"How much did they pay you for her?"

"I know nothing. I don't know!"

"You knew when the boys were asleep. Except one of them wasn't. He saw you with her."

Richard stopped what he was doing, fear evident in his eyes. Just then Jaime walked into the room holding a machete.

"You will tell us now," Paul said.

"I cannot tell you. These men . . ."

"Do not fear cowards who prey on chil-

dren. Fear the ones who love the children." He turned. "Jaime."

Jaime stepped closer. He said calmly, *"You will tell us in a good way or a bad way. But you will tell us."*

Richard backed into a corner of the kitchen.

"Where shall I start?" Jaime asked.

Richard's eyes darted back and forth fearfully. *"Don't hurt me. I'll tell you where the men are."*

Five minutes later Paul was on the phone with the comandante.

CHAPTER

Forty

I shudder to think of how close I came to losing Roxana or what her fate might have been. Far too many children know that their world is not a safe place.

✦ PAUL COOK'S DIARY ✦

Within twenty minutes of Paul's call, Richard was picked up by the police. The comandante had come himself and, with the information Richard provided, they planned a raid.

Paul and Jaime sat up all night in the kitchen drinking coffee, anxiously awaiting news. The call came at six-forty in the morning. Roxana, along with three other little girls, had been found chained in a garage just two kilometers from the Cuzco airport. The police also seized cash and a flight plan. By ten o'clock that morning none of the girls would have been seen again.

When Paul arrived at the Cuzco police headquarters, Roxana was curled up on a couch, her head hidden between her knees. He gently touched her and she jerked, then cautiously looked up. When she saw Paul, she jumped into his arms. He held her tighter than anyone he'd ever held before.

He began to cry. "I'll never fail you again," he said. "I promise."

At the comandante's request Paul took all four girls back to El Girasol. The boys met them in the courtyard, cheering. Pablo signed to Roxana that he missed her. She signed back that she had missed him too.

That night Paul, on his knees, thanked God for sparing the little girl's life, reiterating the promise he had made to Roxana: *He would never fail her again.* Paul climbed into his bed. He looked up into the darkness, and the panic and madness of the last thirty hours dissipated, leaving his mind open to reflection. Only then did he allow his heart the misery of thinking of Christine.

CHAPTER

Forty- One

Another Christmas has come. What brings joy to so many only brings me pain. Still, I hide my feelings from the children. No one has the right to rob children of childhood.

✦ PAUL COOK'S DIARY ✦

CHRISTMAS DAY

Paul sat in his chair sipping cocoa and gazing at the flashing strand of colored lights on their small, potted Christmas palm. The *Christmas Classics Collection* was playing for its third time through, and Roxana sat next to the CD player, her hands spread out over its speakers. She especially liked Burl Ives's *Holly Jolly Christmas*—something about the way it felt.

The December group had been generous and all the children had received new clothing and toys. Paul had gone to Cuzco and purchased dolls for the three new girls who were up in their room playing. Roxana preferred to play alone. The boys were outside breaking in their new soccer ball, their shouts echoing from the courtyard. He didn't know where Jaime was and assumed he had gone off for a siesta.

Paul couldn't wait for the day to be over. He put down his cup. "Oh by golly, have a holly jolly Christmas," he said, shaking his head. He walked over and tapped Roxana's shoulder and signed to her that he was going to his room. He leaned over and kissed her forehead. "Merry Christmas, little one."

He walked the perimeter of the courtyard so as not to disturb the boys' game.

"Hey, Paul," Pablo shouted, "Want to play?"

"No thanks, I'm tired of losing."

Pablo held out his hands. "Hey, it's Christmas. We'll let you win."

Paul smiled. "Maybe later."

He went to his room and shut the door. He sat on his bed; glancing at the picture of his parents. It added to his melancholy. He had called home earlier this morning as he always did on Christmas. It was no surprise, but his mother's condition had deteriorated. And though his father wouldn't say it, they needed him home.

Next to their picture was the snapshot of Christine he'd taken that afternoon when she'd first left him—the sunflower he'd given her lifted close to her cheek, the perfect smile on her perfect lips. It made him ache and he wondered what had possessed him to put it up. Something between nostalgia and masochism, and he considered that maybe there wasn't much difference between the two.

Jaime had given him a book for Christmas—a political thriller in English—and he lay down on his bed and began to read, glad for the escape. He was just getting into the story when there was a knock on his door.

"Come in," he said making no effort to mask his annoyance.

The door opened and Pablo peered inside. "Hey."

"I don't want to play," Paul said.

"That's not what I came for. I have a surprise for you."

He looked up at him, vaguely curious. "Yes?"

"Wait. I'll get it."

The door shut. Paul shook his head, then looked back down at his book. The door opened again and he slowly looked back up.

Christine stood in the doorway. "Merry Christmas."

He sat up, looking at her in disbelief.

She was even more beautiful than he remembered. She wore a light cotton sundress and her hair fell onto her bare shoulders, softly framing her face. Her eyes sparkled with excitement.

"May I come in?"

"Yes."

She stepped inside and walked to him. She glanced at the picture of herself and smiled. She looked back into his eyes.

"I heard about Roxana. How frightening that must have been. You saved her life. But you make a habit of saving lives."

Paul just stared at her. His mind reeled with a hundred questions but settled on none of them.

"I expect you're wondering what I'm doing here?"

"It—crossed my mind."

"I should be with my fiancé on Christmas, shouldn't I?" She held up her hand. She wore his ring.

"What about Martin?"

"Martin." She breathed in deeply. "The thing is, on the surface Martin seemed like a pretty safe bet. Good job. Good family. Everything I thought was important. But the truth is, every relationship is a journey. And no journey is safe. The best you can do is find a companion you care to make the trip with."

"Even if that journey takes you through Peru?"

"Even that," she said.

"Can you do it?"

"I now know I can."

"How can you know that?"

"Because a wise man taught me something."

Paul just stared at her, his eyes glistening with emotion. "And what's that?"

"Love is stronger than pain."

Paul stepped forward and she fell into him, their lips pressed together, their joy as full as the emptiness he had felt over the last two weeks. And both were happier than either believed possible.

"Merry Christmas, sweetheart," Christine said.

"Merry Christmas," he said. And for the first time in more than half a decade, he meant it.

EPILOGUE

In life, as in literature,
all comes full circle.

✴ PAUL COOK'S DIARY ✴

Jessica finally got to wear her maid-of-honor dress. Paul and Christine were married the following March in Paul's parents' home. Within six months they had legally adopted Pablo and Roxana and brought them back to live with them in their home in Oakwood, a small suburb just outside Dayton. Paul's mother died that following June. Paul was at her side when she passed.

✦

I called Christine the day after I returned from Peru. Christine was happy to hear from me and said that Paul had mentioned that I might be calling. She spoke confidently, charmingly, and I witnessed how love and faith can blossom a soul.

I had already started writing their story, and it was a little odd speaking to her—like talking to a character drawn from a novel. I